# Brilliantly Beautiful

ELAINE PATCH

Copyright © 2021 by Elaine Patch

All rights reserved. No part of this book may be reproduced or used in any manner without the prior written permission of the copyright owner, except for the use of brief quotations in a book review.

This is a work of fiction. Names, characters, places, and incidents either are the products of the author's imagination or are used fictitiously. Any resemblance to actual persons, living or dead, businesses, companies, events, or locales is entirely coincidental.

BRILLIANTLY BEAUTIFUL

Cover design by Drew Button of DButton Ink
Editing by Pauline Nolet
Author photo by Scott Patch

ISBN 978-1-7365950-0-8

In memory of my Mimi for her
love of being lazy in the sun,
and my Nanny "Happy Cloud"
who inspired my passion for art.

Until we're together again…this one is for both of you.

## Chapter 1

*Brielle*

"Excuse me, but have you decided on what you want to order yet, as there's others waiting?" The young barista at my local coffee shop interrupts my thoughts with a slightly irritated tone to her voice and a hand placed so firmly on her hip that I notice her knuckles turning a soft shade of white like the snow currently dusting outside.

Do you know that feeling when you're driving along and your mind is totally zoned out for what feels like forever, and then suddenly you snap out of it, only to wonder if you were actually paying attention to the road the whole time? That sums up my current state of mind, and I'm getting huffs and exaggerated eye rolls from everyone around me, who are attempting to satisfy their cravings with the scent of freshly roasted coffee beans as they impatiently wait to get their daily dependency fix of caffeine.

"I'm sorry, yes, I'd like the largest iced chocolate-chip frappé you can make, please."

She's suddenly looking at me like I should be wrapped up in a straitjacket and sitting in a padded room rather than standing here in front of her right now. "You do realize that it's only twenty-nine degrees outside, right?"

Outstanding, it's going to be one of *those* days where I

really need to keep my damn mouth shut, but I just can't control myself with only three lousy hours of sleep under my belt.

"Crap, you're right. I knew when I put on this puffy down coat, knit gloves, and my favorite 'I Love CO Beer' beanie this morning that something was amiss."

"That's an awesome beanie, might I add," chimes in the guy behind me, who's sporting the classic craft-beer-guy-looking beard.

"Thank you." Feeling a little vindicated, I give him a flirtatious wink.

"Ugh, whatever. That will be five dollars and seventy-five cents. Cash or card?"

She's as over me now as I am of her, so I complete my transaction and go wait at the other end of the counter with another dozen people salivating like junkies waiting for their dealer to arrive.

My cell phone suddenly pings with a welcome distraction, letting me know that I have a text.

>**Nicole:** How much do you really love me?
>**Brielle:** More than my sister.
>**Nicole:** You don't even have a sister...
>**Brielle:** But if I DID, it would be more than her.
>**Nicole:** Having one of your mornings, are you?
>**Brielle:** You know me so well. I blame the annoying barista I just had to deal with.
>**Nicole:** If you listened to me and stopped drinking that crap, you wouldn't have this problem, I'm just saying.
>**Brielle:** Yes, mother. Seriously though, what's up?

**Nicole:** If I asked you for a massive favor, would you do it?
**Brielle:** You know I would, no questions asked.
**Nicole:** Perfect, I'll take that as a yes. I'll call you after work with all of the details.

Yikes, she has never asked me for a favor let alone a massive one, but there's nothing I wouldn't do for her. We've been best friends for as long as I can remember, although if you met us together, you'd never have thought that. Nicole is the more introverted, extremely poised, and successful person in our friendship. Myself, on the other hand, well, let's just say that I'm more of a free spirit living life as the adventure it is and trying to see the beauty in everything and *almost* everyone, present company excluded of course.

That's why she's currently an important executive assistant in New York City with a degree in accounting, and I'm a thirty-year-old woman still trying to figure out what I want to be when I grow up. Okay, that's not exactly true, as I'm currently a freelance graphic designer / marketing guru living in Denver (where apparently it can be the end of May and still only be twenty-nine degrees today and probably seventy-five tomorrow).

Don't get me wrong, as I love being creative, I just think I'd rather find a job that was located on a warm sunlit beach somewhere and involved smooth golden spiced rum in some capacity.

"Brielle." They call out my name and place what I hope will be my morning's jolt of energy down on the counter. After Nic's text though, I have a suspicion that I might need to have something a little stronger on hand when she calls me tonight.

Knowing I'm still exhausted from my late-night adventure with my previous project, I decide to get an earlier start this evening on the latest logo design concept I am working on for a local, hip hair salon. These clients have been a blast to work for, as they are open to any ideas I have as long as the rebrand is "bright and banging," using their terms. As I start scrolling through the sea of endless fonts I have loaded in my design software, "She Works Hard For The Money" by Donna Summer comes blaring across the room from my cell phone. Of course, that's my ringtone for Nic, considering how insanely hard that girl is constantly working.

"Hey, Brielle, I'm sorry to call you while you're probably eating dinner, but I just got home from work a few minutes ago." Clearly exhausted, she yawns into the other end of the line.

Looking at my watch, I note that it's already eight at night in NYC. "Okay, I know you live within walking distance of your office, so why are you working so late?"

Sighing heavily, she continues, "Things are crazy at work right now, and it's just been an exceptionally long day. I really hope you meant it this morning when you said that you'd be willing to do anything for me because…I can't do this without you, Brielle."

Suddenly a swarm of butterflies starts flapping their wings at warp speed in my stomach when I hear the concern in her voice and don't have any idea where this is going.

"Yes, of course, now will you please tell me what's going on, as you've got me really worried."

"I heard back from the specialist I saw earlier this week, and she had me come back in today to go over her findings. You know how I've been suffering for so long with endometriosis causing all my horrific monthly pains and swelling, etc. Well, things have progressed, and the doctor thinks that I may also have an additional condition called adenomyosis, so she had me undergo some ultrasounds and MRIs to see what else may be occurring inside. Not only did they show that the endometriosis has spread, but my uterus measures twice the size it should be." She pauses for a moment as if to collect her thoughts, then continues, "She also found a mass on my ovary that has her concerned."

As I'm trying to process all this new information, I sit quietly for a moment, just wanting to reach through the phone and engulf her in a giant bear hug.

"Oh, Nic, I'm so sorry you're having to go through all of this, but I'm also extremely grateful that you finally found a doctor who has listened to you and figured out what's been going on. What is she suggesting the next steps would be for you?"

She goes on to explain to me that based on her current and previous history, her doctor highly suggests that she have a total hysterectomy. Although there's no guarantee that this surgery will make all her pain completely disappear, she feels very strongly that this will dramatically improve her quality of life.

"Oh, Brielle, you have no idea how much I'd love to be rid of all this pain and be able to enjoy myself again." Then she clears her throat like she's trying to hold her tears back.

"I really want that for you too, my sweet friend, and I'm here for you no matter what you decide to do."

"Thank you so much, I really appreciate it. I'm

confident that going through with the surgery is what's best for me. The doctor mentioned that I should do this sooner rather than later and that she has a rare opening in her schedule next week if I was ready, which I am. Of course, this is where you come in."

Without hesitation, I tell her that I'll be on the next plane to New York if she needs me to be there and support her during the recovery.

She makes a hushed, nervous chuckle before she speaks again. "Actually, my mom is going to come stay with me for the first week to help make sure I'm taken care of. The problem is that my doctor wants me to take approximately two to three months off work to let my body totally heal from this major surgery."

Blowing out an exaggerated breath, she continues, "Do you know how I mentioned earlier that work has been crazy? Well, my timing for this leave couldn't be any worse. Unfortunately, we're unable to hire a temp to take my place because of the timing, complexity, and confidentiality of everything going on right now. Look, I know this is way too much to ask of you, but would you be willing to come to New York and take over my position while I'm out on leave? You can live in my apartment with me, rent-free of course. Oh, and you'll be making the same salary I was while you're here, so it's a great opportunity for you to save up for something you may be dreaming about." Nic swallows so loudly into the phone after her tirade of rambling that I can actually hear it. "Brielle, I really need someone in my position that my boss and I can both trust."

For once in my life, I'm left speechless, which is an enormous miracle in its own right. "Let me get this straight, Nic, you want me to get on a plane, move out there with you for potentially three months, and take over your position as an EA in this major firm. A firm and position I know nothing about, except that you work a crazy number of hours for a boss you've been complaining to me about for the past eight years since you've been there. Am I missing anything?"

"Look, I know it's a lot to ask, but if anyone can pull this off and save me, it's you. As for my boss, Kennen, he really is a decent guy once you accept the fact that he can just be a little more complicated to deal with than others at times." A loud sigh comes across the line. "I promise that I'll get you as prepared and caught up as I can before you start, and I'll be at home ready to assist you as you go along. Please, Brielle..." she says with true panic ringing through her voice.

I must be completely out of my mind when I respond right away, but I know in my heart it's what's needed "Okay, yes, I'll do it, Nic, but you'll owe me big time for this one."

"Really? You'll drop everything and do this for me?" Her relief is clearly evident in her tone.

"Why not? It's a new chapter in my ever-changing novel of a life. Just let me know what day you need me there by, and I'll be there."

Crying tears of joy, she blurts out, "You're the BEST, and I can't wait to see you on Saturday. I love you so much."

Three days, that's only seventy-two hours to dismantle and pack up my life here in Denver to start over in the Big Apple. Luckily, after my last disastrous breakup, I let my bastard of an ex keep pretty much everything we had purchased together, and rented a furnished apartment. That just leaves my clothes, a few boxes of personal items, and some treasures I collected over the years, which is somewhat depressing if you think about it long enough.

This is a ridiculous decision for me to make on the spot, but that's what true friends do for each other, right? We're there for each other through the good, the bad, and the absolute batshit crazy.

Standing up from my chair, I head to the refrigerator in search of that much-needed bottle of wine. "I love you too, Nic. Go get my room ready, and I'll see you very soon."

## Chapter 2

Please let Nicole be in better humor today, as she seemed really out of her element yesterday, which is unlike her. She is an amazing assistant, but we don't have time for any type of melodramatics right now. With our major merger coming up, and the board totally up my ass about the so-called "state of my mental health," I can't let anything get in the way of what we need to accomplish. Nicole has been with me since the very beginning when I opened my firm approximately eight years ago. It took us a while to find our stride, but once we did, we became quite the team.

Knowing that I tend to be a difficult person to deal with, I try to keep to myself whenever possible. Most people don't understand what it's like to have a mind that is constantly running and calculating nonstop as mine does. My parents had me tested when I was young, as I was advancing extremely quickly with each milestone that came up, and my IQ at the time was already an astonishing one hundred and sixty.

While other children my age were doing crazy stuff like trying to swing as high as they could before making their death-defying leap off the swing set without breaking their legs, I was busy calculating the odds of said catastrophe based on the angular velocity and speed. I tried pointing this out to them, but they would just laugh at me and run off, saying that I was a weirdo and had "a few screws loose." Needless to say, I didn't make many friends throughout my years of schooling. I advanced through the grades rapidly, making me one of the youngest teenagers at the time to earn my doctorate in mathematics from MIT at the age of sixteen. You might ask how one celebrates such a monumental accomplishment at that age? Well, let's just say it wasn't with champagne. No, after graduation I got my driver's license, and my parents bought me my first car. Most people can't even fathom it when I tell them I graduated college prior to being old enough to drive, let alone being able to drink.

Continuing my education, I earned my CPA status while working back at home for my father at his small accounting firm for six years until he retired. To say I was bored out of my mind was a complete understatement, but he needed my help, and I was barely old enough to work anywhere else. After he retired, I decided to start my own firm focusing on high-profile commercial clients with complex accounting situations, putting me in a position that would challenge my restless mind.

Stirring me out of my thoughts, I hear Nicole knock on my door three times precisely on schedule at eight o'clock, and then she enters, as per our daily routine.

"Good morning, Kennen."

"Good morning, Nicole. Are you ready to get started? As it's shaping up to be another long one today." I do feel somewhat bad that we have been putting in so many hours as of late, but she's as dedicated to this firm as I am and doesn't seem to mind.

"I'm ready. But before we begin our daily briefing, can I

speak with you regarding an urgent matter?"

Her face looks somewhat pained as she says this, which makes me extremely uncomfortable with what she's about to speak to me about.

"Yes, of course." In my head I'm reverting back to my earlier thoughts of anything going on that could get in the way of our current situation.

"I know we don't usually speak about our personal lives, but I've been suffering with a serious health issue for a long time now. After a recent visit with my doctor, she's highly recommending that I have surgery to help alleviate what has been going on and to address a potentially serious issue."

"Really? I had no idea you were suffering with anything. When would you need to have the surgery?"

She's no longer making eye contact with me when she puts the final nail in my coffin. "Next Wednesday." She chances a quick look in my direction. "I apologize, as I know it doesn't give you much notice, but the doctor has expressed an urgency with getting the procedure completed."

I try to clear the lump that suddenly forms in my throat before I continue. "Wow, that's *really* soon, Nicole."

"Unfortunately, there's more…"

Getting up, I start pacing my office, as I can't imagine this situation getting any worse. "More?" I say, a little more pointedly than I probably should have.

"There's also a required recovery period after the surgery that I'll need to take time off for."

At this point I'm afraid to even ask her my next question for fear of what response I am going to get. "How much time will you be needing exactly?"

"Kennen, I think you should sit back down while we

continue this conversation. Also, before you say anything, let me reassure you that I already have a plan in place."

Damn, it's worse than I thought. Reluctantly, I walk back over to my chair and take a seat, as I have a feeling a toxic missile is about to be launched my way. "Please just say what you need to, Nicole, so we can move on from this completely unnerving conversation."

"Right, so she is requesting that I take up to three months off to fully recover, with this being a major surgery. I know everything is in a crucial state around here right now, and that the timing for this—"

"Absolutely sucks," I say quickly, cutting her off.

She cautiously looks over at me. "Yes, that, but I hope you'll understand that I'd never put you in this situation unless absolutely necessary. As I mentioned, I do have an arrangement ready to make sure my absence will barely even be noticed."

The only thing I really heard her say in this whole conversation so far was that she was going to be gone for up to three months. "Please tell me this is some kind of sick joke, Nicole…"

Taking a seat across from my desk, she continues by reminding me how there's no way that we could hire just anyone to come fill in with our current situation going on. But that she has found the perfect person to take over her position while she's out.

"Perfect, right. Might I ask who this amazing person is who will be able to come in and take your place, considering you're the only one who knows every detail of our upcoming merger, our firm, and my situation? And will also be able to do so in the next five days?"

"Her name is Brielle Bisset, and we've been the best of friends since we were little. She is extremely trustworthy, a quick learner, and an extremely talented and successful small-business owner. There's no one who knows me better and how important my work ethics are to me. I know that she'll be willing to continue to do things as you and I have been currently doing them, without any questions asked."

Taking an additional quick breath, she continues, "My plan is to spend this entire weekend putting together all the information she will need. Along with this, she'll be staying with me in my apartment, so we'll have the ability to communicate daily about what things are going on and how to prep for the following day. I really think that this will work out, Kennen. I just need you to continue trusting me the way you have for the past eight years."

A fierce pain starts surging in my head as my new daily migraine begins to pound it's way to the surface. Out of frustration, I slam the pen I'm holding on the desk, making her jump slightly. Looking for any type of relief I can get right now, I begin rubbing my temples and close my eyes for a minute. I know none of this is her fault, and that she is trying to give me a solution to get us through this, but I can't help but feel like this is going to end up in complete disaster.

"I don't know, Nicole; this has corporate catastrophe written all over it. While I know this isn't something you planned for, you've still put me in a really unfavorable position right now. You have been an important representative in this merger with AW Advisors, and I am not sure how they are going to react having to communicate with someone who knows absolutely nothing about either of our firms respectively."

I give her a questioning glance. "Not to mention how our board is going to feel about bringing a stranger in right now, knowing how I react to change in general, let alone such a substantial one for me. You know that they already believe that I am quickly losing my mind, and are trying to prove that I need medical intervention to continue my responsibilities as CEO."

They will not let anything stand in the way of this merger happening, as the payoffs for everyone involved are profoundly lucrative. So they fear that if Austin and his team at AW Advisors catch wind of my "mental instabilities," they will rescind the deal and move on elsewhere. The thought of all this makes my stomach churn.

Keeping my eyes open at this point is excruciating, as the daylight pouring in from the windows feels like lasers slowly cutting open my skull. Maybe I should go back to the doctor to try some medications, but I have no desire to continue being their guinea pig to examine how a mind like mine works.

Being everyone's "curiosity" since I was six years old has been exhausting. I just want to be left alone to continue to develop and grow my business that I've worked so hard to achieve.

Nicole stands, interrupting my thoughts. "Kennen, I can't apologize enough for adding to an already extremely stressful situation. I do understand how much pressure there is from the board to make this merger with AW finish seamlessly, and I promise to do everything I can to make sure that Brielle will be prepared to ensure that."

Very confidently, she places her arms across her chest, looks at me, and continues, "Actually, I think that she'll be a breath of fresh air for you, Kennen. In fact, I think you're going to end up loving her."

Was that a slight smirk I saw on her face when she

finished basically telling me that I need change in my life, and that I would end up loving this change? She has gone totally off her rocker, and I don't even know what to think at this point.

"Nicole, I can assure you that I have no need for the number of changes that are about to take place, nor do I have any interest in loving anyone. I am curious, though, why would Brielle drop her life at the drop of a hat for the next three months to bail you out of your situation, anyway?"

She looks straight at me, totally serious this time. "Kennen, I know that you prefer to keep to yourself, and I understand why, but when you have a true friendship like I have with Brielle, you'd do anything in the world for each other. She knows about the complications I have been dealing with, and there's nothing she wants more than to be here for me so that I can finally get the relief I have longed for. She truly is an amazing person, and all I ask is that you give her a chance to assist us on making this work for all parties involved."

Well, what the hell do I say to that? She's right, I don't understand that level of friendship, as I tend not to let anyone get close to me enough to experience it, nor do I plan to.

"Okay, Nicole, I'm counting on you to make this work, so please don't let me down after all of these years."

I see her sit back down in front of me, slightly more relaxed, thanking me for trusting her with this.

My mind starts running through everything that we are going to have to do to get this to happen. "I will also need you to get all of her details settled with human resources before she can start."

"I'll be sure to get with them this afternoon during my

lunch hour and see that everything is worked out by the end of day today." She smiles at me, trying to calm my nerves, I'm sure.

"When exactly do I get to meet this amazing friend of yours who's going to rescue us from this catastrophe?"

"She's flying in tomorrow morning from Denver, and then I'll spend the remainder of the weekend getting her up to speed on everything. We'll both be in on Monday so that she has a day to shadow me, and we can all meet to put our plan in place."

Oh, this just keeps getting better. What kind of successful business does this Brielle girl have that she can leave it all behind and move halfway across the country for the next few months? I assumed she was living here at least somewhat locally, but then again, you know what they say about assuming things, and I don't typically try to make an ass of myself.

I hope Nicole has made it known to her the number of hours we are going to be putting in, especially in the next three weeks leading up to the merger. If she thinks she will be able to manage Nicole's position and keep up with her current business, she is in for a big surprise.

Sitting back up in my chair, I look right at Nicole, hopefully signaling to her that I am done with this conversation and ready to finally get our normal day started.

"Okay, so are you ready for today's rundown, then?"

Perfect. That is exactly what I was hoping she would say. Man, the thought of starting over with a new assistant in a matter of days, who doesn't understand me the way Nicole does, makes me want to get sick.

"Yes, we're already behind and have a busy schedule ahead of us, so let's get started." With that, I grab the stack of folders she has placed on my desk, along with my favorite pen, and we begin. We spend the next thirty minutes reviewing my meetings for the day, going over reports, and signing any documents that need my approval.

Finished now, Nicole starts to walk away, but right before she opens the door to leave, she turns to me with her eyes narrowed.

"Kennen, please be on your best behavior Monday, and be nice to Brielle. I know how you are, and I don't need you scaring her off on the first day." Then she is out the door before I even have a chance to respond.

Damn, I know I tend to be a little short at times, but does she really think that I would intentionally be mean to someone before I even get to know them? Who am I kidding, I totally would. I've got three days to get myself together and prep for what is going to be the most crucial upcoming month in my career. What I really need to do is find a way to calm this thunderstorm in my head before my meeting starts in half an hour. It's definitely going to be an ibuprofen breakfast kind of morning.

## Chapter 3

*Brielle*

The past few days have been a complete whirlwind trying to get everything wrapped up with my clients, my belongings, and everything else that was my former life. I think I've tried to talk myself out of this situation at least a hundred times. But every time I do, I replay Nic's voice in my head, and how desperate she sounded when she first called to how relieved she sounded before we hung up. Not only do I need to do this for her, but for a potential new start for me. Sometimes it takes an idea this crazy to light a spark so bright that I can't see anything getting in the way of what my future holds.

Luckily on the three-hour flight out there, I was able to get some rest, because in true Nic fashion, she booked me the earliest flight out of Denver, which was at six thirty this morning. I know she wants to get in as much time with me as she can before Monday, but that also meant I had to get up before the roosters started crowing and be in a rideshare by four o'clock a.m. to get to the airport in time for check-in and security.

Considering the double take the TSA agent gave me when he looked at me and then back again at my license, I can only imagine what the state of my hair and outfit looked like this morning. He acted like he hasn't seen someone who has been averaging about three hours of sleep a night for the past seventy-two hours, hasn't had coffee yet, and is in a state of absolute uncertainty with what life is going to look like for the foreseeable future.

I was going to express my thoughts about all of this, when I realized that it could potentially cost me my flight, and I could end up with a totally different version of Saturday than I'd planned. Being locked up in airport security isn't on my bucket list, sorry to say, nor are stripes all that flattering to my figure.

We've just touched down on the runway at LaGuardia Airport in New York, and the pilot announced that we may resume using our electronics, so I grab my phone to text Nic.

> **Brielle:** New York. The eagle has landed.
> **Nicole:** I'm so excited! I can't believe you're HERE!
> **Brielle:** Whoa, tone it down, girlfriend, you're going to have to get some caffeine in me before we get crazy with all of those caps and exclamation points.
> **Nicole:** I'll get you whatever caffeinated cup of death you want on the way back to the apartment to cheer you up, I promise.
> **Brielle:** Now you're speaking my language. I'll meet you at the luggage carousel in about 15.

I really should've thought more about how this living situation was going to play out with her being the early bird to my night owl, but everything always works out in the end, right?

Making a quick stop, I splash some ice-cold water on

my face to try to encourage some energy that must be hiding somewhere deep down in my bones to wake me up before I see her. After scratching half of the skin cells off my face with the infamous cheap paper towels they stack by the sinks, I take a look in the mirror and gasp at how horrendous I actually do look. Now I feel slightly bad for having questioned the poor TSA guy earlier this morning.

It's not like Nic hasn't seen me in worse shape than this before. I seem to recall her holding my hair and cleaning me up as I sang my praises to the porcelain god after a dreadful evening out with my good "friend" Jim Beam. Compared to that, I'm looking like Miss Colorado right now; at least, that's what I'm going to go with, anyway.

Standing up straight, I blow the multitude of stray hairs that fell from my messy bun out of my eyes, grab my carry-on, and pray that they haven't lost my luggage.

As soon as I reach baggage claim, I see her looking as poised and put together as ever, my best friend. "Nic, over here!"

"Oh my gosh. I can't believe this is actually happening, and you're really doing this for me." She quickly scoops me up in a big hug, and once she releases me, I can see a slight shine to her eyes. That's all it takes to melt my heart and remind me that I made the right choice by coming out here.

We wait for what seems like forever for my luggage, which could've made its way around the world and back at this point. Then we head towards the exit to wait for our rideshare to arrive.

If I weren't awake already, the artic-like wind that came blasting at us as soon as the sliding glass doors opened up made sure of it.

"What I can't believe is that I just moved out of

Denver, where it was still in the upper twenties yesterday, to New York, where the temperature is only slightly higher. Couldn't you have lived somewhere in the tropics, Nic?"

She turns to me and chuckles. "You'd be cold on the surface of the sun. So I'm not sure if I lived on an island in the Caribbean that it would've made a difference."

"Touché."

Our driver, Tony, arrived and loaded the entirety of my pathetic life into his trunk, and we were off. Giving Nic a gentle nudge, I remind her that she owes me my morning wake-up juice if she doesn't want me turning into "friendzilla" before we make it to her apartment. Knowing how I am, she quickly asks Tony if he can make a stop at the nearest coffee house drive-thru on the way to our destination. Of course, with the promise of a big tip, he's happy to oblige.

As we pull up to the speaker at the drive-thru, I roll down my back window so I can place my order. They have an advertisement lit up on the menu board for a new "Iced Sea-Salt Chocolate Caramel Frappé," so it's an easy choice for me to make. I place my order, and we pull up to the window so I can pay and grab the heavenly goodness that awaits me. Wouldn't you know that Tony decides to take that moment to break his silence to let me know that I'm crazy to order an iced drink with the wind chills being what they are.

Turning to my right, I look at Nic, who is currently sporting a huge grin. "Stop. Don't even say anything. Apparently, I have a tattoo on my head that says 'please mess with me. I'm a morning person.'" With that, we both burst into laughter and wipe the tears forming in our eyes.

The building where Nicole lives in the financial district is only about twelve miles from the airport, but apparently in New York traffic that means it's about a fifty-five-minute adventure.

Downtown Denver, while big, and crowded in its own right, is no comparison to the level of madness and sheer number of cars and people in this city. Now I understand why Nic spends the exorbitant amount of money on rent that she does, so that she can walk to work and everything else she may need for that matter.

After what seems like a lifetime since my day started, we arrive at her apartment. Actually, "our apartment" for the next few months at least. After we send Tony on his way, and I deduct a star on his rating for being a smart-ass, we gather all my items and head up to get settled.

Her apartment hasn't changed since my last visit, with its gray paint color on the walls and minimal yet contemporary décor. In the small living room sits a simple black couch with two perfectly placed white and silver throw pillows, a glass coffee table, and a glossy white entertainment center.

She has a galley-style kitchen, which may accommodate two people at once if neither of them minds bumping cheeks when opening the refrigerator. Seeing as she lives here alone, it doesn't seem to be an issue for her.

We walk together towards the back of the apartment, where there are two bedrooms, one slightly larger than the other, and a very tiny bathroom. I almost fell over when she told me what she pays in rent every month equals a couple of months' pay for me.

Even though she ends up putting most of her salary into this apartment, I know she doesn't mind since she never goes out and rarely splurges on anything.

After getting my luggage put away in her spare bedroom and taking a shower to wash off all the air travel, I feel refreshed and like a new person. I can tell that Nic's anxious to jump right into my training, as she's sitting on the couch with a bunch of paperwork and a large binder already spread out in front of her across the coffee table.

"Okay, Brielle, are you ready to get started? I have so many things to go over with you and so little time to do it."

Smiling, I relax down beside her, wrapping my arms around her shoulders, just wanting to soak up all her fears and anxiety.

"First, let's talk about how you are feeling with everything you are about to go through. I can't imagine how difficult a decision this must be for you, Nic. I really am excited for you and the potential of a majorly improved life though."

"I'm not going to lie; I'm pretty nervous about going through with the surgery and the long recovery afterwards. Although, I think what I'm most concerned about is the mass that she found on my ovary and the chance that it could be cancerous." She sighs and slumps down on the couch.

"Nic, I have a strong feeling in my heart that it won't be, and I'll continue to pray for that to be the outcome. As for the recovery, your mom and I will be by your side to help you with whatever you need. We will be your 'beck and call girls' and wait on you hand and foot. Don't get any big ideas in your head though that I'll be wearing some risqué nurse's uniform, as you'll have another thing coming...I do have *some* standards." I give her a nudge and a quick wink.

Slowly, a smile gently spreads across her face, and she lets out a quiet chuckle. "Thanks, Brielle. I don't know how I will ever begin to repay you for all of this, but please know that I am beyond-the-moon grateful."

"Don't thank me yet, as I still have to try not to royally screw up your career in the next three months, ugh." I meant that to be a humorous statement, but I suddenly feel a noticeable pressure forming in my chest just thinking about the reality of it all.

Giving her a slight smile, I continue, "Alright, girl, let's get this party started so I can at least pretend to know what I'm doing come Monday morning."

Nicole sits back up, all businesslike, and grabs the binder off the table. "First and foremost, the most important thing you need to understand is how to work alongside Mr. Kennen Davis."

I try to recall all the past conversations we've had over all the years she's been working with him. None of them ever seemed incredibly positive, from what I can remember. "Right. So what is his deal, anyway? You never seem overly excited when you talk about him, yet you've never given me any details."

"Let me preface this conversation with the fact that he really isn't as bad as I've been making him out to be. And the sooner you understand how to deal with his personality and work ethics, the easier it will be."

I quickly squint my eyes at her and then burst out laughing. "You do realize, Nic, that I'm only going to be here for three months. How long did it take for you to get to the level you are at now with him?"

"You're going to have to figure it out quicker than I did with everything we have going on at the office right now. Luckily for you, I have already put in the time and have worked out most of the kinks. You're welcome." She lifts her chin and nose in the air and then winks at me.

"Okay, okay, give me the skinny on this complex boss of yours." I'm ready to keep this conversation moving along so that we aren't here all night talking about some psycho CEO who will probably chew me up and spit me back out on the first day."

"To start with, Kennen is a genius, specifically in mathematics," she says matter-of-factly.

"Aren't they all considered geniuses in today's corporate world?" I say, rolling my eyes at her.

"No, Brielle, I mean he actually *is* a genius. He's had an astonishing IQ since he was just a child, skipped many grades throughout school, and graduated with a doctorate in mathematics from MIT at the age of sixteen."

"Holy crap, are you serious? I'm sorry, but that's crazy smart." I inwardly cringe, wondering what this guy is going to think of me, considering I never even completed college and have no corporate career experience to offer him.

"Yes, and speaking of serious, he is always extremely serious. He's not known to sit around the watercooler with the staff to catch up on the latest reality TV show predictions." Why she's looking at me with her eyebrow raised is news to me.

"Not only that, but he runs everything in his life in a very structured, excessively organized, and repetitive way. He needs his daily routine to be mapped out down to the minute, literally."

I'm beginning to realize why he and Nicole seem to work well together overall, as she has many of the same tendencies, although not to his extreme.

Then there's me...

I blow out a slow breath. "Okay, is there anything else I need to know about him?"

"Alongside his intelligence, his mind runs nonstop with visions of numbers, calculations, etc. It's as though he can't ever turn it off, nor see clearly, which is probably why he is so intently focused on everything he says and does." She briefly pauses to make sure that I'm paying attention to each detail she is sharing with me.

"Moreover, he has recently been suffering with frequent severe migraines. He believes it is just due to the intensity of stress he has been under with the upcoming major merger we're about to go through." Putting her hands on her lap, she looks over to the window for a moment, slightly lost in thought.

Well, that I can relate to, at least. Wait, what? "Um, Nic, did you just say that you guys are about to go through a major merger? When is that supposed to happen?"

Hearing the slight panic in my voice, she refocuses her attention back on me. "I was going to get to that next, but I want to make sure that you have some understanding now of how and why Kennen may react to the significant disruption that my leaving will bring. All I ask, Brielle, is that you are as patient as you can be with him, and not to take anything he may or may not say personally." Her pleading look tells me that this is going to be important for me to do for her.

"Of course, I'll definitely keep that in mind, Nic."

Taking a moment to collect her thoughts, as though this is a conversation she wished she weren't about to be having with me, she begins to fill me in regarding the merger that's about to take place.

"Kennen started his firm eight years ago after leaving his small family business. He did this with the vision of becoming one of the most sought-after accounting firms for major corporations that have extraordinarily unique situations across the nation. Of course, it didn't take long for things to take off once businesses learned of his highly intellectual mathematical and problem-solving skills. Fast-forward to about a year ago when he was approached by Austin Williams of AW Advisors. They are one of the most well-known up-and-coming financial advising companies according to *Forbes* magazine. Since then, we have spent countless hours over the past year meeting, calculating, and negotiating to see this merger come to fruition. They strongly feel that with the combination of each of their companies, they'll become the powerhouse of financial accounting and advising of the country." She smiles proudly at the thought of what this could mean for the firm she works for.

"Wow, Nic, this seems like a monumental merger. It makes sense now why it's been adding such intense stress on Kennen, and yourself for that matter." I rub the back of my head, trying not to get a migraine myself just thinking about all of this.

Stressing the importance of the finalization of this merger for all of them, she lets me know that until it's complete, we have to be extremely careful that any and all information regarding this stays confidential.

"I understand, Nic. Make sure this deal finalizes, and not a peep about it to anyone…or else." I let out a laugh to try to lighten the mood a little bit around here, as this is getting somewhat intense.

"I know, I'm sorry. I feel like I'm about to throw you to the wolves. Unfortunately, there's still more I need to tell you." Biting her bottom lip, she looks down at her lap.

"Somehow this does not surprise me at this point, Nic," I say, laughing internally to myself at the continuing dramatics of this situation.

Continuing, she lets me know that lately at their merger update meetings with the board, Kennen has been considerably more combative and vocal about each of the details. I'm assuming due to all the additional stress on him.

With this, she explains that he's been unable to hide the amount of pain that he's in when one of his unrelenting migraines consumes him while in front of them. Undoubtedly, this is causing a considerable amount of concern with the board, with him being the face and intelligence behind the company. Apparently, they've also been placing intense pressure on him to go back and see his doctor, but he refuses to for some reason unknown to her.

"Brielle, there's so much financially at stake for each of these board members and stockholders that I wouldn't put it past them to do whatever they needed to do to make sure this deal goes through." She covers her eyes with her hands and lets out a slight groan.

I am beginning to understand why she didn't mention any of this to me on the phone when she asked me to come do this for her, as she probably knew I might not have agreed as quickly as I had. I'm already here, though, and I'll need to find some kind of ethereal miracle to get all of us through this before it completely implodes.

"No pressure, I see…" I look at her, my eyes open as wide as they can go.

"Although, as crazy as it sounds, Brielle, I have a feeling that having you take over for me might be a good thing right now."

I'm glad to hear her being positive for once, but I have no idea where she is going with this.

As if reading my mind, she continues, "I feel like with you being a new face around there, you might be able to casually find out if, in fact, the board has any plans that Kennen doesn't know about. Everyone knows who I am, so they tend to stop talking when I come around for fear that I would go back and let him know any office happenings he may be unaware of. You would have to do this quick, though, as word will travel fast that I'll be gone and that inevitably someone would be replacing me."

"Great, so not only do I have to play the superhero and save the company, but I also need to be the accomplice to some sort of deep spying operation?" Oh, this is getting good; maybe I should write a literal "new chapter" in my book of life after all of this.

"Brielle, since when have you not been up for an adventure?" Now she's the one grinning.

"Adventure, right. So when does this big merger deal happen, anyway? I need to know the minimum number of days I have to keep my crap together."

"The final meeting to sign off on the merger takes place in three weeks down in Seaside, Florida, at the AW Advisors office. I was supposed to attend with Kennen, but I'll obviously not be able to travel, being out of the office in recovery. So you, my friend, are getting your warmer destination. For two days, anyway." She gives my thigh a quick pat with a beaming smile.

"Saved the best info for last, did you? Now you're speaking my language."

She can't help but laugh, as she knows she needed to have that cherry on top for me to have some inkling of motivation in this deal. My guess is that I'll probably be spending most of that time in an air-conditioned office, but just being near the salty sea air will recharge my soul, so I'll take it.

A thought occurs to me then. "Wait, I'm surprised that Kennen wouldn't want the final meeting to take place here at your office in the city."

"Kennen, as I mentioned, doesn't like change at all. More so than that is his distaste for traveling. He's made Austin and his team fly up here for every meeting up to this point, so they agreed we would travel down for the final one to keep things equitable."

That's totally understandable and lucky for me that I'm coming in at the end for the trip south to Florida. I can't begin to imagine the size of the smile on my face right now.

"Or," she fires back, as if seeing into my thoughts, "unlucky for you if you don't keep this whole deal from imploding in the next few weeks for me. At which point, we will both be packing, but not for any type of tropical vacation."

Always the buzz killer this girl is.

We spend the rest of the afternoon going through an obscene amount of information, making my head spin faster than a hurricane in warm tropical waters during the summertime.

Apparently, she's also assigned me homework consisting of memorizing daily tasks and how to print out numerous account ledgers, graphs, and reports that Kennen will require on a daily basis. Along with this is a full list of names with pictures of important board members. I must give her credit, as I have no idea how she put all this detailed information together for me so quickly. She keeps reassuring me that she'll also only be a phone call away during the day and free to help in the evenings when I get home.

I am concerned, however, that she is going to be so

worried about what is going on at work that she won't focus properly on her healing. Surely, talking about work is a welcome distraction for her right now, but it's apparent after all our conversations today that it has also been a significant stressor in her life. This is even more reason for me to be here right now and to find a way to successfully help her through this.

We both ended up calling it a night around midnight, as we couldn't keep our eyelids open a second longer before succumbing to sleep. For once, I ended up crashing hard and was able to get an amazing full eight hours of rest before I heard Nic up and about the following morning.

Wandering out, probably looking like a character out of a zombie apocalypse movie, I see Nic eying me curiously with her mouth curled up in one corner.

"Morning, Brielle, you're looking a little disoriented this morning, girl. Were you able to get some rest?"

"Look, not all of us who wander are lost exactly, we're just looking for caffeine." As I say this, I'm heading straight for her kitchen in hopes of finding anything but the horrifically bland turmeric tea she drinks.

Of course, she can't help but laugh at me now. "We're going to have to work on your morning routine, as you're going to have to leave the apartment at seven twenty each day in order to be able to get into the office by seven thirty. It will take you all of thirty minutes to get everything prepped and ready for the day before you have your daily review meeting with Kennen at exactly eight o'clock."

"You cannot be serious right now." I think I might cry at this new realization. I just need to remember that this isn't forever, it's only for three months, or sixty workdays and I don't even want to know how many hours…I can do this.

"Come on, go get ready, and we'll go out and find you some sort of fancy frappé machine to keep here at the apartment so you can get your instant fix from now on. I have a few items I need to pick up before my surgery also, so we'll get a little shopping in this morning, and then it's back to the books, missy."

After I'm ready and no longer looking quite as scary as I did earlier, we head out on our shopping adventure. Nicole does make good on her promise to buy me an amazing frappé maker that I can use to blend my favorite icy goodness to my heart's content. For her we find a large heating pad, some incredibly fluffy long socks, and some supersoft loose-fitting pajamas for her to lounge around in after her surgery.

As we're on the way home, Nicole gets a text from her mom with a list of groceries for us to pick up before she arrives Tuesday morning. So she motions for us to head over to the small local market around the corner from her apartment to grab what we need.

"Oh, Brielle, I'm not sure I can go through with this. I hope I'm doing the right thing here," she's saying as we're checking out with the requested groceries.

"You've got this, girl. Just keep in mind how much better you're going to feel once you're all recovered."

Her lips press together as she looks down at her wallet. "I meant taking you in tomorrow to meet Kennen and handing over the future of my career to you."

Ouch.

"Right, that too."

## Chapter 4

"Brielle, hurry up. We can't be late! You have exactly three minutes before we have to walk out of this apartment." She's impatiently banging on the bathroom door like a crazed landlord trying to collect back rent. All while I'm in here trying to get ready for one of the most important days of my new life here.

I take one last glance in the mirror at my business-style messy bun and makeup and wonder why it takes so much work to achieve the perfect "natural look." Gliding on a pop of color with some tinted lip gloss, I open the door and walk right past her, knowing my timer is rapidly running out.

On the way towards the front door, I grab my freshly made iced chocolate-chip frappé and my satchel and turn to face her.

"Let's do this," I say with a little more gusto than I think she was expecting.

"Wait. What are you wearing?" She's eyeing me curiously.

I look down at my outfit, which consists of navy-blue high-waisted wide-leg slacks, a white graphic tee that says "CRE8TIVE VIBES" in teal, a canary-yellow fitted blazer, and matching high heels. Peering over at Nicole, I see that she's wearing her usual color palate of black, gray, and white in the form of a turtleneck, a blazer, and fitted slacks.

"What?" I say, putting my hand on my hip. If I'm about to take on this monstrosity of an ordeal for her, I would hope that she wouldn't ask me to change who I am and what I look like. I'm in graphic design and marketing, for crying out loud; being artsy is always going to be a part of me.

She catches up and nudges me out the door so she can lock it behind us. "Oh, man, Kennen is going to have a field day with us today," she mutters quietly under her breath.

## Chapter 5

*Kennen*

It's seven twenty, and I've been pacing around my office for the past hour already. I can't believe today is the last day that Nicole and I will be working alongside each other for the next three months. She knows how much I loathe change, and all it took was one unexpected conversation a few days ago to upend everything I have grown accustomed to since I opened my doors here.

It's not that I don't trust her; I do. It's just that I have never even had the opportunity to meet this Brielle person before she starts today. I have no idea who she is, what her qualifications are aside from what little Nicole mentioned, and if I can trust her with my business during this critical time.

Trying to remind myself that this is Nicole's best friend since childhood, my guess is that they would be similar in a lot of ways. Although, it's not that I would know much about friendships considering I have never really had any worth noting.

I look down at my watch again, and just as it turns seven thirty, I hear them walking into the private reception area in front of my office where Nicole's desk is, right on time. Technically, we don't meet until eight o'clock, but

I'm hoping that she will bring Brielle in earlier so that we can all meet before we start going over today's schedule.

Of course, now filled with sheer curiosity, I'm wishing I would have designed my office with glass somewhere other than the back wall, which contains floor-to-ceiling windows. There will be no chance for me to get a glimpse of her before they walk in the way it's currently set up.

A familiar knock at the door immediately brings my attention that way, and I quickly stand up straight and run my hand down my tie to make sure that it is smoothed out perfectly.

Clearing my throat quickly, I reply, "Come in, Nicole."

Nicole enters first, calming my nerves only slightly at the sight of her familiarity. Although I can't get a good reading off the current look on her face right now.

"Good morning, Kennen. I would like to introduce you to Brielle Bisset, who will be taking my place as your executive assistant until I return after my recovery."

After her introduction, Brielle walks in and right up to me with an enormous smile plastered on her face, her hand extended to shake mine. "Hello, Kennen, it's so great to meet you."

Whoa, first of all, she is absolutely nothing like what I was picturing, and the complete opposite of Nicole, in fact. Where Nicole is tall with dark chocolate brown straight hair, dressed in her normal polished attire, and more reserved, Brielle is an explosion of color, shorter, has sandy blonde hair tied up in some sort of knot on her head, and worst yet, she appears to be the overly outgoing type. Great.

Secondly, I notice while she has an impressive sturdy handshake, her hand feels so small in mine and incredibly soft that I don't want to let it go. I'm not sure that I understand what's happening here, but I need to refocus and regain control of myself, so I drop her hand quickly.

"Brielle, it's a pleasure to meet you. Welcome to Future Figures Accounting."

She takes a step back so that she is side by side with Nicole again, keeping her eyes locked with mine the whole time. "Thank you, I'm excited to get started so that we can let our girl here get the relief and recovery she needs."

"Yes, of course. I trust that Nicole has gotten you up to speed on everything that we currently have going on?" I say as I walk back around my desk to sit down.

"She definitely has, and I'm still on total information overload from everything she has shared with me over the past two days." She nudges Nicole in the arm and laughs.

Nicole walks back to the door. "We'll be back in here in twenty-five minutes to start our normal day. I'm going to get Brielle set up on the computer and show her how to prepare your daily schedule." She seems like she can't get out of my office quick enough right now, which makes sense considering what the expression on my face must be relaying to her.

"Thank you, Nicole, I will see you both then."

Brielle starts to walk out after Nicole, but then she turns to me right before she gets through the door. "It's all going to work out, Kennen, you'll see." She gives me a genuine smile, then gently shuts the door behind her.

Taking what feels like my first breath since they walked in, I realize that I am at a total loss for words right now.

## CHAPTER 6

*Brielle*

I'm just approaching Nic's desk after leaving Kennen's office, when I look down at her and see signs of sheer panic written all over her face. "What's wrong, Nic? I thought that went over pretty well considering everything you told me about him, or *almost* everything, anyway."

She's looking up at me, slightly confused. "I don't know what to think, Brielle. I've never seen him react to anyone like that, and I'm hoping this change doesn't send his stress level over the edge. Also, what do you mean by 'almost' everything? I thought I gave you a rather good rundown on his personality and expectations."

I quickly snicker and then clear my throat. "Personality, yes. What you failed to mention is the fact that he looks like a real-life version of Clark Kent, with his strong stature, defined jaw structure, and dark wavy hair. All he'd have to do is trade in the *Men in Black* suit he's wearing for a crimson-colored cape and he'd be screen ready. I don't know what I was expecting, Nic, but it most definitely wasn't that. As your best friend, you should have given me ample warning."

Oh, now I am getting "the look." Whatever she's about to say next should be good, probably popcorn worthy even.

"Seriously, Brielle?" She's shaking her head. "I can't believe that's what you're focused on right now. Besides the fact that he is not my type to begin with, I've never looked at him as anything other than my boss."

Sighing, she points to the chair next to her for me to sit down, signaling that this conversation is officially over. I take a seat and only half listen to her explain how his daily schedule needs to be organized, but to be honest, I can't help but think about our handshake. Maybe it was just my imagination reacting to seeing him for the first time, but it almost felt like a transference of energy slipping from his spirit into mine. Never experiencing anything so intense before, I couldn't take my eyes off his the whole time this was happening. I wonder if he had the same feeling, and that's why he held on to my hand a little longer than you normally would in that situation.

"Brielle, do you have any questions on how to use the scheduling system now?"

Crap.

"No, I think I should be able to figure it out. What else will I need to have prepared for the morning meetings?" Fear hopefully not spreading across my face.

She gives me a reassuring smile. "Great, then you'll also need to organize all of the daily accounting reports for our company and for any of the clients that he has meetings with that day. I would typically go into our system and pull the information myself, but while you are here, I have instructed other staff members to provide that to you by email at the end of each day. Unfortunately, we don't have enough time to teach you the accounting software, as it's on a pretty complex platform."

"Thank you for making this as uncomplicated as you can for me. I appreciate it."

Nic starts back in, letting me know that I'll also be required to sit in on all of Kennen's meetings to take notes, answer his phone calls, and take messages. Also on my to-do list will be the responsibility of booking all his appointments and any travel that may arise.

I feel like I should be able to handle all of this, and I'm so glad she is not expecting me to learn any new complicated software in a day. The only elephant still in the room is exactly how I'm supposed to complete operation "Save Kennen & Finalize Merger," which we can't talk about here in the office. Some things are best left to be discussed over a bottle of Merlot this evening, anyway.

"Got it, Nic. Let's start printing all of these reports and then get today's folders organized, as it's almost time for our eight o'clock meeting with Kennen."

This makes her smile. "Great, I was wondering if you were paying attention to the time. I can't stress enough that things need to run like clockwork around here, and you can't ever be late for anything."

Alright, I see how today is going to go down. There'll be more tests to come, I'm sure. At least I passed this first one, though, so there's that.

We gather up everything we need and stand to go into his office. Nic takes a deep breath as she walks over and then knocks on his door exactly how she did earlier. He calls us in, and I can't help but feel my heartbeat speed up ever so slightly as soon as I see him again.

I'm trying not to make it too obvious to her how much of a reaction Kennen is having on my body right now, because she is going to be watching my every move today. She's obviously already concerned that I'm not focused on the task ahead of me, and what that could potentially mean for her job when she returns a few months from now.

I sit down in the chair next to her, ready to take any notes that will help me for the upcoming days when she won't be here by my side to take care of everything.

She begins to go over each upcoming appointment for the day in significant detail, using the reports and comments that are in each folder. Kennen is sitting with his arms crossed on his desk, listening very intensely to everything she is saying, almost as if he is recording it to his memory. It's fascinating to watch, so of course I do what any other somewhat flustered woman would do…I gawk uncontrollably at him. That is, until he looks over at me sternly when Nic takes a break to switch to her last folder, and he catches me feverishly watching him.

He knows he totally busted me when he turns back to Nicole and speaks. "Does Brielle understand how all of this is put together, which information in the reports will be pertinent to each specific client, and the order in which we go through things during this meeting?"

Clearly, I'm sitting right here next to her, so I'm not sure why he couldn't have just asked me that when he was looking right at me.

Apparently, what I felt when we first met earlier was completely one sided based on his reactions to me thus far. It's probably better to snuff out that flame now before it becomes a wildfire in me that grows out of control faster than I could extinguish it anyway.

Nicole confidently replies, "Yes, we went through all of it together this morning, so she should be prepared and ready to go tomorrow."

He looks right at me, narrowing his eyes slightly. "We'll see."

The rest of the day goes by in a flurry of meetings, training, and quick tours of the overall office, which is considerably larger than it looks when you first enter the space off the elevator.

By the time we're finished making sure everything is set up and ready to go for tomorrow, I'm utterly exhausted and ready to get back to the apartment. Nicole heads into Kennen's office to answer any last questions he may have and to say her goodbyes. I grab my satchel and empty thermos from this morning and look around the space that is about to be my new home for the next few months. The pressure to get all this right is suddenly weighing down on me so heavily that it is hard for me to breathe.

Nicole and Kennen both walk out of his office with looks of concern and a slight sadness to them. As she grabs her things and shuts everything down, I turn to Kennen, trying to be as cheerful as I can.

"I look forward to seeing you bright and early tomorrow morning."

"Brielle," is all he says to me in an irritated voice before he turns back and heads for his office, closing the door behind him with unnecessary force.

What. An. Ass.

My shoulders slump in defeat, knowing this guy is going to be one of my biggest challenges yet.

I find my way back over to Nic, ready to get home and destress a little. "Are you ready to go, Nic?"

She takes one last look at her desk and sighs. "Yes, ready or not, it's time to go."

On the way back to her apartment, we stop by her

favorite local Chinese restaurant for some takeout since neither of us has the energy to cook tonight.

After we get home and get changed into some comfy clothes, we crash on the couch with our take-out containers, and I eagerly start to eat. I know neither of us stopped long enough to take a lunch break today, so she has got to be as starving as I am, but she's simply just moving the rice around in her box.

"Are you alright, Nic? I know this is all a lot for you right now, but this is the last meal you can eat until after your surgery on Wednesday, and you're going to need all of the energy you can get."

"I know you're right. It's just all so overwhelming right now." She leans over and rests her head on my shoulder.

"Do you know how I'm always saying that everything happens for a reason, well, it does, and we just need to trust in the timing as best we can. You have a whole new healthy future ahead of you, Nic," I say, trying to be as warm and assuring as possible for her right now.

"I know you're worried about work, but I promise I'll do everything in my power to make sure that you have a position to come back to in a few months, okay? That is, if Kennen doesn't kick me out of the office before then, HA." I give her a quick nudge.

She gives me a quiet laugh. "Thanks so much, Brielle. I apologize if I have been on edge with you about it. I know you'll do great."

She sits back up, grabs her chopsticks, and quietly starts eating, which brings me some much-needed comfort. We spend the next thirty minutes in silence, finishing our meals and watching some insane reality show she let me put on.

I could really use a strong drink tonight, but instead I should probably get a good night's rest and have a clear head for my big day tomorrow.

"I'm going to head to bed. Try to get some rest, please, Nic."

"Thanks, you too. And, Brielle, don't forget, the early bird catches the worm." She gives me a hug and wink.

"Out the door by seven twenty sharp, I'm on it. Now will you leave me alone so I can go get my beauty sleep?"

I bolt upright in bed after dreaming about being attacked by birds, only to hear the sound of them chirping loudly next to my head. I look at the clock, seeing that it's only six, and I try to figure out what the hell is going on. The chirping keeps getting louder the longer it goes on, until I finally figure out that it's coming from my phone.

"Nic, what the hell?" I yell as I figure out that she has created this obnoxious new alarm for me on my cell that wasn't there previously.

She opens my bedroom door and begins laughing hysterically. "I told you last night, the early bird catches the worm. Get it, *bird?*"

Ugh, it's way too early in the morning for this kind of nonsense. "Got it. Getting in the shower now, mother hen. Speaking of mothers, what time is yours arriving today?"

"She should be here around nine o'clock. Now quit stalling and go get ready."

I'm trying to figure out a way I can get back at her for that stunt as I begrudgingly drag myself into the bathroom to get ready.

About an hour later, I'm showered, dressed, and as ready to go as I am going to be. When I walk out into the kitchen, I see that she has already made me a thermos of my favorite frosty heaven.

"Caffeine in one hand, and self-assurance in the other," she says with conviction as she hands it over to me.

I quickly suck down a huge mouthful, needing to satisfy my fix. "Okay, fine, you're forgiven."

"Glad to see you have toned down your look today, Brielle." She's leaning against the counter with an eyebrow raised.

"What do you mean? I did. These are all pastel colors." Today I'm sporting my "Just Peachy" peach graphic tee with white lettering, a seafoam-green fitted blazer, white slacks, nude heels, and of course my work bun. "Just because I don't have the closet of Morticia Addams doesn't mean I can't be stylish."

Shooting me a death glare, she throws my satchel at me. "Go to work, Brielle."

Walking out of the apartment building, I take in a deep breath of the crisp morning New York air, along with fumes from about a million vehicles passing by. I can't wait for the trip down to Florida for the last meeting to get some fresh seaside air. There...that is the motivation I need to kick-start my first day alone on the job.

I get to the office a few minutes earlier than required thanks to Nic kicking me out before I even had a chance to look at the time again.

Sitting down at my desk, I turn on the laptop and open the email to print out all the reports for the day, then pull up his calendar to see what appointments he has. It looks like he's only got four meetings today, so hopefully that should be manageable. With the reports in hand, I go to spread them out so that I can get them separated into their respective piles. Unfortunately, in the process I knock all of today's clients' folders off the desk, sending papers fluttering through the air like a butterfly migration.

My heart instantly sinks.

I'm frantically running around grabbing papers as quickly as I can, suddenly grateful that Kennen can't see what's going on outside his office right now. When they're all collected, I head back to the desk, sighing at the monumental mess I've made.

I slowly start piecing folders back together, but with the minutes quickly passing by, I'm beginning to panic that I won't get this organized as needed before my meeting with Kennen. Catching a small break, I notice that there are dates on most of the documents, which helps, but this one folder alone has over twenty pages in it.

I work as expediently as possible and get down to the last few pages of the final folder with less than five minutes left. Now complete (and hopefully in the right order), I pause before I grab everything I'm going to need for the meeting. Looking down at my now disheveled outfit, I try to straighten myself up as best I can. I can't even imagine what my hair looks like at this point, but there's no time for worrying about that minor detail.

With everything in hand, I carefully knock on Kennen's door a few times and wait for him to call me in.

"Come in, Brielle."

I inhale a deep breath, put a delighted expression on my face, and walk in. He's standing by his window, half turned, looking out over the city, once again in another black suit clinging perfectly to every toned curve of his body. Just seeing him there ignites a sudden spark down my torso.

Damn, he is most certainly not hard on the eyes, which makes up for his lack of personality, thankfully.

"Good morning, Kennen, how are you today?"

He walks over to his chair and sits down, then leans

back before responding, "I'm as well as I can be, and you? Is everything going okay so far this morning?" His brows furrow together as he tilts his head slightly.

Damn it, did he hear all the commotion I made out there this morning, or is this his way of just being polite and responding to my question? I am going to go for the latter. "Oh, everything is just peachy so far." I smile excitedly at him.

He casually looks down at my chest, suddenly sending a rise of heat up to my cheeks, until he looks back up with a slight smirk and an eyebrow raised. "Peachy, huh?"

Oh my gosh, I didn't even think about the shirt I had on when I made that comment. He must think I am a complete lunatic at this point. I try my best to play it off. "Great icebreaker, right?"

He sits back up and resumes the position he took yesterday while listening to Nic go through all the daily information. "Right. Why don't we get started, then, shall we?"

Fumbling my way through the folder for the first client of the day, I try to remember the key bits of information Nic spoke about yesterday when she went through each one. I try to read through the report as quickly as I can to be able to say anything, but I'm at a loss.

"Brielle, did you have the opportunity to review any of the information in these reports this morning before our meeting?"

I quietly sigh in defeat. "I had all intentions of reviewing them this morning, but it took me a little longer to get everything organized for the first time doing it on my own. I apologize."

"I'll let it slide today, Brielle, but please make sure that you are properly prepared for tomorrow's meeting."

"Yes, I will. Thank you for your understanding."

We continue to go through the basic information for each of today's upcoming clients; then we both stand once it's completed.

He walks over to the door and opens it for me with a stare so intense it sends shivers down my spine. Wow, this guy really lives in a serious state of mind at all times, doesn't he?

I walk towards the door and pause before I go out when he mentions my name. "Yes, Kennen?"

He asks me to walk the client back to his office when he arrives for his nine o'clock meeting, and to make sure that I'm ready to attend and take detailed notes for him.

"Of course, if there is anything else you need before then, please let me know."

He nods and then disappears behind his door again like a stealthy shadow in the night.

When I get back to my desk, I see that I have a missed text from Nic.

> **Nicole:** How's everything going so far?
> **Brielle:** Seriously? I haven't even been here for an hour yet.
> **Nicole:** I can't help it, so please just give me an update.
> **Brielle:** Have you been pacing around the apartment since I left?
> **Nicole:** No.
> **Brielle:** You lie…
> **Nicole:** BRIELLE.
> **Brielle:** It's going…probably about as well as your bowel prep is right now.
> **Nicole:** OMG, Brielle, what happened?

**Brielle:** It just started off shitty, but then it cleared up, so the rest of the day should be good now. Get it...

**Nicole:** What are you, like 12? Now get back to work and don't mess anything up.

**Brielle:** That's the plan, enjoy your liquid diet, and I'll see you tonight.

Our first client of the day arrives about five minutes before the meeting starts. From the notes that I looked at quickly after my meeting with Kennen, it looks like his name is Charles Bishop, the CEO of a new tech start-up that I'm unfamiliar with. Nic's comments in the file also state that they have met a couple of times previously, and that this is supposed to be the commitment meeting for Mr. Bishop to sign a contract with us.

"Mr. Bishop, it's a pleasure to meet you. May I get you anything to drink before we go into the meeting?" I say as I shake his hand. He looks to be slightly older than I am, maybe by about five years or so.

"Please, call me Charles, and unless you've got some Patron Silver hidden somewhere, I'm all set, thank you," he says with a quick wink.

I like this guy already and make a mental note to talk to Kennen about maybe stocking some mini assorted spirits that we can offer clients. It's the little touches that make companies stand out, right?

He grins at me. "I'm sorry, but I don't believe we have met before. You are? I've only dealt with Nicole previously."

"My name is Brielle Bisset, and I'm filling in for Nicole while she's temporarily out on leave." I give him a warm smile.

"Are you ready to get the meeting started?" I continue, not wanting to be late and upset Kennen any more than I already have.

"After you, Brielle." He stretches out his arm towards the door, indicating that he will follow me.

Quickly grabbing my trusty notepad and pen off my desk, I go ahead and knock on Kennen's door. He calls us in and comes around his desk to greet Charles before he has him sit down in one of the chairs in front of him.

Taking a seat in an armchair that he has in the corner of his office over by the window, I get myself ready and notice Charles look at Kennen and then back at me.

"Hey, no one puts Brielle in the corner." With a smirk on his face, Charles taps on the top of the chair next to him, indicating that he wants me to come and sit by him for this meeting.

Kennen watches me like a hawk as I cautiously rise out of my chair and walk over to take a seat next to Charles.

Unable to resist, I turn to Charles and take a chance that he will appreciate my shared movie humor, and with the most dramatic voice I can come up with, I say, "Thanks for sticking up for me and coming to my rescue, Johnny!"

Kennen looks at me, eyebrows raised, like I've completely lost my mind, and he is about two seconds away from firing me on the spot. That is, until Charles bursts out laughing so hard that, one after another, tears begin streaming down his cheeks.

"Oh my gosh, Kennen, no offense, as Nicole is great, but you've got to keep this one around." He's wiping his eyes with the backs of his hands now, trying to calm down.

Kennen clears his throat, wanting to get this meeting back on track. "Right, so about our proposal and client agreement. I thought we could spend the first portion of the meeting going through the data and forecasting reports that we have put together for you. And then afterwards, I would be happy to answer any questions you may have."

Suddenly serious, Charles looks at me and then to Kennen. "Actually, that won't be necessary, Kennen."

I can see the look of panic on Kennen's face, thinking he just lost this potential new client, and if so, most likely because of me.

"Man, I can't remember the last time I laughed that hard, especially with all of the stress of getting this new start-up going. Thank you, Brielle." Charles snatches the pen out of my hand and turns to Kennen. "That sealed the deal for me. Where do I sign?"

They go through the final details and sign the contract, then we all stand up to say our goodbyes, and Kennen walks Charles out of his office. When he returns, he closes his door, sits back behind his desk, and motions for me to sit my ass back down.

Crap, here we go...

"Brielle, what were you thinking? Did you seriously just create your version of a scene from *Dirty Dancing* with a potential new client that we have spent the past two months trying to get on board? You could have cost this company a lot of money just then." He starts rubbing his eyes like one of his migraines Nic told me about is about to surface.

I sigh. "I know, I really am sorry, Kennen. It was very unprofessional of me to do that. I consider myself a rather good judge of character, though, and after our introduction when he first arrived, then him saying that phrase, I couldn't resist." I take in a quick breath then continue, "And I thought—"

He cuts me off. "Let me guess, you thought it would be

an icebreaker?"

I slowly exhale. "Again, please accept my apology. I'll be sure to keep to silent note-taking for the remainder of the meetings today."

As I get up and head to the door to leave his office, he leans back in his chair, both arms on the armrests and his head tilted back. "Brielle, thanks for helping me close the deal today."

"You're welcome. You do have to admit, though, it was pretty damn funny, wasn't it?" I smile, then head out the door, but not before I see the corner of his top lip slightly curl.

Huh.

We get through the rest of the day without any other major issues, thank goodness. I've never had such a stressful day at work before, and this is only day one without Nic.

I'm getting the sense that there is more to Kennen than what he lets on. Outwardly, he acts like he enjoys playing the irritable, demanding CEO role, but I can't help feel like deep inside there is just a regular guy who can't remember what it's like to laugh and have fun every so often.

From what Nic has told me, he's spent the past eight years devoting every moment, thought, and desire into his company. That along with the fact that he prefers to keep himself isolated and not share it with anybody (that I know of, anyway), I can't imagine how lonely he must be.

I open the emails with tomorrow's reports and print them all before I leave so that I can take them home with me to review this evening. Although it's the last thing I want to do tonight, I feel like I owe it to Kennen to take it a little more seriously and be better prepared.

Kennen is on a phone conference that is scheduled for

another thirty minutes, so I shut everything down and clean up my desk. Feeling rude leaving without saying goodbye, I decide to write him a quick note and stick it to his door before I turn and head out.

Walking back to the apartment, I know that a barrage of questions are coming my way. The only real one, though, is how much of today am I really going to share with Nic, knowing her surgery is bright and early tomorrow morning. Then a thought hits me. Kennen wouldn't text her, would he?

## Chapter 7

Well, today has definitely been interesting to say the least. I was really hoping for a smoother transition from Nicole to Brielle, but who am I kidding, as there was no way that was going to happen. I knew Nicole wouldn't be able to fully prepare her in three days' time. I just didn't think today would go down quite like it did.

It still blows my mind that they are so incredibly different, yet the absolute best of friends. Brielle is not like anyone I have ever met, and I'm not sure what to make of her yet. She seems totally out of her element here even though I know she's trying.

I still can't get over the stunt she pulled in our meeting with Charles this morning, and although I will never admit it to her, it really was funny as hell. I'm not sure what their interaction included outside my office before they came in, but I realize now she totally had him pegged right.

When was the last time I laughed so hard that I cried? Hell, when was the last time that I laughed in general? Has it really been so long that I can't remember? Damn, I really am *pathetic*.

My company has consumed my life all these years, and it's all I have been focused on. It isn't as though I'm complaining, because had I not put in the amount of hard work that I did, it would never have gotten to the level it is today. A level that is about to explode once the merger takes place in less than a few weeks.

I must admit, though, it would be a welcome change to have someone by my side other than co-workers to share all of this with. It's too bad I'm so damn stubborn that I won't let anyone aside from my family have any type of relationship with me, or friendship for that matter. The couple of times I have tried in the past have always ended in disaster with someone getting hurt, that someone usually being me.

Nicole has been the closest thing to a friend that I have, come to think of it. Although, we never do seem to share anything regarding our personal lives; it's always just about the business. I was totally shocked to find out that she has been suffering for a long time now. Friends would share that kind of information with each other, though, wouldn't they? What am I saying? Even if we aren't technically friends, as her boss who spends over nine hours a day with her for all of these years, you would think I would have noticed. Thinking about this makes me feel like total shit right now.

Apparently, my once slight barrier against the outside world has turned into a wall so thick that even sunlight has no chance of penetrating it. When she gets back, I really need to try to make more of an effort to pay better attention to her, as it's the least I can do with as much as she does for me.

It's time to call it a night and get home a little bit earlier for once since it's been a long day, and I am completely exhausted. I have a feeling I am going to need all the energy I can gather up to get through another day of Brielle and all the craziness that seems to follow her.

I pack up my briefcase with my laptop and all the documents for the merger that I have already gone through at least ten times. It makes for good reading material, though, in the middle of the night when I'm wide awake anyway. Turning off the office lights, I open my door and notice a sticky note stuck to the middle of it. What the hell? Who would leave a note stuck to my door instead of sending me an email or a text even? When I take a closer look at it, I notice that it reads "I'm 25% funny and 85% bad at math. ~ Brielle." I quietly snicker at that one, pull it off, and put it in my briefcase.

I think I'm going to have to expect the unexpected with Brielle, but maybe that won't be such a terrible thing after all...

After walking the four blocks back to my apartment building, I take the elevator to the penthouse apartment I purchased a couple of years back. It's really more than I need, considering I spend most of my time at the office, but it allows me to have the whole floor to myself where no one can bother me, leaving me in my own little world, as I like it.

The first thing I modified in the apartment after I moved in was the windows. I had to have floor-to-ceiling powered shades installed so that I can block out all the lights and chaos of the city when it all becomes too much. The irony in that is the view is what any normal person would love most about this place.

I ended up hiring a designer to help furnish it, as the whole process was very overwhelming for me. We kept the overall color scheme mostly light, as my mind can't handle an overabundance of color or busy décor. I also had her finish one of the two spare bedrooms as a study and the other as a small home gym for me since I never have visitors anyway.

Laying my briefcase on the desk, I head to my bedroom to get changed into my usual home attire of heather gray sweatpants with a white T-shirt, and then make myself some dinner.

Like a creature of habit, at seven thirty I begin my preparations for the following day by making my lunch, laying out my suit and tie, and shining my shoes. With that all complete, I wash up and then go settle down in my study in hopes of taking my mind off the day with a great novel.

I'm just about to start reading when my cell chimes on my desk with a new text notification. This is odd, considering hardly anyone ever texts me, especially at this time of night. I get up and grab my phone and unlock it to see it is a text from Nicole, interesting.

> **Nicole:** Hello, Kennen, I'm sorry to text you so late. I was just wondering how everything went today? Brielle hasn't said much since she arrived home tonight, so I thought I'd check in with you before my surgery tomorrow.
> **Kennen:** It wasn't a typical day in our office to say the least.
> **Nicole:** I apologize to have put you in this position, Kennen. How did the meeting go with Mr. Bishop? Did he end up signing the client agreement?
> **Kennen:** Actually, I think you should ask Brielle that question.
> **Nicole:** I did, but her only response was to grab a bottle of wine and ask me if we could watch Dirty Dancing on Netflix tonight. I have no idea

what that means, so I figured I'd ask you.
**Kennen:** That sounds about right.
**Nicole:** I still don't understand.
**Kennen:** Goodnight, Nicole, and good luck with your surgery tomorrow.
**Nicole:** Okay, thank you…good night, Kennen.

I toss my phone on the couch and can't help the smile that quickly spreads across my face. I don't know what I like more, the hilarious response that Brielle gave Nicole to her question, or the fact that I kind of wish I were there watching it with her.

## Chapter 8

*Brielle*

It's Wednesday morning, which means it's Nic's big day today, and I'm so nervous for her. I couldn't even imagine being faced with such a life-altering decision as young as we both are.

I got out of bed early so that I could get ready and still spend a few minutes with her before she needs to leave for the hospital. She was in rare form last night, most likely due to the stress of it all. She was relentless in asking me all about work, but I tried to be as vague as possible so as not to upset her even further. While I was watching *Dirty Dancing* and downing glass after glass of wine, she was busy texting on the phone, but I'm not sure who with. She didn't seem overly pleased when she was done, unfortunately, but she didn't mention anything about it afterwards, so I let it be.

When she finally walks out with her hospital bag in hand, I run up and wrap my arms around her in a big hug. "It's all going to be okay, Nic. This is the last day of your old pain-filled life, and the first day of your amazing new beginning."

"I know you're exactly right, Brielle. In a few hours this will all be a thing of the past, and the healing will begin

I'm ready." She gives me a faint smile, remaining in my arms.

A moment later "Momma-T" (that's what I've always called Nic's mom, Tina, since she has always been like a mother to me) joins us in the kitchen, looking like she might get sick with the concern she is obviously feeling for her daughter.

Walking over to us, I grab her arm, pulling her into our now group hug, like a mother bird wrapping her wings around her babies, trying to protect them. I try to will all my strength into them as we stand there holding onto each other. They need my support now more than ever, and I'm honored to be able to be here for them as they have always been for me.

"Is anyone up for a quick breakfast?" I ask, trying to break up some of the tension surrounding us.

Nic looks at me angrily and then pouts. Oops, I probably shouldn't mention food to a starving girl with an angry uterus.

"Sorry, Nic…Momma-T, can I get you anything? It's going to be a long day for you also."

She looks at me with appreciation in her eyes. "Some tea and toast would be perfect, thanks, Brielle."

Making us both some toast, and tea for Nic, I go sit down at the little table in the dining space. "Momma-T, please make sure that you text me as soon as you have any updates today."

"I sure will. And thank you for everything you are doing for Nic. It's very much appreciated." She takes a sip of her tea and gives me a warm look of gratitude.

I grab today's reports from my satchel and start reviewing them, since I spent the evening drowning my sorrows of the day in some very tasty vino and being all starry-eyed watching Patrick Swayze dance instead of working.

Luckily, it looks like Kennen only has two meetings on the schedule, so maybe I'll have some time to start my undercover operation. I would love to have some good news to report to Nic when I go visit her at the hospital this evening. Of course, this also means that I can't create any more unnecessary catastrophes today. I blow out a slow breath and remind myself that I can do this. I'll just put on my invisible cape and with any luck save the day.

Nic walks up behind me and puts her hand on my shoulder. "Wow, look at you working at home already. You'll be just like me in no time at this rate."

"Ha…" I look up at her and laugh. "I just want to be a little more prepared today."

"Brielle, are you ever going to tell me what happened yesterday?"

"Nice try, girl. You just need to focus on you today and don't worry about work. Everything worked out in the end. Just trust me, okay?"

"Okay, fine, but will you please just tell me if we got the account with Mr. Bishop? And then I will leave you alone." She gives me some seriously pleading eyes.

"Yes, we did. And by the way, you're welcome."

Her shoulders start to relax. "Wait, what do you mean you're welcome? I've been working on trying to close that deal for a while now. That guy has been a tough nut to crack."

I have to laugh, which only adds to her confusion. "Let's just say that I sealed the deal for you guys yesterday in record time."

"Okaay then. I'm not sure how you did that, but I guess a thank-you is in order." She looks over at the clock and realizes that it's time for them to head to the hospital and sighs. "Alright, Mom, let's go and get this over with."

I get up and give her one last hug before she leaves. "Alright now, go show your uterus who's really the boss."

"Thanks, Brielle. I love you, my crazy friend."

"I love you too, Nic, and I'll come visit you as soon as the warden releases me from Alcatraz or when I escape…whichever comes first." I give her a wink and a squeeze.

With that, she and her mom are out the door and off to start what is the first day of the rest of her life.

When I get to the office, I notice that the sticky note I left Kennen is no longer there, so I assume he saw it last night before he left. Now, whether he found the humor in it, or it ended up crumpled like a ball in the trash, I have no idea. Maybe I'll start leaving him one every night to see if I can wear him down and be the reason for him to truly smile one of these days.

Luckily, this morning's preparation goes quite smoothly, so I confidently knock on Kennen's door, ready to get this day started. As he calls me in, I can only wonder what his disposition will be today.

"Good morning, Kennen. Did you have a good night?"

He looks straight at me, his eyes decidedly focused on mine. "I have a feeling my evening was less eventful than yours." He quickly clears his throat. "By the way, how is your head feeling this morning, Brielle?"

Wait. What is he talking about? How would he have known that I might be ignoring a slight hangover lingering over my head like a thundercloud ready to burst, when I've only been in his presence for a total of two seconds? Either mind reading is a part of his genius abilities, or...*shit*. As all the pieces start fitting together, I can't help but look away from him, breaking our intense eye contact.

He must have been the one texting Nic last night. But if that's the case, I would think she would have confronted me after he was done filling her in on the day's drama. What if she was too disappointed in me to bring it up? Then again, why did she ask me about that account again this morning? Ugh, why do I feel like I'm still being tested here?

I try to shove all these thoughts into the closet in the back of my mind in hopes that he doesn't try to open that door, and everything comes spilling back out on top of him.

"My head is fine, though I'm not sure why you would be asking me that to begin with." I walk towards his desk and take a seat in front of him, trying to play off like I don't understand what he's talking about.

"Do you know what time it is, Brielle?"

I look at my watch and see that I'm actually two minutes early, so I'm not sure what the issue is. "Yes, Kennen, it's seven fifty-eight. Is there a problem?"

In a rigid voice he replies, "Exactly, our meeting starts at eight o'clock, not at seven fifty-eight."

Wow, who pissed in his Cheerios already this morning? "I'm sorry. Would you prefer that I leave and come back two minutes from now?" Apparently, this answers my question to the effect my sticky note had on him, or worse yet, he can see through my earlier denial.

"It's fine. Let's just get started since you're here already." Then he leans on his desk, resuming his expected position to mentally record my daily dump of information.

"Great, well, let's see, your first appointment is at ten this morning with Robert Smith. Although he wasn't due back in to meet with you until the end of the quarter, he's become aware of a potential money-laundering scheme within his firm and urgently needs to meet with you. All the most recent ledgers can be found in the folder, along with the accounting reports from last month that we completed for him."

I put that folder down and grab the next one. "Your second meeting is at one o'clock with Kari Mallorey, of Kari Mallorey Interiors. She apparently has a new concept for an expansion of her current business that she would like to discuss with you, and how it would affect her overall financial goals and current responsibilities."

I pause and look up at him, noticing his face has gone stone cold and statue-like.

"It sounds like an interesting day for you today, but at least those are the only two meetings you have, so there's that," I say brightly, trying to cheer him up out of his sudden rigid mood.

He rubs his hands down his face, sighs, and then looks back up at me. "You have no idea, and when did this meeting with Kari get scheduled, anyway?"

"She called in yesterday and said it was really important that she see you regarding this matter, and that she'd only be in town for today. I apologize. Was it wrong of me to schedule the appointment?"

He stands up and walks over to the window and stares out at the city, suddenly looking sorrowful. "It's fine. Is there anything else we need to go over, Brielle, or are we done here?"

I hate to even ask this since it seems as though I've once again messed something up by scheduling that appointment. "I was also wondering if it might be possible for me to sneak out of here a little earlier today, so that I may go visit Nicole at the hospital before visiting hours are over?"

He turns to me and puts a hand over his forehead like he totally forgot. "Nicole, right, of course that would be fine. Can you do me a favor and order some flowers for her this morning? We have a corporate account with a local florist, and their contact info should be on the vendors list on Nicole's computer somewhere."

"Yes, I will take care of that for you as soon as I return to my desk. Is there any particular type of flower arrangement you would like me to get, and any specific note that you would like to put on the card?"

"Brielle, you've known her longer than I have. Please just pick something you think she'd like, and put my name on the card. I'm not good at this kind of thing, which is why I always had Nicole do it."

I give him a quick chuckle and then stand up and head for the door. "A man of many words, I see. Don't worry, I'm on it."

If he can't take the time to pick out something special for her and write a sweet note after all she has done to support him over all these years, I'll make sure she gets the biggest, most obnoxious bouquet of flowers they have.

After his incredibly stressful first meeting today, which could end up with the authorities getting involved, I send Kennen my notes recapping everything that was discussed. I think this would be a great time to take my lunch and seek out any gossip in the break room.

I'm in the very back corner of the kitchen area, heating up some amazing homecooked leftovers that Momma-T sent me in with today, when I suddenly hear a couple of girls walk in and take a seat at the long community table to eat their lunches. I keep still in hopes of hearing what they're talking about even though I believe I'm out of sight enough where they wouldn't be able to see me anyway.

"Did you hear that the merger may not happen now?" says the first girl very suggestively.

Quietly, the second girl replies, "Oh my gosh, are you serious? Why not? What's going on?"

"I overheard a couple of the board members saying that AW Advisors somehow found out about Kennen's mental state deteriorating as of late, and now they have some deep concerns about continuing with the merger, with him being the CEO of our company and all."

She continues, "Yeah, so the board is totally freaking out now, knowing that if this falls through, they're going to miss out on a huge payday."

The second chimes back in, "What can they even do about it since Kennen is the one who owns this company?"

"Okay, you have to promise me not to repeat this to anyone…"

"Oohh, this is getting juicy; I promise, just keep going!" The second girl lets out a quiet squeal.

"So they said if Kennen continues to refuse to seek medical help, and any doubts continue to grow at AW Advisors, then at the next board meeting, they are going to…"

Beep, beep, beep.

*Shit,* the microwave timer is going off, not only letting me know that my lunch is ready, but it's also put the girls on high alert that they are not alone.

"Hello, is someone there?" the first girl calls out.

I pull out my phone to pretend I was so engulfed in my social media that I wasn't paying attention to them. I grab my lunch and walk around the corner with my head down, knowing that after hiding out and listening in on their conversation, I'll be eating at my desk today.

"Oh, hey, how are you guys doing?" I try to say nonchalantly like I didn't hear words that could potentially destroy my new boss and the company he's worked so hard to build.

The first girl clears her throat. "We're doing great, thanks."

"So glad to hear that. Enjoy your lunch, ladies," I say as I walk right past them with my face still buried in my phone.

I can't get back to my desk fast enough, and as my ridiculous luck would have it, Kennen is just walking out of his office when I arrive and sit down.

"Why are you eating in here, Brielle, when we have a really nice break room for that on the other side of the office?"

Suddenly, realizing that I'm not even hungry anymore, I close my container and quickly put it back in my lunch bag. I can't even imagine how frazzled I must look to him right now, so I try to sit up straight before I reply.

"Actually, I was just putting it away, as I seem to have lost my appetite."

He's squinting his eyes at me now in question.

Thinking quickly, I add, "Oh, I'm just worried about Nic, as I haven't heard any updates yet, and I thought I would've heard something by now."

"I see, well, let me know if you hear anything. I am going to take my lunch and eat at home today, and then I will be back before my next meeting arrives." With that, he walks out of our area and he's gone.

He seems even more distant than normal today,

especially after I told him about his meeting with Kari Mallorey. However, I don't have time to overanalyze it right now, as I have bigger problems on my hands. Such as why haven't I heard an update on Nic yet, and how the hell am I supposed to save this merger from impending disaster?

Thankfully, and with perfect timing, I hear a ping from my cell:

> **Momma-T:** Hey, sweetie, I just met with Nic's surgeon, and she's in recovery finally.
> **Brielle:** I've been so worried. Why did it take so long?
> **Momma-T:** Apparently, the scope of the surgery ended up being quite a bit more complicated than they had anticipated.
> **Brielle:** Poor Nic. Do they think she will be okay now that they're done?
> **Momma-T:** They are very hopeful that once she heals, she'll feel a lot better, but they can't make us any promises at this point.
> **Brielle:** Understandable. Please give her a big hug for me when you get to see her, and I'll get there as soon as I can later this afternoon.
> **Momma-T:** I sure will. See you soon.

While Kennen is away, I spend the time trying to figure out a plan of how to get him out of this whole mess with the board. I'm so agitated that the microwave interrupted the girls' conversation before I could get the remainder of the information from their gossip session. I'm not familiar with the legalities of the corporate world to know what standing the board has in taking action against the owner of the company. But what I am familiar with is how much it would probably destroy Kennen if this merger fell through, or worse yet, they took this company from him.

I'm suddenly distracted by the distinct sound of high heels clicking on the marble tile down the hallway, coming towards me. I look at the clock and notice that it's almost time for Kennen's next meeting, which is odd since he hasn't returned to the office yet. From what I know of him so far, I know he is absolutely never late.

Appearing like an exquisite model working her way down the runway during fashion week, a tall, redheaded, amazingly dressed woman with legs as long as the Nile River, whom I assume is Kari Mallorey, walks up to my desk.

I stand up to greet her, and Kennen comes around the corner and heads over towards us. Now ignoring me, she turns to him once he's made his way across the space to where we are standing, with a huge grin on her face.

"Kennen, it's so good to see you. It's been way too long." Kari leans over and gives him a quick kiss on the cheek.

"Kari," is all he says to her as he quickly looks over at me for what I am assuming is my reaction to this surprising interaction.

Kari notices and then slowly turns back to me, this time taking a longer look at me. "And you are?"

I reach out my hand to shake hers, but she simply looks at it and then back up to my face, waiting for me to answer her question. "Hello, Kari, my name is Brielle Bisset. We spoke on the phone yesterday. I'm filling in for Nicole while she's out on leave. It's a pleasure to meet you."

"I see you've lowered your standards some since I last saw you, Kennen," she says to him as if I weren't even in the room with them.

Did she seriously just say that? I'm guessing the expression on my face right now must be reading somewhere in between shock and ready to catfight. She must have arrived here by broomstick today instead of a rideshare, that's for damn sure.

Kennen looks over at me with a slightly apologetic look in his eyes, as if he knows how insulting that comment was. "Kari, let's go to my office and get this meeting started, shall we?"

I go to grab what I need to take notes for the meeting, even though I'd rather grab a pencil and poke myself in the eye with it right now, when Kennen stops me.

"That's okay, Brielle. You can sit this one out. Thank you though." He walks towards his office and opens the door for Kari.

As she walks by me, she murmurs under her breath so that only I can hear her, "Yes, Brielle, there's no need for notes when there won't be much discussion going on in there anyway." She winks and then heads into his office with a smug look on her face.

Well, this is certainly an interesting change of events, and I'm at a total loss for words right now. I know Kennen's personal life is none of my business, but I can't help but feel slightly disappointed. Is she really the type of woman he would want to spend time with? I mean, aside from the fact that she is drop-dead gorgeous, her personality is about as desirable as a cauliflower pizza crust. Overall, it looks amazing and as tempting as the normal pizzas, until you take that first bite, and it instantly leaves a vulgar aftertaste in your mouth that doesn't seem to go away.

I really don't want to be sitting out here while they're

both in there doing who knows what, but I also can't call any attention to myself by walking through the office after my encounter in the break room earlier. Maybe now is a good time to think about a plan in case the board does try to do something insane at the next meeting before the merger is supposed to take place.

After an hour of unsuccessful research on the computer and trying to keep my mind from wandering to places it shouldn't be going right now, the door to Kennen's office finally opens, and Kari walks out with him following close behind her.

She smooths her hair and then turns to Kennen. "It's been a pleasure as always, Kennen." When she walks past me, all she does is let out a quick cynical laugh, and then she's gone.

I look up at Kennen, who's now got his hands on his hips and blowing out a slow breath.

"It's been quite the day today again, hasn't it?" I say, trying to lighten the mood.

"It seems to be the new normal around here lately, unfortunately." Then he looks at me with eyes full of exhaustion. "Brielle, why don't you go ahead and call it a day and go visit Nicole a littler earlier, as I don't have anything else pressing that can't wait until tomorrow."

Wow, he must really be off-kilter now, as we all know that no one typically leaves this office until all the day's work is complete. I'm not going to complain, though, as there's currently a fog so thick in the air here now that it would take a serrated knife to cut through it.

"Thank you, Kennen, I really appreciate it, and I know Nic will also."

"Please send her my regards," is all he says before he goes back in his office and closes the door yet again.

After texting Momma-T to let her know that I'm about to head that way, I decide to take another chance and leave Kennen another quick note, and then I head for the elevator, ready to see my "new" best friend.

## CHAPTER 9

*I* feel like my life has recently crossed over into an episode of *The Twilight Zone*, and I have no freaking idea how to get out of it.

How is it that at the most crucial point in my well-established career, everything is suddenly in a downward spiral headed straight for the depths of hell? First, Nicole leaves, next there is Brielle, and then just as my obnoxious luck would have it, Kari enters the madness out of the blue.

What are the odds that Kari would call on the first day that Nicole isn't around to divert the appointment to some unknown date and time? I almost feel like I'm being set up here, but for what, I have no idea. Then she shows up here in typical Kari fashion, and I have to wonder why I ever let her into my life in the first place. Was she always this much of a pretentious snob? I did feel like crap about how Kari treated Brielle, as she has been nothing but kind to me, even with me shoving my demanding personality down her throat. Brielle might be driving me crazy, but she most certainly hasn't been insulting to me, or to anyone else for that matter. If anything, when I take a minute to really think about it, she's probably the most unselfish, giving person I have known. How many people would drop their life in an instant, move halfway across the country, and take on a new career with a complicated boss, just to make sure that her best friend is taken care of in her time of need? Damn, I need to stop being such a prick to her and figure out how to reel in this tempestuous mind of mine a little better.

I really need to refocus and get back to work, as all these distractions are taking my visions and unproductiveness to an all-time new level of intensity. My whole head is spinning out of control like a waterspout on the rough seas, ready to toss anything and everyone aside that may enter its path.

Logging back into my laptop and going through the accounts I have on my schedule to address today, I finally find my groove and spend the next few hours problem-solving and analyzing some complex quarterly data for one of our biggest clients.

Feeling somewhat accomplished again, I pack up my things and get ready to head back home for the second time today. I had to take my lunch break there this afternoon, as I wasn't sure how I would keep myself together in front of Brielle once I found out Kari was on my schedule. Though I didn't end up eating, I did manage to get in a pretty intense workout, which probably assisted in somewhat calming me down both physically and mentally.

When I see another square yellow sticky note on the door, I can't help but smile before I even read it, as I know it's from Brielle, and it must be something crazy. She wrote, "After drinking a whole bottle of wine last night, I swear I instantly became a genius. I must be a real Wine-stein, HA! To answer your earlier question, my head has seen better days. ~ Brielle." Yours and mine both, Brielle. I carefully remove it and place it in my briefcase pocket next to the one she left me yesterday, and walk away snickering despite myself.

## CHAPTER 10

There's an all-organic smoothie shop on the way to the hospital, so I stopped by to pick up one of Nic's favorite ridiculously healthy and grotesquely green creations that she loves. I don't know how she drinks this crap, as there's nothing even remotely satisfying to me about a bunch of blended-up raw veggies with seeds and other natural elements. I'll just stick to being a caffeine junky, thank you very much.

Peeking my head around the door to announce my arrival, I see that she's in her bed, with her mom sitting beside her in a chair.

"Nic, you did it." I walk up to her with a big smile on my face and the smoothie behind my back. "I brought you a present…"

"I am so happy that you are here. Wait, what time is it?" she says, looking somewhat confused.

"It's two thirty. Apparently, I'm out on parole early today for being a good inmate," I sass, giving her a playful wink.

"You didn't get fired, did you? Because I'm not even out of the hospital yet." Her eyes dart over to mine with an unnecessary seriousness to them.

"Will you stop already. Here, drink this, get powered up,

and you'll be back to work in no time."

"Oh my gosh, you are the *best*. I'm starving, and they won't let me have any solids yet." She rips it from my hands like a great white tearing into its prey.

"So, my friend, how are you feeling? I hear the surgery went a little longer than planned." I sit down gingerly on the bed next to her, not wanting the mattress to shift and cause her any additional pain.

"I'm currently feeling fiiine, as they have me on some great meds right now." She gives me a big drug-induced smile, making me chuckle.

"Nice! Care to share some with your bestie?"

"Nope, I earned these bad boys." She points to her stomach, where she currently has an ice pack to help with the swelling. "So how'd your second day go? Hopefully better than yesterday?"

Hmm, that's a good question. Was today actually better, or worse? Okay, worse wins, for sure. I wonder if I should talk to her about it while she is on her "happy pills," as maybe her response will be a little calmer. Then again, I really hesitate to bring up drama when she just had her surgery.

As if reading my thoughts, she continues, "Look, before you say that I just need to focus on my recovery, and don't tell me anything, I assure you that talking about work is a welcome distraction while I wait for the results and start healing."

"Okay, fine, you win. Let's just say that it was a very informative day today in more ways than one."

"Informative, huh, how so?" She takes a big sip of her smoothie.

"Well, let's see, there's the meeting with Kari Mallorey for starters." So much for the relaxed medicated response, because as I look over at her, she almost spits out her entire gulp of smoothie and starts choking on it.

She clears her throat and grabs a tissue from her tray table to wipe her mouth. "I'm sorry, please tell me you didn't just say Kari Mallorey."

"Yes, the one and only," I comment with my chin tilted up and my nose in the air, trying to imitate the stuck-up witch that she was.

"Oh my gosh, how did that appointment even find its way on the calendar? Kennen must have totally freaked out."

It seems to me that he might have gotten his freak on more than out, but that's none of my business. "I scheduled it when she called yesterday, as she said she was only going to be in town for one day, and he had a slow meeting day for today, so I put her on there. Besides, it's not like you *warned* me about her, Nic." Crossing my arms, I glare at her from the sides of my eyes.

"I know you're right. I'm so sorry. She just hasn't been in the picture for a couple of years now, so I tried to erase the memory of her a long time ago." Nicole puts her hands up to her face and sighs.

"She is quite something, that one, yikes." I chuckle. "For whatever reason, I don't think she was very impressed with me, but she seemed very excited to see Kennen."

Nicole's face has suddenly gone shades whiter, like she's just seen a ghost. "Did Kennen actually end up meeting with her?"

"You could say that, I suppose. I wasn't needed in that meeting to take notes, apparently."

"Shit," Nic says and then gets scolded by her mom, who has been casually listening in on this entire conversation the whole time. "Sorry, Mom, but this is a pretty messed-up situation."

Totally curious if she has any dirt on them that she could share with me, I ask her who Kari really is and what their backstory might be.

"Honestly, I don't know the actual story, as Kennen and I never talk about anything if it doesn't pertain to work. However, what I do know is that I was the one who had to deal with the devastating aftermath after that storm blew through town. Whatever went down between the two of them almost destroyed Kennen, and if you think he's bad now, you should have seen him then," she says, laying her head back and closing her eyes like the memory is almost too much to even think about again.

Well, he didn't seem overly heartbroken to me today, so maybe things won't be as bad this go-around? I decide to change the subject. "So, in other news, I made some big progress on our undercover mission today."

Nic looks up at me, hopeful. "Really, already? How on earth did you do that?"

"Well, you see, we were all sitting around the watercooler…" Laughing, I smirk at her.

"Ha-ha, very funny. Can you please get on with the specifics?"

"Let me just sum up what I found out and didn't find out. Apparently, AW Advisors has caught wind of Kennen's current mental struggles, and the board is freaking out that this deal might fall through, so at the next board meeting the members are going to…" I stop speaking.

"They are going to what, Brielle?"

"That's the part I don't know. You can thank the microwave for that," I say very nonchalantly.

"Why do I feel like everyone is just speaking to me in riddles lately? Brielle, what the hell is going on?"

"That's all I know, Nic, really. The mission went bust when my lunch was done cooking. Whatever they are going to do is obviously detrimental to Kennen and how the company moves forward in the future." My shoulders slump just thinking about this again.

"Look, I'm trying to work on a backup plan before the meeting happens on Friday morning, so if you have any thoughts, please feel free to jump in at any point here."

She is suddenly looking lost in thought, so I continue, "Is it possible they could vote him out if they prove him unfit to continue as CEO? I have no idea how all of that works, but I think we need to prepare since this may be their plan."

"This very well may be what they are going to try to do, Brielle, but I do know that he is the majority shareholder, which should make it more difficult for them to pull off. I'm not saying it can't be done, but it would prove slightly more complicated with the timeline of the upcoming merger and any potential fallback plans that Kennen most likely has set up."

I let out a slow breath. "Well, let's hope that they're just going to try to scare him and not actually take any serious actions."

"I'm not sure how we can help him, though, Brielle, as he doesn't seem to want to help himself. The board's concerns over his ability to perform his role as CEO have been brought up a couple of times recently, but Kennen refuses to go seek medical help for his migraines, stress levels, and lack of concentration." Her face is looking fairly strained now.

"Alright, Nic, I think you've gotten enough work talk in

for today, and you need to get your rest. I'll put my creative juices to work tonight and come up with a plan. Don't you worry about it." Giving her a reassuring smile, I walk over to the windowsill in her room and see an exceptionally large bouquet of roses and chuckle.

"Oh, yes, thank you for the flowers, Brielle. I love them." She starts laughing and then grabs her abdomen, wincing, as I'm sure any movement right now is bringing her an unwelcome intense pain.

"I don't know what you're talking about, as they're from Kennen," I say, trying to keep a straight face.

"Nice try. Even though the card did say 'Hurry up and get better so you can get back to work. ~ Kennen,' I know for a fact that he doesn't even know the name of the florist we order company flowers from, or which ones are my favorite for that matter." She crosses her arms and gives me the "you're full of shit" look.

Busted. "In all fairness to him, it was his idea for me to purchase them for you, so give the guy a break. He's trying at least."

Curiously, she looks over at me. "Hmm, defending him now, are we, Brielle?"

"Don't get me wrong, the guy is a complete pain in the ass most of the time, but I can't help but feel that he's just lacking some serious happiness in his life."

"While that may be true, please don't make it your mission to figure that out right now with everything he has going on, Brielle," she says, letting out a substantial yawn.

Mission gladly accepted.

"Alright, let's let you get some rest, girl." Walking over, I give her a careful hug. "Momma-T, let's take a walk to get you some tea and stretch your legs for a little while so Nic can get her beauty rest." Her mom agrees, and we say our goodbyes, allowing her recovery process to peacefully begin.

When I checked in with Nic this morning, she said that they've decided to keep her one more night due to the fact that they needed to keep her catheter in longer, and to keep an eye on her pain-management levels.

By the time I got back home and ate a quick bite of dinner last night, I was totally exhausted. The past few days have completely drained me, and I was really hoping that if I snuck into bed a little earlier than usual, I would be tired enough to just crash. As per usual, though, as soon as my head hit the pillow, my brain decided it was time to start the revolving slideshow of everything going on at the office right now. This makes me wonder what it must be like for Kennen, except for him it's nonstop, twenty-four hours a day, seven days a week. No wonder the poor guy is so short tempered and stressed out all the time.

After lying awake almost the entire night, trying to figure out a plan that will rectify this situation, I still came up totally blank. I know it will come to me when I least expect it to, but I'm cutting it really close, considering the board meeting is tomorrow morning at ten o'clock.

There is no doubt about which of my character tees I want to wear today. It's white with black lettering that simply says "AWAKE-ISH." I top that off with a gray blazer, black slacks, a pair of red high heels, and red-tinted lip gloss as my only pops of color. For some reason I just can't bring myself to even fake bright and cheery today. Not that it matters, as I don't believe anyone in that office appreciates my unique sense of style anyway.

I decide to make a double batch of my famous chocolate-chip, caramel iced frappé today, thinking that I would offer one to Kennen when I got there. If he doesn't end up wanting it, I'd be more than delighted to drink it for him, as I think it is going to be another exhausting one again today.

Deciding to take a chance when I get there, I knock on his door thirty minutes before our morning meeting. As the door slowly swings open, I see Kennen standing there in his usual black pants and white button-down dress shirt, but this time he doesn't have his jacket or tie on yet. His sleeves are also partially rolled up, giving me the slightest peek of what looks like some exceptionally toned forearms. Then there's his hair, which also seems to be in slight disarray, appearing slightly curlier than normal. This instantly makes my thoughts jump to what it would be like for me to be the cause of that. Huh, it's funny how I seem to be a little more awake now than I was just two minutes ago.

I quickly clear my throat and try to force my eyes to refocus back on his. "Good morning, Kennen. It looks like we had similar nights last night." I grin and hand him the extra frappé I made him, which he looks at like I'm trying to hand him a poisoned apple.

"No, thank you, Brielle. I can't drink that stuff. The caffeine only makes the swirling in my mind even worse."

He goes to hand it back to me, but I put my hand on his, stopping him, and sure enough, that electric bolt of energy from the first day shoots straight through my veins, instantly recharging me. Okay, fine, I'm *totally* awake now.

"Please just take one sip, as you wouldn't want to miss out on my famous recipe, now would you?" I give him the biggest, saddest puppy-dog eyes I can muster up.

He lets out a colossal huff, like it's such a burden on him. "Okay, fine, one sip if it will keep you happy and you'll leave me be."

As he takes a long draw through the straw, it is the first time I've taken a moment to look at the shape of his mouth. His lips, full and thick, look like you'd be kissing soft pillows, and my mind quickly imagines what his now cool lips would feel like if they were suddenly pressed against the heat of mine. *Whoa.*

When he's done, he hands it back to me, and I instantly pull it up to my mouth, close my eyes for a moment, and start drinking the rest of it for fear of what words might slip out before I have a chance to calm the sudden need growing inside me.

With the way he's looking at me now, his eyes seem to flash with desire, instantly making the warmth within my body known with an uncontrollable flush.

"What? There's no way I'm going to waste this with the day I'm sure we're about to have," I say matter-of-factly, trying to recompose myself. "Thank you for at least trying it though. What did you think?"

He clears his throat roughly, as if tearing himself away from his own thoughts. "Honestly?"

"Yes, Kennen, honestly."

He gives me a full-on smile for the first time ever and continues, "That was so damn good, Brielle, and in more ways than you will ever know." He turns and walks over to his desk to sit down, apparently needing to put some space between the heat that seems to be mutually building between the two of us.

I take that as my cue to leave and get back to work, but before I go, I suddenly have an urge to talk to him about what I found out yesterday regarding the board and their potential plans. He deserves to have as much notice as possible, and I didn't get a chance to tell him before I left to go visit Nic.

"Before I go, I became privy to some information yesterday that I really feel you should be aware of, but I don't think it's in your best interest to talk about it here in the office." I can see the sudden concern rise to his face. "I was wondering if maybe we could take a walk and find a bench or a little park area to eat our lunches at later and talk about it?"

He considers this for a few moments before he speaks. "Brielle, please don't interpret this the wrong way, but would you be comfortable talking about it at my apartment? I just have a really hard time being out and about in the city without my mind going into overdrive with all the stimuli around, and considering I only slept for about an hour last night, there's no way I could handle that today."

It takes everything I have to hold back my excitement of what it would be like to get a glimpse into the personal life of Mr. Kennen Davis.

"Of course, that would be fine. Thank you."

With that, I turn and leave his office and head to my desk with a renewed smile on my face.

It's lunchtime, and we're riding up the elevator for what seems like forever until we finally reach his apartment, which ends up being at the very top of this building. We didn't say two words to each other the whole way over here, as I think we both felt a little awkward after our interaction this morning.

As the doors to the elevator open right up into his apartment, I'm in complete awe. It's very bright and made up of mostly white tones and natural woods, which I absolutely love. If I had a beach house, this is exactly the color palette I would want, with an added touch of sea-glass blues and greens as accents. The view literally goes around three hundred and sixty degrees, overlooking the whole financial district.

"Kennen, this is incredible." I start to wander into his living room and over to the nearest windows. "This is quite the view. Although, nothing personal, I'd much rather be overlooking the ocean than the city." I give him a quick wink.

"Thank you, though I typically shut the blinds as soon as I get home for the same reasons I mentioned to you earlier about not taking a walk."

"Understandable. But then why would you get the penthouse apartment if you don't even like the views?"

"It was a good investment at the time, and it gives me plenty of room to have everything I need to escape the world while I'm not at work."

I don't know why, but that just brought a sudden sadness to the air around us, knowing he would rather be trapped in his house when he's not trapped in his office.

Smiling, I try to shake it off. "How about a quick tour before we eat lunch and I ruin your afternoon?"

"Of course, follow me."

Lead the way, and I will gladly follow the view in front of me, Mr. Davis. As he shows me his living room, guest bathroom, and a small gym in one of the spare bedrooms, I can't help but notice how extremely tidy he is. There's not a single item out of place or a speck of dirt anywhere. Totally fitting of his personality, of course.

As we approach his bedroom, I can't help but walk right in and look around. My whole apartment in Denver could fit in here. The furnishings and décor are appropriately simplistic and neutral like the rest of the apartment. It all feels a little cold to be a bedroom, without any added personal items or pictures, but to each his own. As I head over to his walk-in closet, I cover my mouth and immediately begin laughing hysterically.

"Nosey, are we, Brielle?" He looks at me curiously. "And what is so humorous exactly?"

"I'm so sorry; it's an amazing closet, but are you out conquering all the aliens that reside among us here on earth when you're not at work? All you're missing is the black sunglasses." I bust out laughing all over again.

"You have a thing for movie references, don't you?" he asks with a smirk.

"I can't help it, too many evenings alone with a bottle of wine and Netflix over the years." I try to calm my laughter down some so I can continue, "But seriously, why all of the black? With your eyes and skin tone, you would look amazing in some blues, tans and maybe even peach."

He can't help but laugh at the last color I mention. Then he looks over at his wardrobe and then back at me like he has never really thought about it before now. "I don't know, it's just another part of the consistency in my life, I suppose. Speaking of color, where's your normal spunk today? You look like you went through Nicole's closet to get ready."

"Ha-ha, very funny. I just felt like all of my color vibes washed out of me last night, along with my ability to sleep."

"I see, well, shall we press on?" He leads me down the hall to what I'm assuming is the spare bedroom, but when he opens the door, I immediately push by him and run inside the room. He stands in the doorway and watches me with amusement as I run my hands up and down the spines of all the novels he has showcased in floor-to-ceiling bookshelves along the whole wall. It looks like a library in here, and knowing him, it's probably organized as such.

After I'm done admiring them, I turn to take in the rest of the space. It's much smaller than any of the other areas in the apartment, but it has all the comfort and personalization that is lacking everywhere else. In front of me is what looks like an amazingly comfortable, maple-sugar-colored leather couch and a lamp. And then a smaller desk is set up on the other side of the room, where all his degrees and awards hang on the wall. I curiously walk up to take a closer look at them and remember Nic telling me how extremely young he was when he earned them all.

Once I'm done admiring his accomplishments, I head back over to the couch, as it is totally calling my name, and then look over at Kennen. "May I?" I say, pointing down at the couch with a gigantic smile on my face.

He chuckles and nods his head. "Of course."

Sitting down, I feel like the couch is molding itself to me and engulfing my body in complete softness. I quickly lean over to take off my heels and pull my legs up, then snuggle into the throw pillow he has sitting by the arm of the couch.

"Oh my gosh, Kennen, this is the most incredible couch *ever*." I close my eyes for a minute, feeling more relaxed in this moment than I have since I moved out here. When I open them back up, Kennen is walking over to me, holding his hand out to help me get up.

"You might need help getting off of there. Trust me, there have been quite a few nights I fell asleep in that exact spot, as I was way too comfortable to move." He lightly laughs.

Great, now I have a vision of him sleeping right where I'm currently sitting, and he wants me to grab his hand? Sitting up, I put my heels back on and then go ahead and grab it to help me rise.

I step back over to admire the bookshelves one more time. "I would totally be curled up on that couch with one of these novels every night."

Kennen walks up next to my side, looks at the books and then back at me. "I didn't know you were a reader."

"I love to read, but I'm more of a romance and thriller kind of girl…I'm not big into reading books about complex analysis." I give him a sweet wink.

He begins to chuckle. "Right. Well, are you ready to finish the tour and eat some lunch?"

"Yes, and, Kennen, just for the record, this is by far my favorite room in your apartment."

With an endearing smile, he says, "It's definitely mine too, Brielle."

We walk out into the hallway until we are back out in the main area of the apartment. He leads me over to the right side of the space, which includes a dining room area and then an enormous kitchen.

"Wow, this is certainly a chef's kitchen. Do you enjoy cooking at least, or is this just for show?" I can't help but walk alongside the island, running my fingertips down the stunning, smooth, white-and-gray-veined marble countertop.

"Let's just say I'm no Gordan Ramsay, but I can hold my own. It's only me though, so I don't get as much use out of it as I would like."

"Trust me, I can relate to that. I do vividly remember

growing up learning how to cook alongside my Italian grandmother and being fascinated the whole time, as she just used her eye to measure ingredients as opposed to any measuring utensils."

The memory brings a special warmth back to my heart. I share with him that we used to make our own cavatelli pasta from scratch and set up our "shop" on her formal dining room table. We would very carefully line up each piece of pasta in tidy rows that would end up covering the whole tabletop. Once they were cooked and combined with the perfect homemade sauce, we would eat them by the bowlful. Although, it's the type of pasta that sinks right to the bottom of your gut like an anchor being dropped once you eat it. I laugh as I remember how full we used to get after that dish.

"Have you ever had it before, Kennen?"

"No, I have not, but it does sound amazing."

"Well, before my time is up here in New York, maybe I can teach you how to make it."

This brings a warmth to his face. "Yes, I'd like that very much."

We grab our lunches and sit down at his dining room table, both laughing once we've pulled them out. Kennen, of course, has a very nutritious-looking salad loaded up with veggies and chicken, and mine consists of a peanut butter and jelly sandwich with a bag of salt and vinegar chips. What can I say, the last thing I wanted to spend time on this morning was my lunch for the day.

After eating in silence and cleaning up our mess, we head over to the living room to, unfortunately, talk business. It's been so great getting to spend time with Kennen being more relaxed and in his own element, and knowing the topic we are about to broach is not going to be a pleasant one, I don't even want to bring it up at this point.

"Alright, let's get this conversation over with," I say with a sigh. "As you are obviously already aware of, the board has concerns regarding the state of your health. While at lunch yesterday, I overheard a couple of girls in the office talking about your situation. One of them mentioned that she heard a board member saying that not only are they concerned, but apparently the team over at AW Advisors has caught wind of it also and are now showing some doubts if this merger should continue to go through as planned. With you being the main representative of the company, I'm sure that you can understand their position on this." I pause for a moment to collect the rest of my thoughts.

Kennen runs both of his hands down his face and looks at me pleadingly. "How the hell did they find out about this, anyway, as it has only been a conversation between the board members and me. Okay, and apparently the gossip twins in the break room."

I wince and continue, "Unfortunately, Kennen, there is more…"

He quickly shoots a serious look over to me.

"According to said board member, since you've made no effort to seek medical advice, and it is affecting your ability to do your job, they plan on taking further action. I don't know exactly what that will be, as the conversation got interrupted, but it doesn't sound good."

He immediately stands up and starts pacing back and forth in front of the couch. "I can't believe after everything I have done for them over the years, and all of the money they have made off of my company, that they would try to do this to me now."

I'm afraid to tell him the next part, but I know it's important that he know. "Kennen, regrettably, it does get slightly worse."

He instantly stops and looks directly at me now without saying a word.

"Whatever they plan on doing, they may have all intentions of doing it at the board meeting tomorrow morning."

"You have got to be kidding me." He runs his fingers through his hair, grabbing at it as his hand makes its way to the back of his head.

"I know. I'm so sorry, Kennen. I'll do whatever I can to help you come up with a plan."

"A plan? What are you going to be able to come up with by tomorrow morning when we don't even know exactly what actions they plan on taking, besides the fact that you've only been here all of a few days?"

I knew this conversation would end up ruining any connection we might have made earlier. "I don't know yet, Kennen, but I'm a pretty creative person, and I know one will come to me." I get a sideways glance at that response. "Let's talk about what they can possibly do to you based on how you have your company set up, for starters. You hold the majority of the shares of the company, correct?"

He looks up at the ceiling and blows out a slow breath. "Okay, you're right. Let's just try to talk out some of the potential scenarios. To answer your question, yes, I do. While this does make it more complicated for them to take a drastic measure such as removing me as the CEO, it's not impossible either. They would have to prove that the issues I am having are preventing me from completing my duties as the CEO, and then have a vote on it. If they didn't get enough votes, they would have to pursue different avenues to complete the same goal. However, if they do get enough votes, I could be finished. I do also have an employment agreement that protects me from scenarios such as this one, basically giving me the option to step down instead and be bought out."

"The part I don't understand, though, Kennen, is why would they want to get rid of you, even if it meant losing the merger and just continuing on as you currently are? You're the backbone of this company, and I wouldn't think that they could retain the high-profile clients you have if your gifts and talents weren't there."

He gives me a half-smile and lets out a quiet laugh. "I might literally be a genius, Brielle, but it still doesn't make me irreplaceable. Apparently, these bastards are getting greedy, as this merger stands to make a ton of additional money for them." He sits back down on the couch and puts his head in his hands, resting his elbows on top of his legs.

Taking a chance, I sit next to him and bring up another question. "Kennen, why couldn't you just go see a doctor? Wouldn't that make them back off you some if they knew you were making an effort?"

By the look he's giving me right now, I know I just went too far. "I'm sorry. I know it's none of my business. I'm just trying to make sense of this whole situation."

"I think we've gone over enough details, Brielle. Let's get back to the office and see what we can put together before my next meeting shows up."

With that, he gets up and motions for us to head back to the elevator to leave. I'm so disappointed and really want to leave here on a better note. "Thank you for sharing your home with me today, Kennen. It really is an amazing space."

"You're welcome, Brielle. Come on, let's get going."

There's a flurry of activity between both of us doing research and getting through the few meetings Kennen has on his schedule today. Unfortunately, none of my brilliant ideas have come to me yet, and I'm very quickly running out of time. There's got to be something we can do to prove to the board that he is still more than capable of performing his duties as the firm's CEO. I feel my own migraine coming on with all this stress, and I have only been working here for three days.

It's currently six thirty, so I decide to call it a night, as I still would like to swing by the hospital quick to visit Nic before I head back to the apartment. I remember Kennen saying that he had a phone conference scheduled at six o'clock tonight with his lawyer, and he hasn't appeared out of his office yet, so I am assuming he might be in there for a while. I'm hopeful that they can get something figured out tonight.

As per recent tradition, I have to leave a quote for him, and since he took me on a tour of his apartment today, I figure I'd go with "The biggest problem with living alone is that it's always my turn to do the dishes. ~ Brielle." I think back to when we were in his kitchen earlier, and I can totally picture us in there cooking together. I really need to make good on my offer of the pasta lesson before my time here is completed. As stressful as it is working here, the thought of not being around Kennen anymore in the distant future brings a sudden disappointment in my heart.

I send Nic a quick text before I head out to see if she needs anything, but her mom ends up replying for her instead. She said that they needed to up her pain medication, which currently has her in a deep sleep. I asked her to give Nic a hug for me when she wakes up, and to tell her that I'll talk to her in the morning after she has gotten some rest.

As I'm walking back towards the apartment, I inhale the most amazing aroma of freshly tossed coal-fired pizza and decide that is exactly what I need for dinner tonight. Following the scent around the corner to the next block over, I find a takeout-only mom-and-pop pizzeria. I step in and order a couple of slices to go, and when I get home and open the box, my mouth instantly starts to water.

Grabbing a plate, I head over to the couch to make myself comfortable while I inhale this delectable greatness. Folding the large slice in half, flavors of homemade sauce, mozzarella, pepperoni, sausage, garlic, and parmesan burst in my mouth. I inhale that piece like I haven't eaten in a year and get up to grab the second one along with a glass of wine. Maybe I should try to eat this one a little slower so that I can really appreciate the finest pizza in the world and not make myself nauseated while doing so.

With a now extremely full belly and a slight wine buzz, I get cleaned up, hop into bed, and fall into an extremely welcome deep sleep within minutes.

It's four o'clock in the morning, and my eyes suddenly open like I've just been awoken by some unwelcome spirit, when I remember the dream I was just having. I was in Florida, lying on the beach, reading a book, when I noticed a shadow appear over me. When I lowered my sunglasses and looked up, it was Kennen staring down at me. Except (and unfortunately, might I add) he wasn't wearing a bathing suit. Instead, he was wearing his usual black suit, white shirt, and black tie. He started speaking to me, except

I couldn't hear what he was saying, and with that I woke up. Okay, so I know that's totally weird and nonspectacular, but I can't help but think that this dream was trying to tell me something.

Suddenly, an idea that will hopefully help rescue Kennen from this impending storm he's about to walk into today hits me so fast that my head begins spinning. It's a risky one on many levels, but at this point it's one I'm willing to take. I lie back down and try to work out all the details in my head before I go and get myself ready for the day. I hope Kennen will trust me on this one…

## CHAPTER 11

I can't get to the office quickly enough to get to work on my master plan. When I get to my desk, there's a sticky note on my computer from Kennen saying that he won't be in until right before the board meeting at ten, as he had to go meet with his lawyers in person. I smile at the fact that he chose to leave me a sticky note, as it makes me think he is paying attention to the ones I've been leaving him.

With my computer fired up, I pull up the database of contacts and say a quick prayer that I can find the cell phone number that I'm so desperately looking for. It takes a little digging, but I'm relieved and totally mortified when I come across his number. It's probably best to go sit in Kennen's office with his door shut, so that no one in the office may overhear my conversation if they happen to walk into our area. I blow out an extremely long breath, pick up Kennen's phone, and dial the number.

When the conversation is over, I push the chair out some, giving myself a big spin, and let out a small squeal. I am currently feeling quite confident about my plan. Now I just need to get Kennen to agree, and the board to take my bait.

When I get back out to my desk, I finish organizing all

the folders and quarterly information that Kennen mentioned he would need to go over with the board, as per their usual update. By the time I have everything ready, I look up to see Kennen walking towards me, looking completely pained and exhausted, which makes this mission I'm on even more important to me.

"Hey, Brielle, are you ready to head to the board meeting?"

As I walk around the desk, he looks me up and down, rubs his chin, then gives me a slight chuckle.

"What? I wore my power suit this morning just for you," I say, with a playful look to my smile. I decided that for this meeting I would need all the power of color I could get, so I put on my fuchsia slacks, a navy blue blazer, and a white tee that simply says "CRAZY BORED" in canary yellow lettering. I knew Kennen would totally understand and appreciate my play on words with this one.

"Kennen, do we have a few minutes to chat before we go over to the meeting?" I need to be able to give him some kind of heads-up if I'm going to get this plan to work.

"Unfortunately, not here. Come on and walk with me, and we can chat along the way."

With that, he turns and starts to walk off as I try to catch up to him. "Kennen, how did your meeting go?"

He looks at me out of the corner of his eye. "Not great, so if you ended up coming up with a better plan, I'd love to know."

I turn my head towards him with a huge smile spread across my face. "Actually, I did."

He pauses briefly right before we walk up to the conference room door. "Wait, you did? What is it?"

"Kennen, I don't have time to explain right now, but I

just need you to trust me, okay?"

"Brielle…" He is looking at me with a slight panic in his eyes.

"Please, Kennen, whatever I do in there, can you just go along with it?" I'm completely desperate and hoping he will follow my lead. "You're going to have to believe me, as this is your best option at this point."

He blows out a slow breath. "Fine, but, Brielle, please don't make this situation any worse than it already is, as this is my life's work we are putting on the line here."

I swallow hard, trying not to think about it that way. "One more thing, once we get in there and sit down, please hand me your cell phone and tell me that you are waiting for an important call that you'll need me to answer."

He gives me a look like I just walked out of an insane asylum. "Right." And with that, he opens the door to where the entire board is waiting for him to arrive, already looking like they are ready to burn him at the stake.

When I walk in behind him, everyone stops and looks at me curiously, and Kennen notices. "Gentlemen, this is Brielle Bisset. She is filling in for Nicole as my executive assistant until she returns from a medical leave."

As we take our seats, Kennen at the head of the table and myself to the left of him, he turns to me and hands me his cell phone. Then he says, loudly enough for everyone to notice, what I asked him to while we were out in the hallway. Phase one complete, too bad that was the easiest of the phases, I think to myself and inwardly sigh.

Kennen starts reviewing the quarterly reports, and you can tell his lack of concentration is totally noticeable today. Of course, I know the reason why, but unfortunately the board doesn't. I look down at my watch and see that I have approximately fifteen minutes before I can put the rest of my plan into action, and now I just need Kennen to hang in there without having a complete meltdown before then.

Once he's done running through all the numbers, the topic of the merger comes up, and I instantly notice the change in the demeanor of the board; then again so does Kennen. With this, he looks like he's ready to chew them up and spit them out, and I see him reaching for his forehead like the migraine from hell is chipping away at his skull with an icepick.

Just then, like an angel sent down from heaven, his cell phone buzzes on the table, and I look at the screen. I quietly stand up and walk out of the conference room so that I can answer the call.

"Hello, this is Brielle, Kennen Davis's executive assistant. How may I assist you today?" Like I don't already know who this is.

"Oh, hi, Brielle, this is Austin with AW Advisors. We spoke on the phone this morning. Is Kennen still in the conference you mentioned?"

"Hello, Austin, I'm afraid he is. I apologize, as you know how these meetings go sometimes."

He laughs. "Do I ever."

"May I have him call you back in about ten to fifteen minutes if that works with your schedule?" Please say yes, Austin.

"Absolutely, my next appointment isn't for another hour. Thank you, Brielle."

"Perfect, thank you."

Once I make sure he has hung up, I run to the break room and grab a mug of hot water from the coffee station and hurry back to Kennen's office to make him some of my special "migraine tea" made up of ginger root and chamomile. It tastes horrific, but it usually helps relieve the pain a little bit when I get mine.

Walking back down to the conference room, holding the cell phone to my chest, making it look like I have the person on hold, I enter the door. From the looks of things, I have a feeling that this ship is already beginning to sink like the *Titanic*, so I clear my throat and get their attention. "Please excuse the interruption. Kennen, the phone call you have been waiting for is currently on hold and awaiting your response if you would like to take it back in your office?" I look right at him, pleading with my eyes for him to just go with it.

"Yes, right, thank you, Brielle." He stands up, and you can see the shock on everyone's face like this is something that is totally unheard of.

We start heading for his office in silence, and I know that I'm about to get an earful once we get back in there. When we arrive, he opens the door and walks in ahead of me. Once I'm in, I go to shut the door behind me, and as I turn back around, he is literally inches from my face with one hand up on the doorway casing and the other on his hip.

He is totally pissed off right now. "Brielle, what the hell is going on?"

My heart starts racing, as I've never been this close to him before. I suddenly get a hint of his cologne, which is made up of a unique light fruity blend, with a touch of mint. I instantly feel an intense heat flowing throughout my body, and want nothing more than to devour him right now.

I take a good look into his eyes, and amazingly, I feel like I can actually see what looks like his eyes moving rapidly as he scans through all the numbers and images running through his mind like he mentioned. It's almost as if he can't really see me, but just the vision of me past everything else. To the average eye you would never notice it from any type of distance, just as I hadn't before either.

I need to focus, as we are on a time limit, so I break my eye contact and walk around him and over to his desk. I grab the tea and a couple of my migraine-relief pills and hand them to him. "Here, first take these, and chase it down with this tea."

"No, I am not taking any medicine, Brielle." He goes to hand them back to me, but I insist.

"Kennen, they are just some over-the-counter migraine-relief pills that I take myself. And I, along with everyone else in that room, can see you are suffering right now, so please take them," I say sternly.

He's so mad right now I think he takes them just to shut me up and move on. After he swallows them with some of the tea, he makes a look of total disgust. "What is this crap? Are you seriously trying to kill me?" He puts the mug back down on his desk and wipes his lips with the back of his hand.

"Another secret recipe. Now can we move on? We are running out of time."

"Who is on the phone, Brielle, and again, what the hell is going on?" He has both of his hands on his hips now. "I have never left a board meeting for anything since day one, so I don't see how this doesn't make me seem crazier than the board already thinks I am."

"Actually, this 'important phone call,' which you're taking while interrupting the board meeting for the first time *ever*, has just put them on notice that you have something in the works. I bet you money they are in there crapping their pants right now. Kennen, you are the CEO of this firm, now start taking a stand and act like it." Okay, that might have been a little more than I planned on saying, but it's true.

He instantly looks at me like I just slapped him across the face.

"Great, now, where was I? Oh, right, my plan, which you are not allowed to freak out on me about, by the way." I take a deep breath. "Can you please take a seat so I don't feel like you are about to pounce on me." Not that I would mind that under different circumstances, of course.

He goes and sits in his office chair, and I stand in front of his desk. "It hit me early this morning after a dream I had about you last night."

He suddenly looks at me curiously with the corner of his mouth turned up and an eyebrow raised.

"I'm sorry, that didn't come out right." Holy crap, did someone just turn the heat on? "Anywaaay, I figured out a way to not only appease the board, at least temporarily, and the team over and AW Advisors, but to also help you in the end."

"Really, and what does this miraculous plan of yours consist of?" He laces his fingers together and sets them on top of the desk and leans over.

Here goes nothing. I stand up straight to compensate for my confidence shrinking by the second. "I called Austin this morning on his cell phone and told him that you had asked me to call him to go over a change in plans with our arrival for the final merger meeting coming up." I try not to look right at him as he is me right now, and then continue, "I mentioned that since all of the details have been settled for the merger, that you've decided to take a brief vacation before the meeting and fly down to Florida a few days prior to get a better feel for his company's hometown. This also allows you to catch up with him for a casual dinner at some point while you're there, to get to know him a little better before you both join forces. I reinforced it with the fact that you thought it was only equitable since you hadn't been down to his office yet the entire time this deal has been in the negotiating process."

He interrupts me. "You did not seriously call him and tell him that I was planning on taking a vacation right before this major merger is going to happen."

"Kennen, you're missing the bigger picture here. This makes him believe that you are making a sincere effort to immerse yourself in his world, and on his territory, all while being confident that there is nothing going on that would prevent you from moving forward with this merger. As for the board, it makes it look like you are taking their advice by taking care of your health and well-being, and leaves them in a tight spot to prove otherwise."

He thinks about this for a minute. "I don't know, Brielle. What was Austin's response to all of this?"

"Honestly, he was ecstatic. He's so excited for you to get a feel for their area down there, and to get a chance to spend some time with you aside from talking shop all of the time."

He looks at me suspiciously, like it can't possibly be this easy.

"He was so excited, he even offered to let us stay in his investment beach house. He just finished renovating it and is about to put it on the market after the merger is complete, when he said he can think straight again."

"What?" He sits up straight now.

"I know, it's crazy, right? Of course, I told him that would be amazing, and we would love to experience his handiwork. Which then got him talking for another twenty minutes about everything he'd just put into this house. By the time we were done, I could tell he had a whole new outlook on any rumors he may have previously heard. I then told him that you would like to confirm everything later this morning when you were finished with your meeting. I scheduled for him to purposely call you while you were still in the meeting, for the reasons I already mentioned earlier."

"So that's who you were on the phone with just now? He hasn't been on hold this whole time, has he?"

"Of course not, I apologized, then told him your meeting was running slightly behind, which he totally sympathized with, by the way, and that you would call him back in about ten to fifteen minutes." I begin feeling slightly better getting this all out in the open now, aside from being physically short of breath.

"Oh, and there was one more thing he wanted me to pass along that he will formally be confirming by email shortly. Their attorneys had a prior, major case come up that requires them to be in court starting the week of the final merger meeting, so they will need to bump it up one week earlier to fit it in before they are unavailable for the foreseeable future."

He's starting to panic again, so I quickly remind him that this also works in our favor, as it gives the board even less time to finalize whatever shenanigans they have planned before the merger goes through.

I grab his cell and hand it to him. "Now, call Austin quick and confirm how excited you are about everything I just told you so that we can hurry up and get back to the chaos that I'm sure is unfolding in that conference room right now."

He looks up at me. "This whole thing sounds completely crazy, Brielle. I have a feeling that the board is going to have an extremely hard time believing that I am taking time off, where I won't be doing any work right before the merger, when I have never taken a single vacation day in the eight years since I started this company."

"That's where I come in, as I will be going with you to make sure that you don't work and you do actually relax a little bit for once, hence benefitting you in the end." I wink and then push the phone at him again.

He lets out a nervous chuckle and rubs his hand along the back side of his neck before he takes the phone from me and calls Austin. Luckily, Kennen is able to cut the call short by saying his appointments are all backlogged now due to his meeting running behind, and that they will talk again soon. He stands up and comes around his desk, taking a hesitant look at his watch.

I smooth out his jacket and look up at him. "Are you ready to go face the firing squad now?"

"Not really, no."

He suddenly grabs one of my hands before I pull them off his jacket, sending little shivers down my body like the aftershocks of an earthquake, immediately causing me to flush all over.

"You're a brilliant man, Kennen. I want you to walk in there as calm and regrouped as possible and tell them what your new plan is. At the end, throw them the curveball that they can expect an email from Austin explaining the revised final meeting date this afternoon, to be sure to send them into complete panic mode."

He gives me a more serious, seductive smile now and brings my hand up to his mouth and then kisses the top of it. "Thank you, Brielle, for everything. I don't know how you did it, but I really appreciate it."

I smile appreciatively back at him. "You're very welcome. I seem to remember telling you I was creative and that it would come to me at some point...so just trust a girl from now on, will you?"

He gently releases my hand as we start heading towards the door. "I most definitely will."

We walk side by side, both with smiles on our faces, ready to go back into this meeting and remind them who is really in charge here.

When we reenter the conference room, there is an extremely heated conversation going on that suddenly silences to the point of where you could hear a pin drop.

Kennen stands at the end of the table where his seat is and very calmly begins to address the board. "First, I would like to apologize for creating such an interruption to our meeting this morning. Unfortunately, it was an important call that I needed to take at that moment, which I will explain further in a few minutes. Most importantly, I wanted to take some time to address the elephant in the room concerning my mental health and well-being. I would like to thank you all for bringing your concerns and recommendations to me, and I apologize if you feel as though I wasn't listening and not taking it seriously. Since I began this company eight years ago, I have poured my entire life and soul into developing this firm to the exceptional level we are currently at today. In doing so, not only have I made each of us a ton of money, but I have also begun to sacrifice my quality of life. You must understand that this company is like a child to me, one that I would do anything to help it not only grow, but to protect it by any measure necessary should anyone try to take it away from me." He pauses, takes a breath, and looks around the table at each board member individually. I can't even begin to express how proud of him I am right now, and it takes everything I have not to burst out laughing watching their expressions change as he does this.

He begins again, "With all of the details for the upcoming merger with AW Advisors now finalized, I have made the decision to take my first, and most definitely earned, vacation, starting next week." He stops as chuckles and murmurs suddenly break out across the room. "Sounds like a joke, I know, but with everything now being in place, this is a perfect opportunity to take my health seriously and get some R & R before we explode back into the market with our new partners. I can assure you that there is not anything medically going on aside from getting some stress headaches, which I know I am not alone with, considering all of the pressure that both of our firms have been under to get to this point in our merger." I'm right there with him on that one.

He then lets them know about the phone call he had earlier with Austin, and how he needed to finalize some dates with him to book his vacation, as they have had a scheduling conflict suddenly arise this morning with their attorneys. When he makes it known that the final merger meeting has been bumped up a week and will now take place a week from this coming Monday, you can feel the tide suddenly shift in the room, like a rip current that has you trying not to panic as it begins to suck you down.

Kennen glances over at me, and I give him a smile and a quick nod in approval of the job he's doing right now. Feeling reassured, he clears his throat and speaks again. "That being said, I have decided to head down to Seaside, Florida, mid next week for my vacation so that I will be in the area for the meeting the following Monday. Since I will need Miss Bisset to attend the final merger meeting, I'm going to bring her down early with me so that she can make sure that I don't spend the whole time working and miss out on what this time is really about for me."

With that, he crosses his arms and asks if anyone has any questions. Crickets, that's what I thought, as I laugh internally at this whole situation. I think they're all in shock and at a complete loss of words for what to do next since this meeting has obviously not gone according to their original plan.

Without giving them an abundance of time to regroup, he addresses them one last time. "Thank you for your time today, gentlemen. I look forward to leading this company into the amazing new journey ahead of us." He walks over to the door and holds it open for me to leave.

When we're back in his office, I reach out my hand to shake his. "Now that, Mr. Davis, is exactly how it's done."

He grabs my hand and pulls me into a twist so that I end up curling into him, my back against his chest and his arm wrapped around my waist. Both of our chests are rising and falling with the adrenaline quickly flowing through us from the excitement of the outcome of that meeting. He suddenly leans over so he's almost touching my ear and whispers, "Oh, I'm not done yet, Miss Bisset."

While still being totally distracted from our amazing, yet intense, moment earlier, I spend the later part of the afternoon trying to book our flights for our trip to Florida. I had to laugh at all the specifics he requested for the flights: it needs to be the latest flight of the evening to avoid the crowds, nonstop only, first class seats (absolutely no argument from me there), his being the window seat and mine the middle seat if it is a row of three, and on the left side of the plane if possible. If you were a travel agent, you might find it all a bit strange, but for me, I know now that it's just what makes him who he is, and I'm really beginning to admire that about him. The only part of the request that I couldn't get to happen is the direct flight, as the closest airport to Seaside is Northwest Florida Beaches International, and there aren't any direct flights out of Newark to get there. Hopefully, that won't be too much of an issue for him though. Once it's all booked, I send him the confirmation emails and begin to prep his schedule for his upcoming time off. My phone pings, breaking my concentration.

> **Nicole:** I'm home finally.
> **Brielle:** Oh, Nic, that's so great. I can't wait to see you.
> **Nicole:** I'm STARVING. Can you please bring some real food home with you so my mom doesn't need to cook tonight?
> **Brielle:** You got it. Any cravings, girl?
> **Nicole:** I was thinking the large grilled chicken salad from All Naturals for me and the swiss turkey sub for my mom?
> **Brielle:** Oh, hell no. We're celebrating tonight, so let me know what you guys want on your handcrafted burgers, and what size fries you'd like, before I leave.
> **Nicole:** Okay, fine, you twisted my arm. What exactly are we celebrating, though?
> **Brielle:** Life, Nic, life.
> **Nicole:** Oh boy, maybe I should skip my meds tonight so that I can drink, as I have a feeling

I'm going to need it.

**Brielle:** HA, good idea. See you shortly.

I'm so excited to tell Nic about everything that is going on now, well, almost everything. I think I'll leave out the part about the energy that seems to be surrounding Kennen and me, as I don't think she would approve of that situation at all. Although, at this point, I doubt it will end up leading to anything anyway, as I'm not sure I'm his usual type, and by type, I mean the Kari Malloreys of the world.

Luckily, his schedule for the end of next week isn't as busy as normal since he was trying to keep the number of meetings to a minimum with the upcoming merger. I rearrange the remaining appointments and try to think of another sticky-note saying I can leave for tonight, but somehow I think "I want you more than I want caffeine, and I can't live without caffeine" might be pushing it a bit. Ugh, maybe I'll just go say goodnight like a normal person and get out of this office before I do something I'll regret.

As I walk up to his door, I gently rest my forehead against it and quietly blow out a slow breath. I feel like his energy is seeping through the wood and passing into me, almost as if he is on the other side waiting. I place my right hand on it, wanting to soak up any amount of this feeling that I can get, but my thoughts are quickly jarred by the door opening. My reflexes are nowhere to be found considering the zone I was just in, and I end up falling forward right towards Kennen. He instantly catches me by the shoulders like this happens all the time.

Oh my gosh, I should have just left the stupid note, as I can't even imagine what he is thinking as he's currently holding onto me so I don't fall. I know I need to break the hold and back up, but I just can't. Feeling his strong hands on my shoulders right now is sending a warmth and protection through me that I haven't felt in a long time.

"Brielle, are you okay? I'm sorry, I didn't know you were on the other side of the door." He's looking at me curiously now, probably waiting for me to say something rather than just standing there.

"Yes, yes, I'm fine, thanks. I was just coming to say goodnight." Maybe it's just me, but it seems like he is suddenly somewhat disappointed that I'm breaking my note-leaving tradition.

"Right, well, have a good weekend, Brielle." With that, he lets go of my shoulders and starts walking by me.

I just don't understand what's going on here. One minute he's acting like he's ready to slam me against the door and show me who's boss in the most seductive way possible, and in the next he just wants to slam me against the door and then leave. And they say women are complicated.

I turn around in hopes of catching him before he makes it too far away. "Oh, and, Kennen."

He pauses and turns back around to look at me. "Yes?"

"Start packing your bags this weekend. We're going on vacation next week, and the only suit you need to be wearing doesn't include a jacket, shirt or tie." I break out my biggest smirk ever and give him a wink to seal the deal.

He clears his throat and rubs a hand down his tie. "Got it."

Walking into the apartment with sacks full of greasy goodness, I see Nic lying on the couch with a heating pad under her back and her favorite soft throw blanket on top.

I place the dinner on the coffee table and lean over to give her a gentle squeeze.

"Nic, it's so great to have you back. How are you feeling, my friend?" I sit alongside her on the side of the couch.

"Actually, I already feel ten times better than I did before. Now I just need to get through the recovery from the surgery." She winces as she tries to sit up extremely slowly.

"I'm so glad to hear that. I knew this would be a great new start for you." I turn back around and grab the hamburgers and fries off the coffee table. "Here, eat this, Nic. It will cure all that ails you."

"That, or it will kill me," she says to me, deadpan.

Ah, I see some things haven't changed in my new Nic. Laughing, I hand her the food and then call out for her mom to let her know that I have arrived with our dinner.

Nic takes a big bite of hers and instantly closes her eyes in delight. "Okay, you win, Brielle. This is totally worth dying for."

I laugh as I get up and go to the kitchen to grab an extremely large glass of wine and come back.

Nicole notices and stops eating. "Oh, that's right, we're celebrating. Although, I'm afraid to ask what." She tilts her head to the side and raises an eyebrow.

"What? Life is good is all." I take a sip of my wine and try not to look at the death stare she is giving me right now. "Look, Nic, you just got home from having a successful surgery, and I may have also just saved your boss and his company from total annihilation today...so yes, life is good." I can't help but have a satisfied smile across my face.

She drops the French fry she was just about to put in

her mouth. "Wait, what do you mean you saved the day? Did you actually end up coming up with a plan?"

"Yes. I. Did," I say proudly.

I can see the panic start to rise in her face, so I quickly add, "And before you ask, no, I didn't do anything illegal, nor did it cost you your position at the firm."

She seems to relax her shoulders some then. "Brielle, you know I am afraid to ask what this brilliant plan is, right, but I have to know what you did." Then she shoves a huge, seasoned, crispy, curly fry into her mouth.

Sitting up straight on the edge of the chair, I tell her how I convinced Kennen to take a vacation right before the final merger meeting to appease the board of their concerns of how he's handling his health, along with quashing any doubts the team at AW Advisors may have had.

Nicole starts choking on her fry, and her mom jumps up to pat her on the back. I seem to be having that effect on her a lot lately, yikes.

After she regains control and takes a sip of her water, she chimes in, "I'm sorry, I could have sworn you just mentioned Kennen and vacation in the same sentence, when he's never missed a single day of work in the past *eight years,* Brielle."

"I know, right. The guy is way overdue for this."

"I don't understand. You've only been here a week, and suddenly you've got him convinced not to work right before the biggest deal of his life is about to take place, when that's all he ever does? I don't know, I'm beginning to think that the board is right to be concerned, as he doesn't seem to be in his right mind anymore."

I'm bothered that she would even say that to me, as if I have put some magical spell on him to lure him out of reality. Although, what bothers me most about what she just said is the fact she's agreeing with the board now. How do you work with someone for such a long time and still not really know them? Maybe like everyone else, she's just never made an effort, thinking it was just how he is, instead of who he is. I've suddenly lost my appetite, so I get up and take the remainder of my dinner and throw it straight in the trash.

Carrying my wine, I start heading back to my room, but before I get there, I turn to Nic with a sorrowful look on my face. "You know, Nic, he's a pretty amazing guy if you actually take the time to really get to know and respect him as though he's no different than any of us. His brilliance isn't a curse, it's an extraordinary gift that makes him who he is, which is pretty damn amazing, if you ask me."

Nic turns her head away from me as though she knows I'm right and has spent all these past years not giving him much of a chance. "It's true, I probably could have made more of an effort." She looks back at me with a gentle smile on her face. "So, vacation, huh?"

I force a smile back at her and then head back to my room to get changed into my favorite worn-in sweats and loose tank top. As I climb into bed with my glass of wine and my phone, I scroll through my contacts until I reach Kennen's number that Nic gave to me right before I started. I take a minute to think about what I am doing, and then decide to go for it:

**Brielle:** I really want someone to look at me the way I look at a travel brochure ~ Brielle

A few minutes later I see the infamous dots appear as he is responding to my message, and I think my heart skips a beat awaiting his reply.

>**Kennen:** Oh, don't worry, Brielle, I'm looking. Try not to dream about me again tonight, though, will you?
>**Brielle:** I'll try, but I never make promises I don't intend to keep.
>**Kennen:** Perfect, neither do I.
>**Brielle:** Good night, Kennen.
>**Kennen:** Good dreams, Brielle.

## Chapter 12

The past four days have raced by so quickly that it all seems like one ginormous blur right now. It's hard to believe that in about an hour Kennen and I will be boarding a plane together and flying to Florida for our vacation. Well, technically his vacation, and I guess a "workcation" for me, not that I mind when working means keeping him distracted.

I spent the weekend helping take care of Nic and getting her settled. Luckily, her mom was able to spend an extra week since this trip came up unexpectedly and wouldn't allow me to be around to take care of her if something came up that she needed assistance with.

Nic is still in shock that this trip is actually happening, as is Kennen, for that matter. He has been in nonstop panic mode, trying to get as much work done as possible since I walked in on Monday. It's understandable, though, as I've made a point to remind him numerous times this week that as soon as we land in Florida, all work stops. Along with the reminders, I also got quite a few aggravated looks, which made me snicker.

Kennen made sure that we left the office in time to get to the airport and have *exactly* two and a half hours to check our bags, go through security, and arrive at our gate, which is where we currently are. Luckily, since it's a later flight, it isn't overly crowded, which is keeping him somewhat calm. He wasn't overly excited when he found out that we would have to make a connection in Atlanta, but at least it is only a forty-five-minute layover.

As he's sitting there typing away on his laptop with his earbuds in, I pass my time people watching. There's no better place to do this than at an airport, and it always amazes me how different each person really is and how they react to their surroundings. Perfect example…the attendant at our gate just got on the intercom and mentioned that our flight is currently running approximately thirty minutes late, due to our inbound aircraft having a previous weather delay. A few people just sighed and went back to their business, and then, of course, there's always that one person. You know who I'm talking about. The one who thinks it's an atrocity for such a delay to be occurring, and she starts screaming at the poor girl behind the desk, who is clearly just the messenger, and demanding to speak to a manager. Unless this poor girl has a connection with Mother Nature, I'm sure there is not much she, or her manager for that matter, can do about it.

Oblivious to everything going on around us right now, I decide not to mention the delay to Kennen, as I don't want to release the kraken and totally ruin that poor attendant's night. If she thinks that last lady was bad, she might go home and never come back after Kennen. Although, I'd be lying if I wasn't a little concerned myself about missing our connection in Atlanta, but I'm going to be positive and focus on the fact that they can usually make up some time in the air. Plus, life is an adventure, right? If anyone knows that, it should be me, considering all these crazy choices

I've been making in the past couple of weeks.

I grab a book out of my carry-on and decide to get comfy for the next hour or so until we board. It doesn't take me long to get sucked right into the plot of this debut rom-com novel and start to have several laugh-out-loud moments. After a while, I look up and notice that Kennen has his chin propped up in his hand on the armrest of the chair and is staring at me with quite the grin spread across his face. I suddenly feel self-conscious, not knowing how long he has been doing that, and why he has that look anyway.

"What, is there something you find amusing?" I speak out, trying to keep a straight face.

"I thought I already cleared this up in our texts last Friday night, when I told you that I am looking?"

Right, the text messages. Hmm, yes, there was some mention of him looking at me, but all I can really think about is the fact that he told me not to dream about him again and then wished me "good dreams" instead of "good night." Does he have any idea what that does to one's sleeping abilities after a comment like that? I start to feel heat rising up my chest, and I will myself to refocus, as he is definitely taking note of my every movement right now.

Thankfully, we are interrupted by a new announcement letting us know that we will begin boarding in the next few minutes. At this, Kennen packs up his gear, then stands to get ready to line up. I gather all my belongings and walk up beside him, waiting for our boarding group to be called.

Once we're settled into our seats in first class, and the rest of the plane is seated and being prepared for takeoff, I notice that Kennen's face suddenly seems excruciatingly tense with a hint of panic.

I turn in my seat to look at him better. "Hey, is

everything okay?"

"Everything's fine. It's just that—" he looks down at his hands, which are now threaded together so tightly that a professional wrestler couldn't even break the hold "—you know I don't care for traveling. Well, the worst part for me is always the takeoff and landing." He continues to look down after he's said this.

Before I can reply, the plane begins to depart from the gate, and the flight attendant starts going through the safety protocols. I quickly grab one of his hands and turn it over so that his palm is faced up.

His face instantly looks right up at mine. "What are you doing, Brielle? I don't need you to hold my hand, if that's what you're thinking."

I give him a dramatic eye roll. "Didn't I mention that one of my friends in high school taught me a little bit about palm reading?" I say, with an excited smile on my face.

He gives me a quick laugh. "Is that so? Why does that not surprise me?"

"Okay, let's see here…bear with me, as I may be a little rusty." I slowly run my finger softly down his palm and notice he sucks in a quick breath. Huh, maybe I'm not the only one who feels this insane energy every time we touch. I continue, "This one here is your lifeline, and based on the fact that it is long, you will have excellent health, but what's interesting is that it splits off in this one area."

"Well, I'm glad to hear that my health is good. Maybe we could have just shown this to the board and skipped out on this vacation?" He gives me a quick wink. "But what does that split you were talking about mean exactly?"

I'm actually pretty surprised about this split, so I trace it again. "Usually, a split on your lifeline tends to suggest a change of direction in life, and before you say it, I don't think it represents taking a vacation."

He looks out the plane window and seems to think about this for a minute, and then looks back over at me. "What does yours show?" He quickly grabs my hand and turns it over, sending heated tingles up my arm.

"Mine also has a long lifeline, thankfully, but see how mine has a break over here where yours splits?"

He nods in agreement.

"Well, that too means a directional change in life, but for me that's just par for the course, as my life seems to change quicker than the weather on a Florida afternoon these days."

At this, he gives me a quick laugh.

I'm about to start explaining his heart line when an announcement from our pilot comes across the speaker, announcing our arrival at thirty-seven thousand feet, and that he is turning off the seat belt sign, so we are free to roam around the cabin if needed. This cracks me up, as where the hell are we going to "roam" exactly?

He gives my hand a quick squeeze, and then just as fast, he lets it go, reaches under the seat to pull his laptop back out, and sets it down on the tray table he's just put down. Crossing my arms, I give him a somewhat scolding look.

He finally senses me looking at him. "Wow, if looks could kill, Brielle."

"You'd better live up the next four hours of travel time we have working on that thing, because as soon as we land in Florida, I'm literally going to be pulling the plug."

He gives me quite the shameless smirk. "Yes, dear."

I know he's just giving me a hard time, but hearing him call me "dear" does something to me inside. I sit back in my seat and try to imagine what it would be like to actually be in a relationship with him. Would we spend all our time bickering back and forth, cracking each other up, or enjoying quiet moments together? If I had it my way, it would be all of the above, as I believe that's what makes up a great relationship to begin with.

I decide to grab my iPad and connect to the free Wi-Fi we get in first class and hop online to do a little research before our dinner tomorrow night. Typing in Austin Williams of AW Advisors to see what I can find out, my screen suddenly fills with tons of articles, websites, and photos of this guy, which I find interesting. I knew his firm was up and coming, but based on these results, his face and name are everywhere. Pulling up an article on *Business Weekly*, I start scanning through it, but it only talks about his firm and the amazing growth they have seen over the past year, which is not what I'm looking for. I need to know "who" this guy really is and what he's like. I need the dirt.

Of course, we all know the best place to find that out is, yup…on social media. Having a feeling he is not the type of guy to keep his account set to private, I open Instagram and type in his name, and after a few quick swipes, there he is. I click on his account and start scrolling through all his pictures, tags, and comments. He looks to be a similar age to me and is definitely throwing off some major Chris Hemsworth vibes, with lighter hair, blue eyes, and barely enough scruff to potentially call it a beard. I instantly smile. What is the deal with all these "financial" guys lately looking like they belong on a spread in *GQ* magazine? The marketing side of me can already picture the upcoming photoshoots with him and Kennen to announce the merger of their firms, and I can't help but laugh about how much more business they will probably attract from them.

Kennen suddenly clears his throat and looks at me curiously. "What exactly are you doing, Brielle?"

Busted.

"I'm doing some research for when we go to dinner tomorrow night with Austin, why?"

"Research…right." His look suddenly seems to have a little edge of jealousy to it as he very slowly turns his focus back to his laptop screen.

Well, well, well, this just got interesting. Maybe I should mess with Kennen a little bit here, but I decide not to push it any more than I already have in the past two weeks.

"Yes, research," I say plainly. "Since this dinner is supposed to be an all-casual, no-business get-together, I thought it would be a good idea to find out some of his interests, likes, etc. so that we all have something to talk about."

He starts to chuckle. "Okay then, so what have you found out so far that would be pertinent to our knowledge of him exactly?"

"Let's see, from what I can tell, he is definitely quite the social butterfly, somewhat egocentric, likes to go on adventures in the outdoors, he seems to prefer blondes, and, oh, it looks like he's really into whiskey."

His left eyebrow arches up. "Is that so? You can tell all of that about him after looking at his social network feed for all of five minutes?"

I hold my head up. "I told you, I'm usually a good judge of character."

Our conversation ends when we are approached by the flight attendant asking us if we would like a beverage. "Excuse the interruption. Would either of you like a complimentary glass of champagne or something off our premium cabin beverage list perhaps?"

Oh my gosh, she is my new best friend, sorry, Nic. "Yes, a glass of champagne would be wonderful, thank you." I turn to Kennen. "Would you like some also?"

He looks up at the attendant. "No, thank you, but if I could please have a glass of water with lemon, I would appreciate it."

"Of course, sir." She gets our beverages, hands them to us, each with a napkin underneath, and then moves on to assist the passengers sitting across from us.

"Water, really?" I ask Kennen, wondering if this guy ever lets loose every once in a while.

"Like your famous iced cup of crack, I also can't drink alcohol, as it too sets my mind into a swirl of unbearable madness, and in the end it's not worth paying for it." His face seems somewhat somber with this statement.

My heart breaks for him a little bit at his mention of this, not that there is anything wrong with not drinking alcohol, or caffeine for that matter, but for the fact that he can't even indulge in some of life's enjoyable pleasures every once in a while without causing him such distress.

I try to lighten the mood, so I continue, "Well, if it makes you feel any better, I'm a truthful drunk, which tends to get me into trouble at times." I give him a wink and then pick up my glass of champagne, holding it up to him, ready to toast.

"Here's to a well-deserved vacation, and according to our palms, a long life filled with whatever changes it intends to throw our way."

He smiles at me warmly and picks up his water; then we clink glasses and take a sip (or a gulp in my instance).

Kennen goes back to working on his laptop, and I decide to do some research on whiskey, as I feel like this could be a good conversation topic with Austin tomorrow.

As I start doing my search, I realize there are so many types that I need to narrow this down a little bit somehow. I locate the website of the restaurant Austin suggested we meet at and pull up their online liquor menu. It looks like for whiskeys they have several, ranging from your common Jack Daniel's, Crown Royal, and Jameson to what seems like, based on the cost, your finer whiskeys like Blanton's Original Single Barrel Whiskey and Yamazaki 12-Year-Old Whisky. This is certainly helpful, so I open another browser and start looking at tasting notes for each of them and then start jotting down some information about each in my notes app. Trying to memorize this by tomorrow night might prove to be challenging, but I am going to give it my best effort to impress Austin.

A short time later, the pilot comes back on to make an announcement, letting us know that we are going to begin our descent into Atlanta. Unfortunately, we are still around thirty minutes late, which only gives us fifteen minutes to get to our next gate and board the plane. As we start putting away all our electronics and personal items into our carry-ons to store them beneath the seats in front of us, Kennen looks at his watch and then back up at me with a renewed panic in his face.

Reading his mind, this time I speak up. "By the way, how do you feel about running?" I suddenly look down at my feet, remembering that I still have my high heels on from working earlier today.

Following my eyes to my feet, he throws his hands in the air and then starts laughing, like really laughing for the first time since I've met him. "Now this I have got to see."

I start laughing alongside him and try to figure out exactly how I'm going to pull this one off. I have faith and determination though, and I will not let some three-inch spikey heels stand in my way, damn it.

We are close to landing now, and I can see him tensing up again, so this time I decide to just take his hand in mine, not caring if it bothers him or not. As we start to experience some turbulence, he gives me a slight squeeze, and I squeeze him back slightly harder, which then turns into a game of who can squeeze the hardest. I suddenly feel like I'm back in high school, which makes me laugh yet again.

Before we know it, the plane has safely landed on the runway, bringing a much-needed sense of peace to Kennen's previously rigid face. Once they open the door of the plane, we head out of the Jetway and begin running, people looking at us like we are bank robbers escaping from the scene of the crime. I'm struggling to keep up with Kennen with his long strides and my not-so-perfect footwear, so he slows down slightly and grabs ahold of my hand.

Of course, our plane landed in Terminal E, and our next flight is in Terminal A, so we are booking it down there, trying not to take people out on our way. As we finally turn the corner of our new terminal, Kennen suddenly yanks me out of the way of one of those carts that ride around giving people who need assistance lifts to their gates. In doing so, I end up losing my balance and twisting my ankle just enough that it will probably still be a little sore in the morning, although it did save me from a nasty fall.

I stop for a minute, not sure how much pressure I can put on it, when we hear the final boarding call for our flight in the distance. Before I even know what's happening, Kennen scoops me up effortlessly, like I'm a bag full of groceries that he's carrying home, and takes off running again.

We reach the gate just as they are starting to close the door. "Please wait. We're supposed to be on this flight," I yell, since Kennen is now noticeably out of breath. Thankfully, they pause and meet us back over by the podium to scan our boarding passes. Kennen very carefully sets me back down on the ground so that he can retrieve his and I can retrieve mine. After we hand them over and are ready to get on the plane, Kennen once again picks me up and carries me all the way down the Jetway and to my seat on the plane. At this point, it seems like every pair of eyes on the plane are peering at us now with the grand entrance we've just made.

The male flight attendant for first class approaches us with a big smirk on his face. "Newlyweds, are we?"

Oh my gosh, the look on Kennen's face is priceless.

He quickly replies with a serious yet condescending tone to his voice. "No, we're not married. She just had a near-death airport transportation experience and might have sprained her ankle in the process."

I quickly put a hand over my mouth to keep myself from laughing my ass off as the attendant's eyes shoot open as big as saucers.

"Oh, my goodness, I'm so sorry to hear that. Let me go get you some ice in a bag to put on it, unless you'd rather get off the flight and go to the emergency care center back in the airport?"

"NO," we both boldly shout at the same time.

I can tell by the look on this poor guy's face that he already thinks this is going to be a long late-night flight. "I'm sorry—" I look over at his nametag "—Derick," I continue, "we didn't mean to yell. It's just that our flight was late, causing us to sprint all the way down here from

Terminal E in less than fifteen minutes in these crazy heels. Then I almost got ran over, hurting my ankle in the process, leaving my personal Superman over here running the rest of the way while carrying me. We'll be sure to behave the rest of the flight." I wink, hoping that I can win this guy back over.

He starts laughing. "Fifteen minutes, huh, that might be a new airport record." He gives us a smile. "Let me go get that ice for you, and I'll be right back."

Kennen looks over at me with a raised eyebrow. "Personal Superman, really?"

I lean over right next to his head and whisper in his ear, "Yes, my very own hero." I slowly move my mouth over the slightest bit and give him a gentle kiss on his cheek, then carefully pull away, keeping my eyes locked on his the whole time.

I notice him swallow hard, and I could swear that his eyes seem a slightly darker shade of cerulean blue than they were just a minute ago.

Interrupting our moment, Derick comes back over with the ice bag for my ankle. "Here you go. Please let me know if you need anything else. In the meantime, please buckle your seatbelts for takeoff, thank you." Then he walks off.

After we buckle up, Kennen carefully pats my leg and motions for me to turn towards him and put my leg up on his lap. Luckily, my legs are short enough where it fits in the space we have between us. Then he gently removes my shoe and asks me for the ice bag to put on my ankle. I give a slight wince when he first puts it on, but more because of the sheer coldness of the ice than the injury itself.

He looks at me with concern. "Are you okay, Brielle?"

"I'll survive, and I'm sure I'll be good as new by tomorrow," I say, and give him a reassuring smile. "Thank you for coming to my rescue and carrying me the rest of the way."

With a sly grin he looks at me. "You're very welcome, as it was definitely my pleasure." He looks out the window as the plane starts pulling back, and begins gently rubbing my leg, causing me to close my eyes and finally take a few calm breaths after that whole insane fiasco.

Once we're at altitude, Derick comes by and hands Kennen a pillow to put under my ankle, and takes our drink order.

"Derick, we'll have two glasses of champagne and one glass of water with lemon, please."

"My pleasure, let me get those for both of you." He prepares them, then puts all three glasses on my tray table, since my leg is preventing Kennen from putting his down, and moves on.

Kennen pointedly looks at me. "I thought I was clear enough earlier that I do not drink alcohol, Brielle."

I start laughing. "You were. Don't worry, these are both for me," I say, picking up the first glass of champagne, and take a long sip. "The pain will be gone in no time now."

He shakes his head and starts laughing. "Ah, I see. My apologies for the wrongful accusation."

I figure now that I have his attention and sympathy for the duration of the flight, it might be a good time to try to coax some information out of him about his personal life.

"So tell me, Mr. Davis, along with you clearly being a mathematical genius and a real-life superhero, are there any other powers or talents that I should know about?"

"Hmm, let's see, for powers, I also have a photographic memory, which comes in handy quite a bit of the time. As far as talents go, well, I guess you'll have to wait and see."

He gives me a big grin and a wink when he's done speaking.

Okay, so we're going there now, are we? Little does he know he just opened up a can of worms. I grab my glass of champagne, down the rest of it, and place the empty glass behind the remaining full one.

"Keeping me in suspense, now, are we?" I say while giving him the most seductive smile I own.

His reply is instant. "I like it that way, as it tends to prolong the excitement." He's looking at me right now as if he's got X-ray vision, undressing me as he looks from my face down to my waist and up again.

I'm glad I have a blazer on top of my shirt so that he can't see the effect he is currently having on me right now. I take another sip of champagne, hoping that it will cool off the flames rising inside that are about to melt me to the core.

Kennen grabs his water and starts to take a long sip, and I can't help but watch him. How is it possible that you can make something like sipping a drink as sexy as that?

Oh yeah, it's time to get nosey. "So, Kennen, tell me, where is the craziest place you have ever utilized or thought about using these talents you mention?"

He lets out a few coughs like his water suddenly went down the wrong pipe.

I start rubbing circles on his back. "Are you okay, or do you need me to give you mouth-to-mouth?" Why stop the flirting now that I've started?

He clears his throat, his eyes suddenly burning with desire. "My office," is all he says, and then waits for me to reply.

Oh, right, he is answering my question that got him all worked up to begin with. When I think about this, it begins to cause a sour taste in my mouth, as of course he would say office since that is where he probably last shared his talents, with Kari nonetheless.

With my delay in response, he continues, "And thought about not utilized, many times, as a matter of fact."

Okay, so maybe they didn't have sex during that meeting, then, but as he just confirmed, he has definitely been thinking about it. Why is it that all the gorgeous women get to have men fantasizing about them? What about us normal, everyday cute and funny women? I grab my drink and start taking another long sip to add to the slight buzz that is currently forming.

"So," he says, looking at me with great curiosity, "what about you, Miss Bisset?"

Before I even think about what I am saying, I blurt out, "Your office as well, actually."

He quickly raises his left eyebrow, and I happen to notice the rise and fall of his chest, as he is suddenly breathing a little heavier now.

"Is that so?"

Oh. My. Gosh. Did I seriously just say that out loud? Why can't I be a happy drunk instead of a truthful one? It's too late now, so I decide to just keep going and dig myself into a bigger hole.

"About five days ago to be specific," I say point-blank and then finish off the rest of my champagne without looking at his reaction, hoping this will shut me up for a few minutes.

He seems to think about this for a moment, carefully considering his response. "Huh, great minds must think alike, then." He waits for me to turn and look at him before he goes on. "I have to be honest with you, Brielle, I have never been so outrageously pissed off and fiercely turned on all at once like that."

Wait, did he just say what I think he said? His craziest thought was about him and me in his office, not Kari? Okay, I need to just take a deep breath and refocus for a minute, as this is not where I thought he was going with that.

"While we're being honest, I was kind of hoping that you would have backed me up right into your office door and—"

He cuts me off. "You have no idea how much I wanted to do just that, remind you who was the boss that day, with you taking control of my career like that, but that's just it, Brielle." He looks out the window for a minute and then back at me with a slight pain in his demeanor. "I am your boss, and it would be totally inappropriate and most likely end in disaster."

Ouch, I instantly feel sober with that proclamation. Professionally inappropriate, probably. End in disaster, why? It's not like co-workers can't date and have happily-ever-afters.

He sees me wince and tries to recover. "I'm sorry, I didn't mean it to sound like that." He rubs a hand across his forehead. "I'm not really good at this sort of conversation to begin with, hell, conversation in general, as you may have already figured out." He looks at me apologetically. "Brielle, as much as I love us flirting with each other, we probably should just keep it at that so neither of us gets hurt, okay?" He begins to rub my leg again.

I grab the ice pack and gently pull my leg off his lap, resting it in front of me again. Then quietly I reply, "Of course, Kennen, I understand."

We sit in silence for the remainder of the flight, and I

suddenly feel the soreness of my ankle and the stress of how the conversation ended start to settle in. Once we've arrived at the gate in Florida, I carefully stand up and grab my carry-on and get ready to exit.

He puts his hand on my arm to stop me for a moment. "How's your ankle? Do you need me to carry you again?"

There's no way I could be in his arms right now, so I will suffer through whatever pain I need to at this point. "It's feeling somewhat better, so as long as we take it slowly, I should be fine, thank you."

He looks at me somewhat regretfully. "Of course, luckily this is a much smaller airport, so it shouldn't be as much walking for you."

We take our time getting over to baggage claim and gather up our suitcases, then go outside to wait for our rideshare driver to come get us. Unfortunately, it's another forty-five-minute ride to Seaside from here, and it's already really late. Once the driver arrives and we get settled into the car and head off, I can feel the tiredness gently creeping in.

Luckily, our driver is quiet, as most are at this time of night, and I lean my head against the window and slowly start to drift off to sleep.

After what seems like only five minutes, I hear Kennen calling my name, and when I open my eyes, I realize my head is currently resting on his chest, with his arm wrapped around me.

"Brielle, I am sorry to wake you, but we're here."

I slowly sit up, trying to refocus, and see that we are in front of a stunning three-story beach house. That is from what I can tell, anyway, with the limited light currently shining on the front porch and a few interior lights.

We get out of the car and then walk up to a smaller

front porch, where I enter the code Austin gave me for the lockbox he put on there. As we enter the foyer, there's a charming stairwell to our left with treads and risers made from natural-colored reclaimed wood, white board-and-batten walls, white spindles, and an amazing handrail that looks like it was custom made with long pieces of driftwood. Right in front of us is an accent wall made of hundreds of beautiful oyster shells and a narrow driftwood accent table.

As we walk to the right and a little further down a short hallway, there is a doorway on the left with a smaller room currently staged as a simple home gym with white walls on one side and mirrors on the other, an exposed wood ceiling, free weights, and a yoga mat. As we continue walking, we pass a full bathroom, and then it opens into a game room fully equipped with a bar area, a billiards table, a skeet ball game, and a pinball machine. If you can't have fun in this space, then you must have some serious issues. The back of the room has a fully stackable sliding glass door that opens the whole space up onto a back porch, which gives you private beach access right to the ocean in between the dunes.

I so desperately want to go run onto the beach, but I'm exhausted and ready to get settled into a bedroom by this point. I look over at Kennen, who is slowly turning around and taking in everything in this room.

"I can't believe how great this space is, and it's only the first floor."

He laughs. "Yeah, when you said beach house, I don't know why, but I was thinking more cottage-like than house for some reason." Then he nods back towards the front entry where we first came in. "Let's go check out the rest of the house quick and then head to bed, as it's been an extremely long day for both of us."

In agreement, I follow him back to the stairs and take a deep breath. While the throbbing in my ankle has lessened to a dull roar compared to what it was earlier, it's still somewhat sore, and the thought of climbing up two flights of stairs seems like quite the task.

Kennen notices my reaction to them and turns around so his back is to me as he kneels down on the first step. "Here, climb on. I'll give you a lift." As if he has eyes in the back of his head, he chimes in, "Brielle, just get on my back. I know your ankle isn't healed yet, and the stairwell is too narrow for me to carry you the other way."

Is he seriously offering me a piggyback ride right now? Oh, what the hell, I'm too tired to argue at this point. Quietly snickering, I take off my heels, climb on his back, and then wrap my arms around his neck. He carefully rises and then walks us up the stairs to the second level. Aside from some undercounter lights in the kitchen, the rest of the space is filled with darkness, requiring us to locate some wall switches and turn a couple of them on.

The kitchen is the first area to the right and is equally as impressive as the one in Kennen's apartment. However, this one contains some coastal touches like the incredible seashell backsplash and exposed driftwood shelving, giving the all-white kitchen a welcome warmth. The kitchen opens to the living and dining room areas, with a long island and barstools dividing the spaces. I love the open floor plan, but what I'm most enchanted by is the wall full of French doors that has the most spectacular view of the ocean just past the deck.

I can't help myself, so I grab Kennen's hand and pull him alongside me out through the doors onto the covered deck, which is furnished with an outdoor seating area and an outdoor dining/grilling area. "Oh my gosh, Kennen, isn't this the most amazing sight you've ever seen?" I smile widely at him.

He glances over at the ocean for a moment and then back at me with a soft smile on his face. "Not quite, but certainly close." He lifts his hand and tucks a few loose strands of hair behind my ear that the ocean breeze blew out of my bun. "Come on, my little Ula, we still have one more level to explore."

Curiously, I look at him. "Ula, what exactly does that mean?"

"Gem of the sea, or sea jewel." He winks and then leads me back over to yet another set of stairs, resumes his position, and carries me up to what I assume is the final level.

There are two average-sized bedrooms on the end towards the front of the house, with a jack and jill bathroom connecting them. Between them is a den area with two larger master suites situated on the ocean side of the home. The layout of both suites is identical, aside from them being the flipped version of each other and the different décor. With further exploration we realize that both rooms also open to a shared covered deck by way of French doors like the second floor. We take a quick peek out there and see yet another astonishing view of the ocean. Hung between each post are curtains that are pulled back (but could be let down for privacy), an extremely comfy-looking chair with an ottoman, and the most spectacular bed-sized swing you could ever imagine. I'm in complete awe of this house and feel so blessed to be able to experience it for the next week while we are here.

"Why don't you pick which room you'd like, and I'll go back downstairs and grab all of our luggage."

"Thank you so much. I'm really sorry I can't help out more."

"I would have done it for you anyway, Brielle, so there's no need to worry about it. You need to get your ankle elevated, so go hop on one of the beds and relax for a few minutes." Then he heads out and down the stairs as the gentleman I know he is, but for some reason pretends not to be.

I head back inside and end up picking the suite that has seashell décor and the most mesmerizing oil painting of the waves above the headboard, two of my favorite things. The other room is a little more masculine and decorated with nautical ropes and an incredible oil painting of a ship in rough seas. Both rooms have white walls with the most exquisite paneling and trim package. It's obvious that Austin spared no expense with the renovation of this house, and I can't even imagine how much he will end up selling it for.

Taking off my blazer, I hang it up in the walk-in closet and then go stretch out on the bed. I snuggle my head into a bunch of pillows that are so fluffy they feel like a pile of feathers. A few minutes later, I hear Kennen making his way up the final flight of stairs and then calling out to me to see which room I ended up in.

"I'm in here," I say loud enough so that he can hear me from where he is.

He takes one look at me when he walks in with my luggage and laughs. "Comfortable, are we?"

"I think I'm in heaven and may not move for the next few days," I say, with a huge smile as I roll onto my side and watch as he places my things over by the closet.

"It looks like it, go get some rest, and I will see you in the morning. Good night, Brielle." He smiles and goes to shut the door.

"Good night, Kennen, and thanks again for everything today." With that I reluctantly sit up and make my way off the bed to unpack and get ready for bed.

Once I'm all washed up and have taken some ibuprofen, I try to turn my mind off to get some much-needed rest. Unfortunately, I think my forty-five-minute catnap and my typical late-night mind shenanigans have other plans for me, again.

Quietly, I get out of bed and open the French door out to the deck and head outside so as not to wake Kennen in the room next door. I decide to walk over to the edge of the balcony and sit down on the edge with my back against the post. Looking out over the sea, I take a deep breath, trying to fill my lungs with the welcome fresh, salty sea air. There's a gentle ocean breeze this evening, blowing against my arms and legs, cooling me just enough so that I'm not overly warm.

I continue to watch the waves gently rolling in and right back out again, reminding me of how much I enjoy being at the beach at night. There's no chaos of the crowds, just the peace of the quietness, and the only light around is coming from the moon reflecting off the ripples of water.

Glancing over at Kennen's room, I see he's got the drapes pulled closed, but through the cracks it looks as though he's got a dim light on somewhere in his room. Knowing him, he's probably sneaking in time working on his laptop that he's not supposed to. This makes me internally chuckle, as I've never met someone so passionate and dedicated to his career before. Well, I take that back, as Nic is also very much like that. Okay, fine, so maybe I'm just a slacker in that department.

I decide to try going back to sleep again, as I need to

have energy for our dinner coming up with Austin. Before I do, I grab hold of my cell phone and send off a quick text.

> **Brielle:** I do my own stunts…
> **Kennen:** "A true hero isn't measured by the size of his strength, but by the strength of his heart." – Hercules
> **Brielle:** Nice try, but I'm not sure I'm buying that one, Superman…
> **Kennen:** You can't blame a superhero for trying, right?
> **Brielle:** Don't ever stop trying. Now stop working and go to bed.
> **Kennen:** Wait. How would you know if I'm working or not?
> **Brielle:** You never asked me what my superpowers were, now did you?
> **Kennen:** So, X-ray vision then or psychic telepathy?
> **Brielle:** You may never know…goodnight, boss.
> **Kennen:** Touché, good dreams, Brielle…

I blow out a slow breath, as this man drives me insane. How am I supposed to survive the next week with him without anyone else around for the most part? I really need to get a hold of myself. Now totally flustered, I bury my head in the pillow and will myself to go to sleep, and thankfully shortly after, I get my wish.

## CHAPTER 13

What the hell am I doing here, and by here, I not only mean this crazy vacation, but with Brielle? I can't seem to control myself around her, and I know I need to, being her boss. "Boss," yeah, she didn't seem to take my comment regarding that matter very well on the plane earlier. I didn't intend for it to come off harshly, or that it was more to do with us personally not being able to work versus us working together. I just felt like it was the right thing to do in this situation. Could we even possibly have a lasting relationship, though, if the work part of it wasn't an issue? We are noticeably different types of people, but it's a scientific fact that the opposite ends of magnets attract, right?

I have only ever had one serious relationship in my life so far, and we were somewhat similar people, and look where that left me. A heart so broken that even years later there are still cracks running through it. I told myself that after Kari destroyed me, I wouldn't let anyone inside again. So then why can I not stop thinking about when I was carrying Brielle through the airport with her body pressed against mine, her arms wrapped around my neck, and how perfect she felt just being there, letting me take care of her?

Hell, just the simple act of her tracing the lines in my

hand while she was doing my "palm reading" shot a connection so intense throughout my whole body that it took everything I had not to pull her out of her seat and into my lap so I could feel the warmth of her body on mine. Now here we are, the only thing separating us is a single wall, some furniture, and my stubbornness about not giving us a chance.

Between these thoughts of Brielle and all the numbers regarding this merger running through my mind right now, I'll be lucky if I am able to get any sleep tonight. The good news is I don't think Brielle put anything crazy on our vacation agenda for tomorrow except for our dinner with Austin.

I put my laptop away and try to get comfortable so that I may sink into slumber, but of course my revolving mind has other plans. Maybe I do need to find a hobby to try to distract my mind somewhat and get some much-needed peace. More importantly, maybe I need to find someone not something.

Looking at my watch, I see that it is only five o'clock. Of course it is, because that is the exact same time I have been waking up every day for at least the past ten years or so. I press my palms into my eyes, trying to relieve some of the pressure on them from the exhaustion. The last time I checked before falling asleep, it was two o'clock, so a whole three hours, wonderful. Trying to fall back asleep is completely pointless, so I decide to get up and try to get my daily workout in before Brielle gets up.

Carefully, I open my bedroom door and head down the stairs as quietly as possible, as I have a fairly good assumption at this point that Brielle is not a morning person. I go into the kitchen, hoping that there are some glasses around so I can fill one with water and take it with me down to the first floor where the gym is. Luckily, after opening a few cabinet doors, I find a water bottle, which is perfect.

I have to say, I'm impressed with the attention to detail Austin put into this remodel. With further investigation I find the kitchen is fully stocked with all the utensils, plates, glassware, and cookware that you would need had you been living here. He must be trying to sell it as a totally prepped potential rental or vacation home property.

Before heading downstairs, I notice that there is a generous fruit and nut basket on the corner of the kitchen counter that has a card on it with Brielle's and my name, and a welcome message from Austin. That was nice of him, especially since there isn't a lick of food in this house, and we didn't have a chance to go to the market last night when we arrived.

Down in the gym area, I begin with some stretches to try to loosen up all the tension built up inside me right now. As I begin using the free weights, I realize that my arms and back are reasonably sore from carrying Brielle while running in the airport and up three flights of stairs here last night. Don't get me wrong, though, it's not as though she's heavy because she is the perfect weight, actually. It's just that I definitely exerted myself more than I would have on any other given workday. I decide at this point that I should probably focus on cardio today instead. The problem is there is no treadmill, which is how I usually get this part of my workout in, but I guess why would you need one living here, literally on the beach?

Passing through the sliding glass door in the game room

area, I walk down the path that leads to the beach. It's still pretty dark out considering the sun hasn't risen yet, but this is perfect for me so that I don't have to be distracted by other people when I am trying to stay inside my own mind. As I start finding my pace, I can't help but feel a part of me start to actually relax a little bit. The sand is extremely soft and seems to be soothing my feet as I go.

I have no idea how far I ended up running, but when I get back, the early morning light is beginning to softly rise against the horizon. After refilling my water bottle, I decide to go out onto the back deck and watch the sun rise and fill the sky with the most beautiful rainbow pastel colors. It's moments like these that I wish I could control the distractions in my mind for a few minutes, just to be able to see and appreciate this without the moment being clouded over.

With the morning light beginning to overtake the day, I decide to go back in and head upstairs to get cleaned up. As I approach the bedroom, I hear the shower running in Brielle's suite, which I didn't expect for at least another hour or so based on how late we were up last night. Knowing she is a caffeine crack addict and there's not a trace of that in this house right now, I go in my room and grab my wallet and flip-flops and head back downstairs to the entrance of the house and decide to go get her one of the "chippy" beverages she likes. I remember her mentioning that everything you may need around here is within walking or biking distance, so I take a deep breath and head out the door.

This is way out of my comfort zone considering I hardly ever go out into public places, especially in areas where I have never been before. Besides the office and my apartment, I very rarely go anywhere else. Hell, I even get all my to-go orders and groceries delivered to avoid it all. Something inside me really wants to do this for Brielle though, so I start heading down the road to where the main area of town is. I eventually end up in front of a specialty coffee shop with white shiplap siding, and tables adorned with blue umbrellas that already have customers gathered around them out on the patio. As I head inside, I am instantly hit with the amazing aroma of freshly brewed coffee. This is another reason why I don't venture out much, as it's somewhat torturous inhaling these scents and not being able to enjoy them.

Once it's my turn up at the counter, I'm instantly greeted by a very bubbly woman who seems more than happy to be here at work right now. I look up at the menu boards and then back down at her. "Good morning, maybe you could be of some help to me, please, as I'm not exactly sure what I should be ordering."

Her smile is welcoming, and she's not at all annoyed by the fact that I'm holding up the rather large line forming behind me. "What type of beverage are you craving this beautiful morning?"

"My girlfriend likes the iced frappés made with chocolate chips and caramel, I think. Is that something you are able to make for me?"

She lightly blushes. "What a sweet boyfriend you are to run out and get this for her. Yes, of course, I'll get that ready for you. Is there anything else I may get you today?"

I raise my eyebrows, just realizing what I said to her and what she said in return. "I'm sorry, I meant to say my co-worker. We're not dating or anything. Maybe I'm the one who should be drinking that this morning, yikes." I look over at her and see her stifle a laugh. "That will be all for this morning, thank you very much."

"Of course. After you pay here, you can pick it up at the end of the counter down there. Oh, and what name shall I put on there for you?" She tilts her head with the cup in one hand and a Sharpie in the other.

With a sudden smirk on my face, I reply, "Ula, please."

Her eyes suddenly shoot to mine after she writes it on the cup. "A gem of the sea is she, this co-worker of yours?" She gives me a wink and then proceeds to complete my transaction.

I quickly clear my throat and can feel my own cheeks flushing now. "Right, that she is."

When they finish preparing my order and call out, "Ula," I grab the cup of devil's juice and head back to the house, trying to erase the embarrassing moment I just shared in that coffee shop.

When I get back, I head back upstairs to the kitchen, where I find Brielle cooking what smells like oatmeal. Wait, where did she get that from, anyway? I take a seat at the island and put the frappé up on the countertop.

When she turns and sees me sitting there with it in front of me, she walks over with a big smile on her face. "Oh my gosh, Kennen, did you get this for me?"

I laugh. "Good morning to you too, Brielle, and yes, this is for you." I slide it over to her, and she grabs it immediately and takes a long sip.

Excitedly, she comes around the island and gives me a quick kiss on the cheek. "You're the best. Thanks, boss." Her whole face is lit up as she heads back over to the stove.

As she starts drinking again and begins stirring the oatmeal in the pot, I try not to pay attention to her lips as they curl around the straw, so I try to change the subject. "So where did you get the oatmeal from? I didn't find any food around here this morning when I was exploring."

She puts the cup down and turns off the stove after finishing up the oatmeal. "I actually packed some in my suitcase, as I figured there wouldn't be anything here before we had the chance to go to the market in town." Then she grabs a cutting board, one of the bananas, a few of the strawberries, and some of the walnuts out of the basket and begins chopping them up.

With everything prepped, she passes one over to me and then grabs her own bowl and drink and sits beside me at the island. "Thanks again for my frappé. I really appreciate it. Although, if I'm being honest, based on what you've told me about yourself, I'm pretty surprised that you ventured into town without me." She nudges my arm with her elbow and gives me a big smile.

I look over at the drink and then back at her. "Well, it was definitely a first, and most certainly a last."

She's looking at me with concern on her face. "Why, did something go wrong while you were out?"

Without saying anything, I turn the cup around so that the name on the label is now facing her. I wait for her reaction to see if she understands what I'm getting at here.

By the look on her face now, I believe she does. "Ula…Kennen, no, you didn't?" She starts laughing hysterically. "Let me guess, the barista who works in a small seaside town knew exactly what that meant, didn't they?"

I put my face in my hands as the memory of the encounter starts flooding back to me. "That wasn't even the worst part, but yes, you are correct. She knew exactly what it stood for."

She puts her hand on my shoulder, trying to calm her laughter down from a solid roar to a soft giggle. "Hmmm,

I guess I owe you a little more than a bowl of oatmeal, then, huh?"

I look back over at her as seriously as I can, even though I am starting to find the humor in all of this because of how contagious her laugh is. "Something like that," I say, deadpan.

"Whatever you want, just let me know." She gives me one of her sexy winks and then gets back to eating her breakfast.

"So it sounds like I'm going to the market solo this morning, then?" With that, she starts laughing all over again and grabs our bowls to take them to the sink.

I stand up as she comes back around to grab her drink, and I trap her back against the island, putting both of my hands on either side of her. "Seems like someone is quite the comedian this morning." Getting as close to her face as I can without actually touching her, I hear her take in a deep breath. I close my eyes, and instead of kissing her, I back up a little bit, grab the drink, take a sip of it, and then walk away.

"I'm going to take a shower," I call back, leaving her there still struggling for breath as I run up the stairs, taking them two at a time. This needs to be a cold shower this morning, as I don't think I can handle any more heat in my life right now.

Since Brielle left to go shopping and explore the downtown area, I figured this was my chance to get caught up on a little work. If she finds out that I'm doing this, she will probably throw this laptop so far out into the sea that it would become encrusted with barnacles like some long-lost buried treasure.

Opening my business email account, I see that there are over sixty new messages since I checked it late last night. I sigh, knowing this is why I can't take a week off. It would take me twice as long as my vacation was just to catch up. I try to answer all the ones first that don't require me to do a bunch of research and/or calculations, and then dive into the more complicated ones. I get through almost all of them when I get a text from Brielle.

> **Brielle:** Hey, I am at the market. I forgot to ask you if you are allergic to anything that I should be aware of.
> **Kennen:** Women.
> **Brielle:** Now who's the comedian?
> **Kennen:** I'm learning from the best…
> **Brielle:** Don't you forget it either. Alright, I'm going to grab some groceries here, and then I'll be on my way back.
> **Kennen:** Hey, I totally forgot to ask how your ankle is today. Do you need help getting the groceries back here?
> **Brielle:** I'm good as new, mostly in part to the amazing care I received after my injury. Also, I took one of the bikes Austin told me he had at the house that has three big baskets on it, so that helps.
> **Kennen:** Only the best for you, Miss Bisset…

I think it's time to pull the plug on work for now and let my laptop cool off for a little while before she gets back and probably inspects it for any potential heat radiating off it. Maybe I'll try to catch a quick power nap also, since we have our "nonbusiness" dinner tonight with Austin, and I'm beyond exhausted at this point.

With everything put away, I lie down on the couch in the living room so that I can hear Brielle when she gets back with the groceries. It makes me feel bad that I didn't even ask her about her ankle before she left. I was in such a state after my coffee adventure this morning, which makes me wish even more so that I didn't have such a hard time in everyday social situations.

Putting my hands behind my head, I close my eyes, blow out a slow breath, and thankfully within a few minutes I fall asleep. When I wake up, Brielle is next to me on the edge of the couch, just watching me.

I sit up, somewhat startled, and run my hands through my hair. "Hey, I'm sorry. Are you ready for me to help you carry the groceries up?"

She's looking at me like I'm crazy. "Kennen, are you feeling okay?"

Now I'm confused. "Yes, I'm fine. Why?"

"I was just wondering, as I called for you several times when I got back, and you didn't reply. Also, you look exhausted. Did you end up getting any sleep last night?"

I suddenly feel a warmth growing in my heart, knowing that she's concerned about me. "Not much less than I normally get, I suppose."

She's looking at me sympathetically now. "How many hours of sleep do you get on a normal day, and how many did you get last night?"

I laugh at that question. "Well, let's see, on a normal night I usually get around four, maybe five if it's a good day. Last night, or shall I say this morning, I got three."

"Yet here you are still functioning, and without caffeine nonetheless. You really are a superhero." She stands up and puts out her hand.

I look up at her. "What?"

"What you need is some good old beach therapy. Come on, let's go get our bathing suits on and head out to the beach and get some salt in that soul of yours."

I take her hand and stand up, then let go of it. "Brielle, I'm not really much of a beach guy, and I already spent my morning running on it, so do you mind if I sit this one out?"

She seems to think about this for a minute, and then she looks over at me. "Kennen, do you trust me?"

Oh, great, the "I am not getting out of this" "do you trust me" question again. I close my eyes and put my hand on my head. "I do, Brielle, but can I join you another day if I promise to go sit out on the deck and read a book while you're out there getting your beach fix?"

Looking somewhat disappointed, she continues, "Okay, fine, but you'd better stay out there and rest until I come back in. Oh, and if I catch you on that laptop again, I am going to hide it from you until the meeting on Monday. You've been warned."

She strides past me and up the stairs to get changed, and I follow her to go grab a book and sit outside on the deck in that comfy-looking chair. Maybe, with any luck, I will fall asleep again, maybe.

A short time later I notice Brielle walking out onto the beach with a bag in hand and a cover over her bathing suit. She looks up to make sure I'm actually out here, and then waves. Waving back at her, I watch as she disappears, probably finding a spot near the dunes where I can't see her from this angle. I must be crazy not to be down there with her right now while she's wearing a bathing suit. Aside from her T-shirt and shorts today, I haven't seen her in anything other than her work clothes, which expose practically no skin on her aside from her neck and a peek at her collarbone every once in a while. It's probably best that I'm up here, though, as it's taking all of the willpower I have to keep my hands and lips off her anyway. I grab my book and try to focus on the words, but they are running as fast through my mind as the numbers currently are.

Approximately two hours later, I finally see her making her way back up to the house, so I get up and go inside to see if she's hungry for a late lunch. When she gets up to the kitchen area, I notice her skin is already illuminated with a golden glow from the short time she spent out there today.

"Before you ask, yes, I stayed outside and read my book the whole time."

She looks at me questioningly and then begins to laugh.

I walk behind the counter and open the refrigerator to see what she ended up buying earlier at the market. It looks like she picked up everything we need to make some salads, which will be perfect for this warm afternoon, and nothing too heavy to spoil our appetites for dinner later this evening.

"I was thinking of making us some salads for lunch. Are you hungry?"

"I'm starving, so that would be great, thank you." She gives me a smile and then heads upstairs to go change.

After getting lunch prepped, I decide to take the salads out to the deck since there is an amazing late afternoon breeze going on right now.

Sitting down across from me, she speaks up. "This view would never get old. And this house is even more incredible in the daylight. I just can't get over it."

I start mixing up my salad and look over at the ocean. "I must admit, even though I'm not really a beach guy, this place is definitely growing on me." I turn to see Brielle smirk and then take a bite of her salad. "What?"

She puts her fork down. "I have a hard time understanding how you're able to focus and function living in NYC, as even I have a hard time dealing with it all." She looks over at the ocean, closes her eyes, and takes a deep breath. "This is my dream in life. To live somewhere like this where I can breathe in fresh ocean air, clear my mind, and fill my soul with the healing salts of the water."

Her passion for the ocean inspires me to think about what she is saying. It really is peaceful here, which one would think would be in my best interest with the everyday life that I lead inside my mind. It makes me think about my life in the city and how sheltered I am there. I go into the office and then home to my apartment, then repeat. Although, my experience this morning should let me know that it wouldn't matter where I lived, as I would still have trouble dealing with society in general.

I look back at her and smile lightly. "I'm not sure I could function any better here, Brielle, based on my earlier coffee house incident."

She moves her hand across the table and laces her fingers in between mine, causing my pulse to begin racing with the intimate connection. "Kennen, it's day one in a new state, a new town, and a new house. Give yourself a little credit. Just the fact that you were kind enough to go venturing out to make sure I had my caffeine this morning, after an extremely long day yesterday, seems like amazing progress if you ask me." She gives my hand a gentle squeeze and then lets go of it to start eating again.

Maybe she's right, as I hadn't thought about it that way. The odds of me doing something like that in the city are pretty much slim to none.

I decide to change the subject before it gets any deeper than it already has. "So how was your visit in town today?"

You can see her eyes instantly light up with this question. "It was amazing. I explored quite a few of the local shops and found some places I would love to take you to before we go back." She looks down at her food and then back up again. "Everyone here is so warm and welcoming; it makes you instantly feel at home."

I smile at her excitement and passion for the simple things in life. "Give me a day or two, and I would really like for you to show me, Brielle."

"Oh, that reminds me. I haven't gone over our itinerary for tomorrow with you yet."

Oh man, I have a feeling I should prepare myself for whatever crazy vacation madness she is about to unleash on me.

"Before you say anything, just hear me out, okay?" Her eyes suddenly glint in mischief.

Great, it's even worse than I expected. I sit back in my chair and cross my arms against my chest. "You shouldn't have said that, as now I'm totally panicked…"

I can't help but smile with how fast she suddenly starts laughing at me.

"You're a seafood guy, are you not?"

Well, this sounds like a loaded question, but I answer anyway, knowing I should probably just say no. "Yes, actually, I love seafood." Now I'm saying a prayer, hoping that she just has plans to take us to some amazing local seafood restaurant, which I could handle.

"Great! Well, I made a reservation for us early tomorrow morning, and we will need to take a rideshare out of here by six o'clock to get to the dock in time." Then she casually takes another bite of her salad.

Somehow, I don't think a morning reservation at a dock interprets into us eating at a seafood restaurant, *shit*.

I raise an eyebrow at her. "Why exactly are we going to a dock, Brielle? I'm assuming we are not going there to pick up some fish to bring home for dinner."

She stands up and grabs both of our now empty bowls of salad and continues, "Close, but not exactly. I want our dinner tomorrow night to be even fresher than that."

Fresher than that? What the hell is she talking about?

Noticing my confusion, she pauses before she walks back inside the house. "Oh, and make sure you wear a bathing suit and sunglasses, Captain Davis, as you and I are going on a private sportfishing charter over in Destin to catch our dinner for the evening."

Oh my gosh, she cannot be serious. I haven't been on a boat since I was a little kid, and it was a canoe, so I don't think that technically qualifies as an actual boat. Hopefully she's a good fisherman because I think the biggest fish I ever caught was a guppy, which means we will be pretty hungry after our "feast" tomorrow night.

I give her a dirty look, causing her to laugh even harder this time, and then she walks inside, leaving me out here trying to figure out how not to disappoint her tomorrow.

When I go back inside, she's sitting on the couch with her legs curled under her just like she was at my apartment. The sight of this makes me reminisce about that afternoon and how amazingly comfortable and at home she looked in my study.

As if she's jumping right into my thoughts, she chimes in, "The only thing that I would change about this house is this space right here." She looks around, runs her fingers lightly down the white fabric of the couch, and then looks back at me with sincerity written on her face. "It needs your dreamy couch, and some built-ins on the wall over there by the TV, filled floor to ceiling with books."

I take a look over to the wall she mentioned. "I couldn't agree more. Should we make a bet now that Austin isn't much of a reader?"

"Right, and you can tell all of that just by taking a quick minute to look at a room he remodeled?" Tears begin shimmering in her eyes as she begins laughing uncontrollably.

"I blame you. It's your fault."

"Oh, is that so? It seems as though I'm rubbing off on you, Mr. Davis, and if that's the case, you'd better get ready for quite an adventure."

I can only imagine what that adventure would entail. Too bad I'm allowing my sheer stubbornness to get in the way. Looking down at one of the decorative pillows next to me, I decide to pick it up and throw it right at her.

"Yes, you are. Now will you please stop corrupting the gentleman that I was previously?"

She gives me the classic "oh no you didn't" look and then grabs the pillow and chucks it right back at me, hitting me right in the head.

"Gentleman, huh? I can't believe you just threw a pillow at me." Suddenly giving me a serious look, she continues, "I'm going to call HR, as this is workplace violence."

Noticing her nibbling on her bottom lip, trying to fight back the fact that she can't let out the laughter that I know is building inside her right now, makes me want to jump across this couch and do something that I know HR would definitely not approve of. I can't help but chuckle at this, as she's throwing the whole working relationship back in my face again, though this time literally. I think about this for a second before I respond with my next smart-ass remark.

"Luckily, as the CEO, I have to give my approval and sign off on any HR complaints before they can be processed to the full extent of the law."

She suddenly rises and walks over to me. Then she straddles my lap and puts one arm on either side of me against the back of the couch, as I did to her earlier this morning in the kitchen. My chest starts to rise and fall with rapid breaths, as I have no idea where she is about to go with all of this.

Leaning over and placing her mouth along the edge of my ear, she whispers, "If that's the case, Mr. Davis, then why are we wasting precious time worrying about our working relationship instead of working on the one with such intense heat currently burning a hole straight through both of us?"

She slowly removes herself from my space and begins walking away towards the stairs that lead to the third floor. "I'll be in the shower, getting ready for dinner, if you have a change of heart." She gives me the sexiest grin and then quickly heads upstairs.

Any guy in his right mind would never turn down an offer like that, especially from her, but then again, I don't think I have been in my "right mind" since birth. I need to hold strong, at least until after her three months of working for me is up and Nicole returns. This makes me wonder, though, where will she go after she's put in her time filling in, back to Denver maybe? It doesn't seem like she would want to stay in New York, which instantly brings a sudden ache to my heart. What the hell is wrong with me...

Standing up, I decide to head upstairs to start getting ready myself. When I get in front of our rooms, I can hear the water running in her bathroom, and I let out an embittered growl. I go and crash down on my bed, covering my face with a pillow, hoping that maybe by smothering myself, it will put me out of this torturous misery.

Taking a few deep breaths, I decide to go out onto the back deck to get some much-needed fresh air for a few minutes. I walk over to the railing and take in the scenery before me. There are a considerable number of people out on the beach today. Some soaking up the warmth of the sun, kids splashing around in the ocean, and others walking along the amazingly soft white sand. The sea breeze seems to be bringing me the calmness I desperately need right now.

When I turn back around, I notice that Brielle has her curtains open, which allows me to see straight into her room. She must still be in the bathroom, thankfully, as I don't see her in there, and I would hate for her to think I was being some sort of creep.

I head in to get myself ready for this dinner with Austin in a couple of hours, trying not to stress myself out about hanging out with him in a casual non-work-related setting. Each time I have been around him has been in meetings at my office, not in a crowded restaurant or talking about anything other than the merger. Hopefully, having Brielle there will make this go way smoother than it would if it were just him and me.

Hopping in the shower, I start wondering what Brielle will think of the new outfit I bought for this dinner based on her comments about my *Men In Black* wardrobe, as she called it. When she looked up the restaurant online, she noticed that it was a higher-end restaurant with a jacket requirement for guys. So much for our casual dinner, but maybe he's just trying to make a good impression, and I can't knock a guy for that. Although, in all honesty, I'm not much of a casual dresser, anyway, as I feel more comfortable in my power suits. I ended up calling a local men's clothing shop in the city last weekend, and they set me up with one of their personal stylists. After talking through my thoughts and sizes on some new suits and casual outfits with him, he ended up putting together a handful of options for me to go through and brought them to my apartment for me to look at. Every now and then there are a few benefits to having money, as there was no way I was going to go out and about shopping as stressed out as I have been lately.

The hot water is running down my face, and I wonder if Brielle will be wearing one of her trademark tees with a jacket and slacks, or if she will be in something else. I almost lost it when I saw what she wore the day of the board meeting. Luckily, none of those guys seemed to notice her brilliant play on the words "crazy bored" like I did. I have to say that I look forward to seeing what the shirt of the day will be, along with what note, or text more recently, she will leave me each night. Just thinking about it brings a grin to my face.

After I'm dressed and ready, I look in the mirror and barely recognize the man in front of me. I have to admit that just a simple color change does seem to calm my overall appearance. It's just something I will have to get used to.

Noticing we only have thirty minutes until we need to be there, I decide to go check on Brielle to see if she's ready yet. As I walk up to her door, I take a deep breath, remembering what she said to me earlier before we came upstairs. Of course, my mind would go right back to that moment, so I rub a hand down my face and decide to go ahead and knock before I need to go take another shower.

"Come in, Kennen. I'll be out in a minute."

I walk in her room, and I'm instantly hit with aromas of sweet summer flowers and tropical fruits and notice that she is still in the bathroom. "Brielle, we really need to get going. We're supposed to meet Austin there in thirty minutes."

I hear her laugh. "Don't worry, it's only a ten-minute walk from here, so we have plenty of time." The water begins running for a minute like she's washing her hands as she continues, "I can't wait to show you the amazing dress I found at this local shop in town that has a custom-made clothing line. As soon as I saw it, I knew I had to have it. Although, I might need a raise to help pay for it, in case you're wondering."

I hear her laugh after that last part, but what I am more focused on is the fact that she said she is wearing a dress. When the light goes off in the bathroom and she appears in front of me, I think the beating of my heart pauses for a brief minute. Who is this person, and where the hell did Brielle go?

She stops a few feet away from me, giving a little twirl with the biggest smile plastered on her face that I have ever seen.

"What do you think? I feel like a mermaid in this dress, and I absolutely love it."

Whoa. I'm at a total loss for words, and I can't control my eyes from continually staring at her. First of all, her hair is spilling down her back with curls that look so soft I just want to run my fingers through them. And since she's never once worn her hair down since I've met her, I didn't realize how long it really is.

Next, let's talk about this dress for a minute, because

the word amazing doesn't even begin to do it justice. It's a sleeveless, extremely form flattering, somewhat shorter style dress falling about four inches above her knees. The entire front is made up of fabric pieces running in a herringbone pattern from top to bottom, giving the appearance of "scales." This, with the iridescent navy blue and sea green shine and long curly hair, most certainly gives her a classy, chic, modern mermaid vibe.

The last thing that I'm trying not to focus on is the amount of skin and legs I'm currently seeing. She's not one of those ultra-skinny model types, as she has the perfect amount of curves that I would love to get lost in right about now. I would much rather skip dinner and find out what else she's wearing under that dress tonight than go out into public and have to control all of the urges that are already building inside me. Apparently, with the heat rushing through me, and the hardening in my slacks, my body seems to agree with me.

Realizing I have spent way too long admiring her at this point, she starts to lightly chuckle at the fact that I haven't responded to her question yet.

I clear my throat and finally speak. "I think you look like the most stunning mermaid I have ever seen, Brielle."

I see a flush start to come over her body, and she gives me an amused smile. "Seen many mermaids, have you, Kennen?"

I raise an eyebrow at her; then she takes a step closer and continues, "I'm sorry, it's just that it's the nicest compliment I've ever gotten, so what I meant to say is thank you. I really appreciate it."

If that's the nicest compliment this amazing woman has ever gotten, she hasn't been with the right man yet, apparently. She deserves more compliments than I have been giving her, that's for damn sure, and I wish that I could be the one giving them to her from now on.

All of a sudden, as if she is just noticing my appearance, I watch her eyes wander up and down my body as her mouth curls into a smile. "Wow, Kennen…look at you. It's like you just stepped out of an old black-and-white movie and ended up in a 4K colored version instead." She stares at me as she continues to assess my new outfit. "That sand-toned jacket really makes your skin glow. And the navy-blue slacks and pale sea-glass-colored shirt bring out the similar tones in your eyes, like how the ocean's color changes along with its depths…it's incredible."

Closing almost all the distance between us, she reaches up and starts loosening my tie, undoing the knot, and pulls it off my neck to throw it over on her bed. Then she begins unbuttoning a few buttons and opens my collar some, her fingers lightly brushing my skin in the process. I slowly swallow, trying not to show what an unbelievable reaction I'm having to her right now.

She glances up at me with a flirty smile. "There, now you look like the perfect version of casual chic, Mr. Davis."

I don't know what it is, but when she uses my formal title like that, it turns me on even more so than she already does. I have no idea how the hell I am going to get through this night out with her.

"Thank you, Brielle. Are you ready to go now? We're getting close on time."

She gives me a pouty face and grabs the lapels of my jacket. "Are you sure you wouldn't rather skip dinner and stay here tonight?"

"Look, this dinner tonight was all part of your grand scheme to save my job, my company, and this merger, remember? So, no, it's time to go, Miss Bisset."

"Okay, fine, you're right, but are you ready to act casual and not talk shop tonight?"

I blow out a slow breath. "Yes, I believe so."

Reading the sudden tension in my face, she grabs one of my hands in hers. "Just follow my lead tonight, Kennen, and let me help you get through it, okay?"

Little does she know I would follow her to the stars and back if that's where she led me. I give her an appreciative smile. "Thank you, Brielle, I will."

## Chapter 14

We get to the restaurant and check in at the hostess desk; then she leads us to a table on the outdoor veranda, where Austin sits waiting for us. When he sees us arrive, he reaches for my hand and gives me the same firm handshake I remember from our last meeting. Then turning to Brielle, he grabs one of her hands and brings it up to his lips to kiss the top of it before speaking.

"You must be Brielle. It's a pleasure to meet you in person finally."

Finally? He's only just spoken to her for the first time last week and only once since then, and he makes it seem like they've been in communication with each other for as long as we have been working on this merger. I know this is a casual dinner tonight, but this seems like a little much to me.

She smiles graciously at him for a long moment. "Thank you, Austin, it's my pleasure to meet you also."

As she walks over to a chair on our side of the table, I pull it out for her, causing her to grin up at me. "Thank you, Kennen."

Once we are all settled, our waitress brings our menus over to us and asks to take our drink order if we are ready. Before Brielle or I can reply, Austin turns to the waitress and orders us each a shot of Blanton's Original Single Barrel Whiskey to start us off. I go to mention the fact that I don't drink alcohol, but sensing my disagreement with the order, Brielle gently kicks my leg under the table and tilts her head, silently telling me to just go with it, as this is one of his favorite things. Is it normal that we can already read each other's minds after such a short period of time?

She turns to Austin now. "Austin, we can't thank you enough for letting us stay at your house. It is absolutely incredible." With a beaming smile she continues, "I'd love to see the before pictures of it, as I'm amazed at the vision and attention to detail you clearly put into the renovation."

I know she is only trying to get the conversation going, but I can tell his ego has already moved up about ten notches with her compliments, and he starts getting into all the details of the project and how much money he invested in it.

Finally breaking their conversation for a moment, the waitress returns with a tray of our three whiskey glasses and sets one in front of each of us.

Smiling at Brielle and me, he begins a toast. "Here's to our future business and to new friendships." He finishes off by winking at Brielle, which really makes my skin crawl. Look at this guy, he only met her a little while ago, and he's already flirting with her.

We all raise and clink our glasses, and as he begins to take a long sip, we are interrupted by his cell phone ringing in his pocket. He takes it out and looks at the name on his screen, then back at us apologetically. "I really apologize, guys, but I've been waiting on this call all day. Would you mind if I take it quick?"

Brielle jumps in rapidly. "Not at all, Austin, go ahead. We all know how that goes."

Well, that's interesting, because I know if I were to do the same thing, I'd probably be receiving the death glare right now.

He finishes off his drink quickly before he gets up and walks away from the table, answering his phone. Once he's out of sight, Brielle instantly grabs my glass of whiskey and downs it in three quick gulps, then places it back in front of me. I look at her with signs of complete shock on my face.

She glances at me amusingly and starts laughing. "What? I'm just taking one for the team." With that, she drains her glass next, and her eyes quickly pinch together as she swallows the liquor. "Whoa, that stuff is pretty intense. I can already feel it burning its way slowly down my chest like a wildfire."

With her mention of chest, my eyes can't help but slowly move down from her face like they are tracing the path that the liquor is currently taking. I have to make a conscious effort to look away once I reach her breasts, with the way she is filling out this dress tonight. I suddenly notice her eyes blaze with desire as she totally catches me doing this.

I blow out my cheeks to try to recompose myself, as I see Austin returning to the table. He sits back down and apologizes, then takes note of our now empty glasses.

"What did you guys think of the Blanton's? It's amazing, isn't it?"

Sensing my hesitation, Brielle jumps in to save us yet again. "Yes, it is. You could definitely smell some vanilla on the nose and taste the incredible notes of citrus and oak on the palate."

Austin and I both look at her in amazement as if she were some whiskey sommelier, and I know she is most definitely not. Amazing at online research, yes, but whiskey connoisseur, not so much.

Austin chimes in, breaking my thoughts, giving Brielle an enamored smile while leaning his chin in his hand. "Brielle, I think I'm in love. I had no idea you enjoy your whiskey as much as I do."

Brielle quietly chuckles, and it's my turn to tap her leg under the table. She recovers remarkably quickly though. "I suppose you could say that, although I do enjoy all types of liquors and wines, actually."

Thankful for the waitress once again coming to the table, this time to take our dinner order, we end the whiskey conversation and all take a minute to look over the menu.

With our orders placed, we begin talking about the town and what it's like living down here as opposed to living in the city. Brielle carries the conversation with ease, adding in her contagious humor when appropriate. And I chime in here and there to make sure that I am contributing to the casual conversation I've been instructed to have.

Brielle stands up, slightly off balance, causing her to lightly bump into the table as she excuses herself to use the restroom. Once she is gone, Austin looks at me a little more seriously now. "Kennen, no offense, as Nicole is a very intelligent woman, who is very good at her position with your firm, but Brielle is something else altogether."

"I've been told that several times lately, actually." I look directly at him, wondering where this conversation is going to go.

He smiles and looks over at the ocean for a minute and then back at me. "Can I ask you a personal question, Kennen?"

Great, here we go. "Yes, of course."

"So what's the story? Are you and Brielle seeing each other, personally I mean, or is this just a working relationship you guys have going on?"

He's either just being curious as a future partner of mine, or he's trying to find out if he can make a move on her. My guess is the latter. There's a part of me that wants to tell him that we are seeing each other outside of work, but I know that is not professional, and this could be a test of some sort that he's giving me.

I sit back in my chair to seem as casual as I can right now. "Brielle is an amazing woman, but she is strictly my executive assistant until Nicole gets back." There, that tells him there's nothing going on right now, but may also somewhat imply that there may be something there after Nicole returns. I thought that answer was the best of both worlds and pretty much the truth also.

He makes a drumming noise on the table with his hands and then sits back in his chair, smiling at me. "That's great to hear, thanks, Kennen."

Well, apparently, that plan backfired, as he didn't see the same message in my last statement that I did.

Just then, I look up to see Brielle approaching the table, looking a little flush and unsteady on her feet. My guess is those two glasses of whiskey on an empty stomach are kicking in, which makes me appreciate her even more, knowing that she did that for me.

She sits down and looks over at us. "Sooo, gentlemen, did I miss anything exciting?"

Of course, Austin leans over the table towards Brielle, giving her a lopsided grin. "Exciting, well, in a way, I suppose, it just depends on how you look at it."

Brielle smiles politely, but I can tell that she's confused. And when she looks over at me, I'm glaring at Austin. I try to give her the best smile of reassurance that I can come up with and decide to let his cockiness go, so as not to start anything tonight that would cause any unnecessary tension.

We continue with casual conversation until all our meals are finished; then Brielle notices a live band setting up in the corner of the veranda. You can see her eyes instantly light up with excitement.

She looks over at Austin. "They have live music here?"

"Yes, and the bands that usually come in to perform tend to be pretty amazing."

Once they start playing, I can see Brielle swaying to the music in her seat, with her eyes closed, which brings a sudden warmth inside me to the surface. I love seeing her so relaxed and in her element.

The song "Lady In Red" by Chris De Burgh begins to play, and she turns to me. "Oh, my goshhhh, I love this song! Kennen, would you like to dance with me?" I love that she asked me first instead of Austin, but there is no possible way in hell that I'm dancing in public.

"I'm sorry, but I'm not really up to dancing right now, Brielle, but thank you for asking." I look at her apologetically, hoping she understands why I'm refusing.

She smiles at me sweetly and pats my leg. "Of course, no worries."

Austin wastes no time chiming in—shocker. "I'd love to dance with you, Brielle, if you are still looking for a partner, that is?" He finishes with the most seductive smolder I have ever seen a guy try and actually pull off.

Brielle grins at him and then quickly looks at me as if to get my permission. I don't know why, as I have told her several times now that our relationship can't be anything other than professional, but I do appreciate the gesture, so I give her a slight nod that only she would notice.

Looking back at Austin, she stands up, making sure to hold onto the table this time for support. "That would be great, thank you, Austin."

She walks around the table, swaying slightly, and he gets up to meet her. He puts his hand on her lower back to lead her to the dance floor area, but not before looking back at me with a shitty smirk on his face, like a dog marking his new territory, I suppose. I have never wanted to kick somebody's ass as much as I want to kick his right now. Damn it, I should have just danced with her, and I wouldn't have to sit here suffering as they begin to slow dance.

As the song goes on, you can see that they are deep in conversation as they move to the rhythm, but they are far enough away where I can't hear or see anything they are talking about. I rub my hands down my face, never feeling so torn in my life as to what I should be doing right now. I know I need to be professional, but my heart, and apparently my current jealousy, is telling me otherwise.

After a couple of additional songs, they come back to the table, both smiling and laughing, adding to my current internal raging.

I look down at my watch, just wanting this night to be over already, and Brielle notices.

"Austin, tonight has been great. Thank you so much for your hospitality. But after our long trip yesterday, I think I'm ready to call it an evening if you don't mind." She gives him one of her amazing smiles.

"Of course, I totally understand. It's certainly been my pleasure."

He pays for our dinner, and then we all get up to leave. I shake his hand and say goodnight; then he walks up to Brielle and gives her a kiss on the cheek, making my blood boil even more.

"Goodnight, Brielle, I hope to speak to you again soon, as I've really enjoyed our time together." With that he turns and begins walking to the front of the restaurant.

"Are you ready to go now, Brielle?"

She looks at me as though she can see right past my running visions and straight into my ever-revolving mind, trying to figure out what I'm thinking. "Yes, I am. Let's go."

As we leave the restaurant and turn towards the road, she turns to me with her mouth curving into a smile. "Would you mind if we walk back to the house on the beach instead?"

This is my time to redeem myself for not dancing earlier, so I agree without hesitation. As she begins walking, I notice that her poor body is still probably fighting off the poison of the whiskey she consumed. The breeze is a little cooler tonight, and I can tell that she must be chilly, as she begins rubbing her arms up and down. I stop walking and take off my jacket to wrap it around her, just wanting to bring her some warmth.

"Thank you, Kennen, I really appreciate it." She's looking up at me like she wants to say something more, but for whatever reason, she chooses not to.

As we resume walking, she begins speaking again. "Well, I think tonight went rather well, don't you?"

"I think it went about as well as it could have, I suppose." I turn to look at her. "So what did you think of Austin now that you've had the opportunity to meet him in person?"

She looks down at the sand and then back up at me with a serious expression, making me wonder how she is about to respond. "Let's see. How do I say this..."

I'm internally praying that she doesn't say that she's attracted to him and may want to see if there is anything there, as I will probably lose my mind.

"Holy crap, I totally pegged how he would be on the plane, didn't I?" She suddenly bursts out laughing and stops walking for a minute to try to control herself.

Totally relieved, I join her in laughter and can't help but smile. "Yes, Miss Bisset, you sure did."

Trying not to laugh for a minute, she keeps going. "Wow, I mean, he's a nice guy and all, but definitely not my type, as his personality would completely wear me out."

"So what is your type of guy exactly?" I look at her, genuinely curious. "You haven't mentioned anything about past relationships, so I'm just wondering what your preferences are."

With this she starts walking again. "I prefer a guy who is confident, but not overbearing, someone who likes to have fun yet also likes to relax, someone who accepts my faults and still loves me, and also does the same for themselves." She pauses, her eyes now searching mine. "Mostly, I just want that ultimate, unbreakable connection and bond with someone who wants to share this crazy journey of life with me."

I think about all of that and realize I'm probably not even close to what she mentioned. "That all seems reasonable, I suppose, and you haven't been able to find this amazing guy yet?"

"Let's just say that my past track record with men hasn't exactly been stellar." Walking over to the edge of the water, she looks out over the ocean, deep in thought. "People can just be so hurtful and selfish sometimes." She looks back at me, and I nod in agreement as I walk up next to her. "One minute you think, this is it, my life has finally come together, and I'm going to share it growing old with this amazing person. And then you're on vacation celebrating your engagement, and you catch the bastard making out with some wannabe snow-bunny tramp on a ski lift when you go inside to warm up." I notice that she has a tear forming in the corner of her eye, and she quickly wipes it away and turns back towards the ocean.

Unfortunately, I totally understand how she feels. I gently lay my hands on her shoulders and turn her so that she is facing me now. "Brielle, listen to me; you deserve so much more than what that piece of shit did to you, as it's pretty obvious now that he didn't truly love you." I slowly run my hands down her arms and grab ahold of her hands.

"You're an amazing woman. Even with your crazy T-shirts, caffeine addiction, and off-the-wall harebrained ideas." I give her a quick wink. "It's jackasses like that who give the good ones out there a bad name. So just know that he did you a favor, Brielle, and I know your Prince Charming is out there, making his way to find you as we speak."

Giving my hands a light squeeze, she looks up at me curiously. "Maybe that's just it, Kennen. I've spent endless years looking for my Prince Charming when I should have been looking for my superhero instead." Her face is so sincere as she says this, it's completely melting my heart right now.

I swallow heavily and look away for a minute, not sure how to respond to that. When I look back over at her, I say the first thing that comes to my mind because she deserves anything other than silence right now.

"Brielle, I'm sorry I didn't dance with you earlier…it's just that, well, you know how I am in public, and I didn't mean to disappoint you." Great, now I sound like a mumbling idiot after she basically just told me I'm the type of guy she wants to be with. I inwardly sigh, wishing for once that the right words would come to me.

With her irresistible smile beaming at me right now, she brings my right hand to her lower back, then lifts our other hands to my chest. "I'd rather dance with you right here, Kennen."

"There's no music, so how are we supposed to dance exactly?"

"Close your eyes, and I want you to tell me what you hear right now."

I laugh. "I don't hear anything, Brielle."

"That's because you're not *really* listening."

Okay, apparently, she wants me to take this seriously, so I make every attempt to calm the chaos of my mind enough to listen for any sounds that I should be hearing right now.

Like an overnight fog that clears its way in the morning, I begin to hear what she's talking about. "I hear the ocean, but mainly the waves as they break against the shore." I feel our bodies begin to gently sway.

Upon opening my eyes, I see her looking up at me. "Keep going. What else do you hear?"

I try to keep the distractions flooding my conscious at bay a little longer and continue listening. "I hear the wind whistling against my ears, and what sounds like a seagull squawking in the distance."

"Perfect, there's just one thing you are missing from all of that, and it's the most important."

She nestles the side of her head against my chest and continues rocking as if we are in time with the movement of the waves. "Silence, Kennen." I rest my chin on the top of her head as she continues, "Beautiful moments also happen in the lack of any sound at all."

I lift my head and slowly breathe out, hoping more than anything that she can't feel the thunderous pounding going on inside my chest right now.

She looks up at me just as the wind blows one of her long curls across the front of her face. I wrap it around my finger, wanting to experience how soft it is, then gently place it on her back where it was before.

Cupping the side of her face with my hand, I lean my head down softly against her forehead. Barely loud enough for me to hear it myself, I whisper, "I'm so sorry, Brielle, I just can't."

She looks up at me with a shine in her eyes. "You can't, or you won't?" She leans her head back away from mine. "I am beginning to think this isn't just about us working together anymore, and that it's more to do with this…" She traces around my heart with her finger.

I think she might be right, so I nod in agreement and then step away to create some space.

She folds her arms tightly around her stomach and glances at me. "Was it Kari?"

I'm sure it's pretty obvious based on my expression that she knows the answer.

"What did she do to fill you with so much pain that you'd rather push people away instead of embracing them?"

Picking up my shoes, I nod over to hers, hoping that she will do the same so we can continue walking. She follows my lead and then catches up with me.

I look ahead as I share with her how the difficulties of having a complex mind like mine tend to scare most people off, ultimately making it hard for me to be social and involved in relationships. I also try to explain that Kari initially came to me for a consultation, seeking advice for the interior design business she was thinking of starting, and how that one appointment led to several appointments, and she started showing some intense interest in me.

Brielle lightly chuckles. "Intense is definitely how I would describe her after our encounter."

"Don't get me started, as I'm still pissed off about that." I clear my throat and then continue, "Anyway, the meetings turned less about work and more about the attraction, and well, I'm a guy, one who has never had any female lust over me like that before. Especially someone who looked as she did and seemed to be so like me personality wise."

I look over at Brielle to see her staring at the sand as she's walking.

"She was very business focused, she wasn't the emotional type, and she always knew what she wanted. Everything about her was very black and white."

Brielle cuts in, "So is that the type of woman you want, then?"

"I thought so at the time." I feel a sadness suddenly come over me. "Everything started happening so quickly. My business was booming out of control, and I had Kari convincing me that she was so in love with me, that we needed to move in together to take it to the next level. That's when I bought the apartment and had her decorate it for me. She had absolutely no problem spending my money as if it were her own, and I honestly didn't even care. Money is nice to have, but it's not why I continue to grow my business. I do it for the challenge that it brings my chaotic mind."

We end up in front of the beach house, so we stop

walking, and Brielle turns to me. "I can understand that. What happened next?"

I put my hands on my hips. "To make a long, painful story short, she ended up just using me to launch her business with all my money, my name, my contacts, and my inexperience with relationships. Once her business took off even faster than mine, she ended up leaving me for some other guy she had apparently been seeing on the side the whole time we were together." I look over at the ocean now. "It destroyed me, Brielle. My heart had never experienced anything like that before, and although it's been years, it's never fully healed."

Brielle walks up to me with eyes full of understanding and sympathy. "I'm so sorry she caused you such pain, Kennen." She gently places her hand over my heart. "It will heal when you're ready to allow it to, you'll see." Then she takes off my jacket and hands it back to me before heading back down towards the water. "I'm going to stay out here for a few more minutes before I head in, so go get some rest. We have our next adventure tomorrow." She gives me a light yet tired-looking smile.

"Goodnight, Brielle."

When I get into my room, I hang up my jacket and put my shoes away, then start unbuttoning my sleeves. I decide to walk out onto the deck to see if she's still out there, which she is. I can't help but lean against the wood post and watch her. It looks as though she is combing the shoreline, looking for shells, stopping to bend down every couple of feet to pick one up and then gently place it back down again. She does this for several minutes until she finds what must be the perfect one, and then she puts it up to her ear for a moment like she's listening to its life's journey. When she's finished, she closes her eyes and holds it out in the palms of her hands, almost as though she is making a wish.

The evening breeze is still lightly blowing the soft curls of her golden hair behind her, and she's lit only by the light of the half-moon in the sky above. This is a moment when I absolutely love having a photographic memory. So I take a snapshot in my mind and store it away, knowing this is one photograph I will be pulling out on a daily basis.

A moment later she sets it on the edge of the water and stands there until it gets pulled back out to sea. She waits until it's no longer visible, and then she begins walking back to the house. I return to my room in a hurry, not wanting her to know I was encroaching on a part of her private moment that she needed.

Hoping that my business isn't imploding while I'm gone, I decide to pull out my laptop for a little while to catch up on my emails. I get settled on the bed, and once I sign in, I see that there aren't any new emails in my inbox, which is unusual. Maybe the word finally got out that I wasn't going to be in for the next week, so they are giving me a break.

Great, now what am I going to do? I was hoping that it would take up more of my night by getting some work done. I decide this might be a good time to go online and learn some information about local sportfishing before our "next adventure" tomorrow.

I'm deep into reading about the different species of fish that are common around here this time of year, when I hear my phone receive a text. Knowing it's my funny quote of the day from Brielle, I can't help the instant smile that suddenly widens over my face.

**Brielle:** Did you know that a banana is 105

calories, and a shot of whiskey is only 80, see…I chose wisely.

**Kennen:** Actually, you technically had two shots, so…

**Brielle:** Damn it. So much for breakfast…

**Kennen:** Did you know that silence is better than bullshit?

**Brielle:** Best one yet.

**Kennen:** Thanks for sharing your silence with me.

**Brielle:** You're welcome. Now get off your laptop and go to bed, Mr. Davis.

**Kennen:** I'm not even working.

**Brielle:** You were earlier. Goodnight, Kennen.

**Kennen:** Good dreams, Brielle…

# CHAPTER 15

*O*h, my gosh, who's brilliant idea was it to drink two forty-six percent abv glasses of whiskey on an empty stomach the night before I need to get on a boat and rock along the sea all day?

I drag myself out of bed, completely afraid to even look in the mirror at this point, knowing the horror that awaits me. So, instead, I get the shower turned on and step right inside. Not even checking the water temperature before I get in, I let out a resounding yelp when a million miniature icebergs suddenly pierce my skin. I quickly jump over to the other end of the shower, trying and failing to get out of the water for a minute. Well, I suppose that's one way to sober up…

There's a sudden loud knock on my bedroom door, and then Kennen's voice calls out to me, "Brielle, is everything okay?"

It takes everything I have to not start laughing, considering the massive pounding going on right now in my head. "All good. Sorry about that!" I try to yell as loud as I can, as the sounds echo off every wall of this shower like Ping-Pong balls.

I pick out the sexiest bikini I brought with me to go fishing in today. My guess is that based on Kennen's reaction to seeing me in that dress last night, this might be just enough to torture the hell out of him as payback for having to drink his whiskey (which, in turn, resulted in this morning's madness).

It has a tropical print with a white background and green palm leaves, with a cut that sits higher on the thigh. I think I'll also wear my favorite short frayed denim shorts and my "Resting BEACH Face" white tank top with green lettering, tied up on the side in a knot. To finish off my look, I decide to wear a white baseball hat with my hair pulled up in a pony coming out of the back.

Grabbing my beach bag, I put a couple of towels, suntan lotion, and my aviator sunglasses in there. As I head down to the second level, I notice Kennen sitting at the island in the kitchen, drinking a glass of water and eating an apple. He stops mid bite when he sees me, slowly finishing it off, and then swallows hard as I notice his Adam's apple creep down his throat. With that bite consumed, he puts the apple down and then starts laughing. Let's see who's laughing here shortly, buddy.

I walk around the island and stand next to him, putting my bag on the countertop, all while giving him a pointed look. "What on earth is so funny?"

"Good morning, Brielle, how's everything going?" He's trying to contain his amusement as he continues, "Sounded like you had a sobering shower this morning."

"Ha-ha, you're hilarious." I cross my arms against my chest, trying to portray the seriousness of the situation that's nowhere to be found. "Just remember that this is all your fault, because if I didn't have to pick up your slack, my head would be a little more pleased with me this morning." Then I give him a little smirk. "Just remember, Mr. Davis, payback's a bitch."

I climb up on the barstool, causing my already short shorts to slide up my thighs even higher. And of course, like a hungry predator in the ocean, he takes my bait and notices.

He clears his throat before he speaks up again. "I'll remember that, thanks."

I slap my hand down on the counter with a force that makes him jump, and then I get back up. "Great, now that that's settled, let's grab some drinks and head out."

My arm lightly brushes his as I walk by, suddenly covering me with goosebumps and prickles of heat. So much for this being only about torturing him…

As he gets up and takes another look at me, he starts chuckling. Noticing my confusion as to why he's laughing yet again, he comes over to me. "Where do you find these shirts, anyway, Brielle?"

"I actually designed an entire line of them for a company out in Colorado last year, and they gave me one of each of the designs I made as a thank-you." I give him a pouty look. "What, do you not like them? I can stop wearing them and put on a plain shirt if you prefer."

He hooks his fingers into the belt loops of my shorts, pulling me towards him. "No way, Brielle, those crazy shirts are one of the things I like most about you." He gives my hips a quick squeeze and then heads out of the kitchen to go downstairs to the front door.

Well, we'll see if he wants me to put this shirt back on later or not. I smile to myself and then bound down the stairs after him.

We arrive at the marina, and I notice a small snack bar / bait and tackle shop open, and I'm praying they have some sort of caffeine in there to get me going. Not that the shower didn't do a good job of that already this morning. I walk up to the window, and there sits an elderly gentleman who looks like he has spent most of his life out at sea, with his tan leatherlike skin, his bleached white hair, and a name tag that reads "Captain Ahab."

I'm in love with this guy already. "Good morning," I say. "*Moby Dick* fan, are we, or just an inside joke?" I give him a smile and a pronounced wink.

He lets out a rough cough before speaking. "Ha, both." And then he smiles back up at me. "Reader or trivia expert?"

I start laughing. "Reader, definitely a reader."

"I knew I liked 'cha the moment I saw ya." He stands up. "What can I get for ya, my dear?"

"Any chance you have any coffee in there and a cup of ice?"

He points over his shoulder, then goes and gets the coffee and a cup of ice for me. "Here ya go, my dear, on the house."

I give him an enormous smile. "Thank you, Captain, your kindness is very much appreciated." I start to walk away, and then turn around and blow him a kiss, causing his cheeks to instantly flush a rose-tinted hue. Hey, even an old sea captain needs to be flirted with every now and then to keep his spirits up.

I walk back over to where Kennen is standing further down on the dock and see him shaking his head with a huge grin.

Once I get closer to him, he chimes in, "I'm not even going to ask what that was all about."

"What?" I walk right up to within inches of him. "You're not jealous, are you, Kennen?"

"What, of Captain Ahab over there? I think I'm pretty safe." He starts laughing.

Did I just hear him right? "Hey, how did you know that was his name?" I look up at him more intensely now.

He continues laughing until he sees my face. "You can't be serious?"

"I've never been more serious before in my life." And then we both burst out into thunderous laughter, causing our eyes to fill with moisture.

I calm down enough to pour my coffee into the cup of ice, take a quick sip, and then nod my head to the other end of the dock. "Alright, Mr. Genius, let's go see how much you know about fishing."

When we get towards the end, I locate the boat we are looking for. As we approach, a girl who looks a similar age to us steps off the boat and onto the dock to greet us. "Hey, guys, you must be Brielle and Kennen. Welcome to the *Wee Three* fishing charter." She extends her hand for us to shake. "My name is Captain Allie, and I'm excited to take you guys out today. Watch your step and climb aboard."

Kennen climbs on first and then reaches out his hand to help me board. Once we're all on the boat and get all the rules and regulations out of the way, we get everything organized, and Kennen helps Captain Allie untie the ropes that tether the boat to the dock. Kennen and I stand off to the side as she pulls us out and away from the marina and heads towards the Gulf.

She looks over at us and smiles. "So, Kennen and Brielle, huh? You actually look more like Ken and Barbie." Then she starts laughing. Sensing our confusion, she continues, "I'm sorry, I just had a thing for Barbies when I was little, and I couldn't help myself."

We give each other the "this could be an interesting trip" look and tentatively smile back at her in return. I really love how all we need to do is glance at each other to know what the other is thinking.

Kennen and I are both scoping out this boat, and it's incredible. With its longer hull and sleek high-end finishes, it has everything on it that you could ever want or need.

Kennen turns to Captain Allie. "So I noticed that this boat is built by Pursuit. Which model is it?"

"This is their 385 Offshore model, coming in at just under forty feet in length. And with the triplets on the back, she pushes out a maximum of one thousand and fifty horsepower."

He looks over at the stern to check out the motors again and then smiles at her. "It's really impressive. I've never been on anything like it."

"Thanks, it's a family boat that my sisters and I share for our charter business, hence the *Wee Three* name she bears." She seems to be lost in a thought or memory after saying this.

I decide to chime in, "So, Captain, how's the mahi mahi and wahoo been biting out here recently?"

"Actually, we're just getting into high peak season, so we have a pretty good chance of hooking some today."

The thought of catching some this afternoon makes my mouth water, and my adrenaline starts pumping. "Are we going to be using ballyhoo for bait, then?"

Kennen shoots a look over at me with an eyebrow raised. "Sounds like you have done this a few times before, Brielle."

Captain Allie and I both start laughing as if going along

with some inside joke. "Once or twice maybe."

She looks over at Kennen. "Alright, you, come on over and steer for me for a little while so my first mate and I can go get the poles rigged and the outriggers down to start trolling." She looks at me and gives me a wink.

With amusement in his eyes, Kennen starts shaking his head and then goes and takes a seat in the captain's chair to take over for her. I have to say, seeing him sitting there behind the wheel in a formfitting white T-shirt that stretches across his chest, a black swimsuit (of course), and aviator sunglasses is like viewing a Nautica ad, and pretty damn sexy. I try to refocus and go to the stern with the captain to start rigging up the bait on the rods so we can get them down in the water.

Now ready, Captain Allie takes over, relieving Kennen of his duties. "That was really cool. Thanks for letting me fill in for you, Captain…so what's next, then, ladies?" He claps his hands together and begins rubbing them back and forth.

I turn to him. "Now Captain Allie will troll us along until we get a bite. In the meantime, you can come up on the bow of the boat with me and help me look for seaweed lines and birds, both of which will increase our chances of that happening."

He looks over at Captain Allie, and she looks back and forth between us and laughs. "Exactly what she just said. Just do me a favor and don't fall off the boat, as I wouldn't want the sharks to get you."

He puts a hand up to his forehead. "Sharks, right."

I start laughing as I walk back out onto the deck to begin my plans to seduce him. I start by slowly removing my tank top and shorts to get ready for a long day out on the water.

Kennen stops short when he sees me and lets out a slow breath. "Seriously, Brielle, are you trying to give me a heart attack now that we are miles away from shore and the nearest doctor?"

"What? I'm just getting comfortable. It's about to get pretty hot out here, and I also don't want to end up with any crazy tan lines."

While biting his bottom lip, he stalks up to me so quickly that he's only inches away from me when he arrives a moment later.

"The stifling heat in hell won't compare to what it feels like out here right now, Brielle." Then he runs his fingers over one of the straps on the top of my bathing suit. "Tan lines, huh?"

I am so flustered right now, I don't know who is torturing who more at this point. I need some space for a minute, so I clear my throat. "I'll be out on the bow if you want to join me." After which, I quickly make my way out to the front of the boat and take a seat, letting the breeze blow a cooling calmness over me. Closing my eyes, I take in deep breaths, letting the salt fill my lungs and clear my mind once again. I get so in the zone that I don't even hear Kennen arrive until he is suddenly sitting right behind me, straddling his legs on either side of mine, with the sudden warmth of his chest on my back.

Oh, my gosh, there's no way I am turning around if he took his shirt off, as I might actually fall off this boat then. Even though in reality, I have dreamt about what he looks like without anything on, more times than not as of recently.

He lightly brushes his lips on my ear and whispers, "You may have started this fight, Miss Bisset, but I *am* going to win the war."

Little does he know how I respond to challenges.

I turn my head slightly and smile at him. "Don't forget that on this boat, you're in my territory now."

He knows I'm right, and blows out a slow, warm breath next to my face. "Good thing I stayed up last night memorizing everything I could about sportfishing, then."

I chuckle. "Let's be clear here, studying and doing are two different things when it comes to fishing, Mr. Davis."

I carefully get up and start walking back to the side of the boat, trying with everything I have not to look at him as I do.

He calls out, "Where are you going? I thought we were hunting birds and weed lines?"

"Oh, I'll be right back. I need to grab my suntan lotion. I forgot to put it on this morning, and I don't want to burn, remember?" Then I walk around the boat before he has a chance to respond. Let the war begin...

When I come back with the lotion in my hand, I can't help but take in the sight of the back side of him as he is sitting there. He obviously never misses a workout because every muscle in his arms, neck and back is toned and cut to a bodybuilder's perfection. I suck in a deep breath and go and sit back down in front of him between his legs where I was previously. Just not as close this time, leaving a little bit of space separating us.

I begin to rub some of the suntan lotion slowly up and down my arms, then across my chest and up my neck and face. Squeezing out some more, I smooth it across my stomach and do the same for each of my legs. He swallows hard, letting me know that he is paying attention like the good soldier he is.

I place the bottle of lotion over my shoulder. "Can you please do my back for me, since I can't reach it?"

"Only if you do mine also," he says, snickering.

Gladly. He doesn't need to ask me twice. "Of course, all's fair in love and *war*, right?"

He pulls my ponytail over to the side, then grabs the bottle and squirts some out on my back. At first, he's touching me so lightly like he's afraid to; then I feel him let out a slow breath and start to rub harder. I lean over and close my eyes, placing the side of my head on my arms, allowing him better access to my lower back.

He laughs quietly. "Comfortable, are we?"

As he starts rubbing it lower on my back, it takes everything I have not to let out a groan of satisfaction, as it feels amazing having his hands gliding across my skin right now.

I slowly open my eyes. "I'm just making sure you have access to the areas you need."

"Maybe you should turn around, then, Brielle," he says, giving me an extremely seductive smile.

I quickly sit up and walk around him, feeling the heat quickly rising throughout my body. "My turn, Mr. Davis."

Starting at his neck, I slowly make my way down his shoulders and then massage it into the mountains of muscles on his back. With additional lotion in my hands, I rub it from his lower back across to his hips, making sure my hands reach across the front side of his body some.

"Okay, all done. Do you need help with the front also?" I say very sweetly, just to tease him a little more.

He clears his throat. "No, thank you. I think I can take it from here."

That's what I thought.

I carefully stand back up, and when I do, I see what looks like a good seaweed line approaching on the port side of the boat.

I immediately call out to Captain Allie, pointing in the direction I see it, and then start heading towards the back of the boat, calling out excitedly to Kennen as I'm walking.

"Come on, Kennen, let's see what all of that memorization got you, as things are about to get interesting."

When I get to the helm by Captain Allie, I see her fish finder lighting up like the skies during a hot afternoon Florida storm.

She smiles and looks at me. "Are you ready for some action?"

I laugh. "I was born ready to fish. Bring it on."

Kennen rounds the corner of the boat, and when I hear one of the outrigger lines snap, I yell, "Fish on!" I run to the back, grabbing ahold of the rod, and start reeling it in to set the hook so we don't lose the fish.

I glance over at Kennen, who is standing there looking like a lost puppy. "Kennen, get over here. I need you to start reeling in this fish so that I can help Captain Allie start bringing in the rest of the lines to get them out of the way."

He runs over and grabs the rod from me and begins to crank the handle on the reel.

I look up at him. "Okay, so I'm not sure if you've ever been sportfishing before, but what you want to do is reel the rod down and then slowly pull the rod back up with your other hand and then repeat the process. If the fish starts to take off, let it take out some of the line and then start over again."

He looks over at me, half excited, half panicked. "Okay, thanks, got it."

Once Captain Allie and I get the rest of the lines in, I go back over to where Kennen is fighting his fish. After about fifteen minutes of reeling, we finally get a good look as to what is on the end of his line. Clear as day, you can see that it's an amazing mahi mahi with its colors all lit up with bright blues, yellows and greens.

I rub his back. "You're doing awesome, Kennen. You have a killer fish on your line. Keep going."

He looks over at me with an enormous smile on his face like a kid on Christmas morning and then refocuses back on what he's doing, bringing the fish up to the edge of the boat. We get the fish in the boat, and I have Kennen hold it up so that I can take some pictures with my phone. I love seeing how excited he is right now, and it brings an added warmth to my heart knowing this is probably the most exciting thing this poor guy has done in an extremely long time.

I turn to Kennen and give him a big high five. "So there's a rule about catching your first sportfish, you know."

He laughs. "I'm afraid to ask what that is."

"You have to jump overboard for a quick swim."

He puts his hands on his hips. "Seriously?"

"Yup, and watch out for the sharks while you're in there."

With the boat stopped from when we brought the fish in, I walk Kennen over to the tuna door on the back of the boat and open it up for him, motioning that he can jump off the back.

He shakes his head and then laughs. "Okay, fine, I'll jump in quick so as not to break any traditions."

He hands me his sunglasses, then dives off the back of the boat and swims around for a few minutes, never venturing out too far. As he's climbing back up the ladder—extremely slowly, might I add—Captain Allie and

I look at each other, and I can feel the flush creeping up my face.

"Yeah, I know…"

He walks up to me, with water dripping down every curve of his chest, runs a hand through his hair, then grabs his glasses out of my hands and puts them back on. "You're up next, my Ula."

Damn it. I hate it when he's sexy and sweet at the same time. It's just not right.

We spend the next couple of hours trolling the crystal-clear, sea-green waters of the Gulf of Mexico, waiting for another bite. As we're chatting, I hear some birds off to our left that are diving into the water with great force. I point them out to Captain Allie, and we start heading over that way. As we get closer, we start to see a bunch of flying fish jumping in and out of the water alongside the boat, signaling there are monsters lurking nearby.

Suddenly, we hear a loud ping, and the spool of line on the reel goes peeling off insanely fast and doesn't stop. My heart starts pounding, as I have a feeling it's one of my favorite fish to catch on the end of this line.

I run over to the rod and grab it to start reeling, and for every little bit of line I get back in, it races out and takes twice as much with it. It's pulling so hard that I have a feeling I'm going to need backup.

With a slight strain to my face, I look over at Kennen. "Can you grab the fishing belt and quickly put it around my waist, please, as I think there's a beast at the end of this line."

Captain Allie hands him the belt, and he quickly comes

over and puts it around my waist, then helps me get the rod set in the belt holder. The battle continues for another forty-five minutes, and just as I get it closer to the boat, thinking it's tired, it takes off, pulling me so hard I lose my balance and hit the edge of the boat.

"Kennen, quick, wrap your arms around my waist and anchor me down before I go flying off the side of this boat and out to sea with this fish."

He starts laughing until he looks at me and it registers how serious I am right now. I'm momentarily distracted from the fish as I feel his body suddenly hugging tightly around mine, that is until I hear a bunch more line peel out and I realize I stopped reeling it in for a few minutes. It's taking everything I have to refocus, so I start reeling and pulling the rod up as hard as I can, my arms getting considerably weaker by the minute.

As I start breathing heavily, Kennen notices and speaks up. "Hey, are you okay? Do you need some help?" He squeezes me a little tighter, letting me know he's there if I need him. "What kind of fish do you think is on the line, anyway?"

I laugh as I keep reeling, my face scrunching up in exhaustion after each repetition. "Oh, there is definitely a very large wahoo on the end of this line, and I am not stopping until he's on our dinner plate tonight."

Kennen laughs at this. "Here, why don't you keep reeling, and I will pull the rod up so that you can give your left arm a break."

Good idea, as this fight could go on for another hour if the fish so chooses.

I look back at him and smile. "Yes, that sounds like a good plan. We could be at this for a while."

He puts his left arm on top of mine, and then we start

working together, me reeling down, causing us to bend over slightly, and him pulling us back up with the rod. We easily find our rhythm, and it feels so right, and absolutely incredible, that it makes me think about what it would be like if we were doing this in bed instead of out here on the water.

Stirring my thoughts, Kennen leans down and whispers close to my ear, "Brielle, I'm not sure how much longer I can help you with this."

I lean my head up against his chest so that I can see him. "You can't seriously be tired already, after I've been fighting this beast for well over an hour now."

"I'm fighting my own beast right now, Brielle, and I'm not sure how much longer I can do that. So please hurry the hell up and get this damn fish in the boat." He leans into me even closer, allowing me to feel his hardness against my lower back, causing me to realize the ache currently growing between my own legs.

I put my head back down and start reeling as fast as I can. "Got it. I'm on top of it."

He blows out a long breath. "Yes, that's exactly the problem." Then he lets out a small growl so quietly that only I can hear it.

I think I just need to be quiet and get this fish boat-side ASAP.

We fight it for another excruciating twenty minutes and then finally get it up on the boat. It's by far the biggest wahoo I have ever caught, and I'm so excited that I turn around and give Kennen a big hug and then high-five Captain Allie. She takes a bunch of pictures for us, and then we put it in the fish box with Kennen's fish from earlier.

Once everything is cleaned up, we make our journey

back to the marina, Kennen and I both totally exhausted and fairly frustrated in more ways than one.

## Chapter 16

We stopped by the market on our way back to the house to get some additional ingredients we needed to make our fresh fish dinner tonight. And then we both took a few minutes to take quick showers and get cleaned up before we started cooking.

When I take my first bite of wahoo, I close my eyes, soaking up how amazing the flavor of freshly caught fish really is, especially with the amount of work that went into catching this one.

Kennen notices my reaction and grins. "I totally agree with you there. This is the best fish I have ever tasted in my life…even though I thought for sure it was going to be the death of me." He takes a bite and then gives me a playful yet seductive wink.

You and me both, buddy.

After eating mostly in silence, we get up to clean the mess we made in the kitchen. He washes and I dry, once again falling into our groove as "teammates." By the time we're done, it's late, so we both agree to call it a night and walk up the stairs together.

Before going into his room, he turns to look at me. "That was the most fun I've had in, I don't know how long. Thank you, Brielle." Then giving me one of his dimpled smiles, he walks in and gently shuts the door behind him.

I walk over to his door and raise my hand to knock on it, but instead I lower my arm and gently rest my forehead on it, closing my eyes for a minute. I take in a quiet breath and then head to my room, lost in my thoughts and the mixed-up feelings that I have towards this man.

After slipping into bed with hopes of getting some rest, I end up lying there for over an hour just tossing and turning. As tired as I am, I'm also incredibly sore after putting in so much effort with that fish earlier, so I decide to run a hot bath to try to soothe away the pain.

Digging in my toiletry bag, I pull out my natural oils and decide to put a few drops of lavender in the bath to help relax me. I place my bathrobe next to the tub and go to put my hair up in a bun only to realize that my scrunchy is all the way downstairs, and I'm too lazy to go get it. Grabbing the next best thing I can find, which is a pencil I have in my carry-on bag, I twist up my hair and shove it into place. The steam coming off the water rises like a smoke signal of relief that my body so desperately needs, so I carefully slide in so that only my head is above the welcome heat of the water.

I've been relaxing in here for over an hour when I suddenly hear a few concerning yells coming from Kennen's room. I immediately jump out of the tub, trying to quickly dry myself off, throw on my robe, then run over to his room, and knock on his door.

"Kennen, is everything alright? Are you okay?" Sudden panic fills me to the core.

"It's okay. Go back to bed, Brielle. I'll be fine," he calls weakly through the door.

When another somewhat quieter yell comes out, I burst

through his door to find him curled up on the floor, wearing only a pair of sweatpants and holding his head between his legs. I rush over to him, throwing my arms around his back, and look up to see his bed is totally covered in papers, folders, his briefcase, and in the middle of all the mess is his laptop—signed into his email, of course. If he weren't in so much pain, I would totally kick his ass right now.

I look down at him with fear probably crossing my face, and start rubbing his back, trying to soothe him any way I can. "Kennen, will you please tell me what's wrong so I can help you?"

He tilts his head up and puts his hand on his forehead, rubbing profusely. "It's just my head and another insane migraine. I'm sorry if I woke you."

Putting my hands under his chin, I look him in the eyes and notice the distance and chaos that has clouded them over once again.

I give him a gentle kiss on his forehead and then stand up. "Don't move. I'll be right back."

When I get back to his room, I'm armed with a couple of the migraine pills I carry with me everywhere and the peppermint and lavender oils from my stash that I took out earlier. I go into his bathroom and fill a glass with water and bring it to him, having him take the pills. He doesn't even argue with me this time, so the pain he's feeling must be pretty intense.

I climb on his bed and try to organize the papers enough to get it all into piles, shut down his laptop, and put it all in his briefcase. While I'm getting everything in there, I notice yellow in the side pocket. Being the nosey person I am, I open it up to see that he has saved each of the sticky notes I left him since I started, causing me to instantly clutch at my heart. With his bed now cleared off, I turn down the covers, prop up a few pillows on the headboard, and climb in, grabbing the oils off the nightstand on my way.

I look down at him. "Come here, my superhero. Let me take care of you," I say, and pat the bed in front of me.

He slowly stands up and looks at me in his bed. "Brielle, I'm sorry, but this is definitely not happening, and especially not right now."

Oh, my gosh, men, always thinking with the wrong damn head.

I give him a light chuckle. "I didn't mean it like that; now will you just get over here and lie down between my legs."

His eyebrows shoot up just as I realize what I said.

This is only getting worse the more I talk, so I grab another pillow and put it between my legs and chest and point for him to lie down. "You. Here. Now."

He starts to laugh, and then he winces with the pain that must be causing him.

After he climbs into bed, he rests his head down against the pillow and crosses his arms. I grab the peppermint oil, pour a few drops on my fingers, and begin rubbing his temples, trying to bring some much-needed relief at his pressure points.

He tilts his head and looks up at me. "What are you doing, and why do I smell like a candy cane exactly?"

I give him a scolding face in return. "Will you please just be quiet and close your eyes so that I can help alleviate some of the throbbing from your headache."

Putting his head back down, he closes his eyes and then snuggles into the pillow. Once he's comfortable, I go ahead and start rubbing his temples again. Then I move across his forehead and slowly start to move my fingers down the sides of his neck and then to the back of his head. I remain in silence so that I can focus all my energy into bringing him some peace, then move his arms so that they are now resting on top of my legs. Grabbing the bottle of lavender oil next, I pour some into my hands, take a deep breath, and then place them down on his chest and begin massaging it gently into his skin. I inch my way up towards his neck and then back down over his upper torso in bigger circles, then grab one arm at a time and massage them also.

Once I'm done, I gently place his arms back across his chest and then start on his head again. I do this for about an hour longer until I finally hear him lost in sleep.

I lie there very still for a little while longer, then extremely carefully get up from behind him and get off the bed. I go around the room and bathroom, turning off all the lights, and decide to go climb into the chair and ottoman that are in the corner of the room. I don't feel comfortable leaving him in here by himself tonight in case he wakes up in pain again, so I curl myself up and use the throw pillow to rest my head against, close my eyes, and drift off to sleep within what feels like seconds.

I awake to a noise in the room, and I slowly start blinking my eyes open, trying to figure out where I am and why it's so bright in here already. Kennen comes and sits down on the ottoman in front of the chair I'm in, with a gentle smile on his face.

"Good morning, sleepyhead."

Visions of last night are coming back, reminding me of why I'm currently curled up on a chair that isn't the most comfortable and is probably the cause of the current massive kink in my neck.

I sit up towards the end of the chair and place my legs down in between where Kennen's are, rub my eyes, and stretch my arms out above my head.

Letting out a yawn, I look over at him. "What time is it?"

He grins. "It's ten o'clock."

My eyes shoot open in surprise. "Are you serious? You should have woken me up. Now I feel awful that I've been in here being lazy, while you've probably been up for hours already."

He tilts his head down, laughs, and then looks back up at me. "Actually, I just woke up myself."

I feel better now, knowing that I'm not the only one who slept in, until it hits me like a crash test dummy slamming into a brick wall. "Kennen, do you mean to tell me that you just slept for ten hours?" I lean over, wrapping my arms around his neck, and give him a big hug. "Oh, my gosh, this is so amazing; how do you feel?"

"I don't think I've slept that much in one night ever, actually." The corners of his mouth suddenly turn up. "I feel amazing. Thank you so much, Brielle."

I lower my arms, putting them in my lap, and smile back up at him, completely beaming. "It was my pleasure, Kennen. I'm thrilled that you got some much-needed rest and are feeling better."

He curiously looks up at the top of my head while pulling out the pencil I used last night to hold my bun in, and then holds it in front of us with a questioning eyebrow. "Should I ask?"

I give him a small huff. "This is what I like to call a 'Graphic Designer's Scrunchie.'"

This makes him chuckle, and then he starts gently shaking out my hair so it's now falling down the length of my back. "I love your hair when it's down, Brielle. It's really beautiful."

I start to lightly flush at his compliment, and the way it feels having his hands in my hair. "Thank you. Feel free to play with it or wrap it around your fists anytime you wish." Then I give him a playful wink.

He quickly clears his throat. "Don't tempt me, as I just might." His smile turns mischievous.

The thought of this causes my mind to wander to places I know it shouldn't considering he's mentioned several times now that we are only doing the flirting thing.

Before I can think any more about it, both of his hands are cupping my face, and he's looking at me in the most tender way. "No one has ever taken care of me like that before, Brielle, nor have they even cared enough to. You are the most selfless, caring, amazing woman I have ever had in my life."

He leans in close enough so that our faces are only breaths apart, keeping his eyes focused on mine the whole time. "According to some people, I may be crazy, but the one thing I am not is stupid."

He gently runs a thumb over my bottom lip and looks down at it and back up at me again. "And I would be stupid not to let you into my heart, Brielle, no matter how scared I really am."

I'm suddenly struggling to find my breath as my heart begins pounding heavily in my chest. Then, before I can say anything, he closes his eyes and lightly presses his warm lips on mine.

His kisses start off slow and gentle, until neither of us can control the urging desire that has been consuming us over the past couple of weeks. Then a quiet moan escapes me as he parts my lips with his tongue. The heat currently raging inside me instantly begins spiraling downward, awaking every nerve ending along the way.

With one swift motion he slides his hands down, lifting me forward until I'm straddling him. His mouth suddenly leaves mine as he slowly begins to kiss his way along my jaw, his breaths sending shivers up and down my spine. Bringing one of his hands back up, he gently pulls on some of my hair, causing my head to tilt back, giving him better access to my neck and collarbone. With his other hand, he carefully begins to slide the top of my bathrobe off the side of my shoulder, softly kissing me on the newly exposed skin.

He raises his head, slamming his lips back on mine, and then stands up, lifting me with him as he walks us over to his bed. I'm set down quickly with a force that tells me he's definitely done playing our flirting-only game. Before he climbs into bed with me, he slides his sweatpants down and takes them off, completely revealing himself to me.

*Oh. My. Gosh.* If the cardiac arrest I'm about to have doesn't kill me, I think what I'm about to experience just might. It's like the Greek gods sent this man down to earth just to torture my soul out of existence.

I place a finger in my mouth and bite down on my nail, trying to control the fact that I'm ready to devour this man right now.

As he climbs onto the bed, he straddles me with a passionate determination in his eyes. Goosebumps suddenly make their appearance as he runs his fingers down the edge of my bathrobe until he reaches the belt, lightly grazing my skin along the way. Then, as if he were savoring a present he was about to open, he begins to slowly untie the knot. Once it's undone, he carefully opens both sides, then quickly looks up at me, his eyes instantly turning from flirtatious to feral.

He blows out a slow breath. "Brielle, please tell me you haven't been sleeping less than ten feet away from me all night without anything on under this robe."

I sit up, placing my hands out behind me for support, causing my bathrobe to slide all the way down to the bed. "What's a girl to do when she's soaking in a steaming hot bath and hears a cry for help?" My lips curve up in one corner. "I jumped out, threw on this robe, and came rushing over. There wasn't any time for worrying about what clothes I may or may not have neglected to put back on beforehand, Mr. Davis."

Smiling at me, he brings his face extremely close to mine so that I can feel the warmth of his breath as he continues, "That hot bath of yours has nothing on the amount of heat you are about to experience once I'm inside you, Brielle."

This time it's my turn to grab him by his hair and pull him towards me, crashing my lips against his with everything I have.

He places a hand on my lower back, then lifts my leg and carefully adjusts us so I'm now lying down against his pillows with him on top of me. Feeling our bodies now skin to skin causes the heat between my legs to quickly turn to moisture.

Painstakingly slowly, he begins kissing down my chest and to my stomach, causing me to almost lose my mind. I rub my hands up the curves of his back and shoulders, needing us to be face-to-face and, more importantly, to have him inside me.

Once again reading my nonverbal cue, he slides back up

to my face and kisses me with more passion than I have ever experienced at any point in my life.

Then he carefully lifts himself up and climbs off the bed as he heads over to his suitcase to grab a condom and put it on. Before I know it, he returns, positioning himself back on top of me.

Resting his elbows on either side of my head, he puts his hands back on the sides of my face, gently caressing my cheeks with his thumbs. "Brielle, if we do this, please promise me that you won't break my heart. For as connected as I feel to you already, I know it would completely shatter."

I softly put my hand on his racing heart and gaze directly into his eyes. "I promise."

He shifts his hand behind my head, slightly raising it, and places his lips against mine so quickly, the dizziness it causes makes my head spin. He lifts himself slightly and then positions himself inside me, our souls instantly connecting with a bond so strong that I can't even tell whose body is whose. Our eyes remain locked with every movement we begin to make.

As his motions begin to increase, he fills me so completely that it doesn't take long for him to push my desires over the edge and take him down along with me. After a few moments, he eases himself carefully back on top of me, both of us left breathless and shaking.

He's looking at me so intensely right now, almost as if he's observing me in a whole new light. "Brielle…I see you, only you, and absolutely nothing else."

"Really?" I feel a shine beginning to form in my eyes, as I know exactly what he means by this, and how important a statement that is.

His heart is pounding so fast in his chest right now that

I can feel it battering against my own. "My mind has never been so clear, and my eyes so calm, I..." He buries his hands deep into my hair and then kisses me so softly on the lips without finishing his sentence.

"So now that you can really see me, am I still what your heart really wants?" I run my fingers down his cheek and back to his heart, wearing a big smile.

He grabs my hand in his. "You have no idea how much, Brielle. This is the most incredible moment of my life, and I'm so glad that it's you I'm sharing it with."

I know it's not possible that I could already be madly in love with this amazing man, but my heart seems to be swelling so quickly, telling me otherwise.

Kennen gets up briefly to go clean up and then comes back and slides in the bed, curling up behind me. I know it sounds cliché, but we really do fit together perfectly. As he snuggles his head into the pillow behind mine and wraps his arms tightly around me, his broad biceps provide a welcome secureness and comfort.

After a while of remaining wrapped up together, Kennen speaks up. "Do we have to move, or can we just stay like this for the rest of the day?"

"As much as I would love nothing more than to do that, if you don't get some caffeine in me soon, you may see a total other side of me that isn't quite as pretty as this."

As soon as I say that, his stomach lets out a loud growl. "Well, apparently if you don't feed me soon, I won't have enough energy for any more rounds later." He leans up and playfully bites my ear.

I sit up and quickly slip out of bed. "Oh, I'll make sure that you are refueled and ready to go by tonight, don't you worry, Mr. Davis." And with that I give him a wink and let him watch as I sashay my naked body back over to my room to get ready for the day.

We're currently walking into the downtown area, and of course, our first mission is to find a frappé for me, as it's already lunchtime, and I might transform into some hideous monster if I wait any longer.

With a keen sense of smell, like that of a shark, I quickly track down the coffee shop that Kennen must have gone to previously based on the look of his face right now.

I laugh as we approach the door, and turn back to look at him. "Let me guess, is this the same one you went to last time when you were apparently traumatized?"

"Please don't make me go in there again, Brielle, especially now."

I'm not sure what that means, but he's definitely bringing his ass in there now. I grab ahold of his hand and pull him towards me. "Don't worry, I'll protect you." Then I give him a quick kiss on the lips and pull him through the front door.

This place smells like heaven, and I think we just might hang out here for a few hours instead of walking around town. I inhale a big whiff, and it takes the edge off until we get to the counter and are greeted by a very welcoming woman.

"Good afternoon, what can I get for you today, miss?" She smiles, then seems to notice Kennen standing behind me, causing her eyebrow to rise at him as she lets out a quick chuckle.

Hmm, either I'm about to find out what ended up happening after all, or he's going to spill it to me later on. I place my order, and Kennen kindly pays for the drink for me. As we begin to make our way down to the other end of the counter, I realize she never asked for my name.

I stop and catch her attention to ask her if she needs it, and she replies with, "You're all set, hun. It will be out in a few minutes." And then she gives me a playful smirk.

Kennen looks like he'd prefer to be anywhere but here right now, making me feel *somewhat* bad for torturing him like this. I walk up to him and place my hand in his back pocket while we wait, hoping a quick squeeze of his amazing ass will cheer him up some.

A few minutes later I hear a guy call out, "Ula, iced caramel chocolate-chip frappé."

Kennen instantly runs his hands down his face, and I start laughing so hard I almost wet myself. I walk up to the counter and grab my drink and then turn to see the woman who helped us earlier start laughing also.

She calls out to me, still laughing, "I'm guessing you're the girlfriend, right?"

Oh, he's definitely going to have to fess up later, but for now I walk down and lean over the counter to give her a high five.

I walk back over to Kennen, who now has his hands on his hips, pretending to look completely annoyed. "What the hell, is this a conspiracy or something?" He starts shaking his head, causing me to laugh even harder.

"So I'm your girlfriend named Ula, huh?" I take a sip of my amazing drink and then motion for him to lean down some so I can reach the side of his head.

I position myself extremely close to his ear so that he can feel my breath on him when I speak. "Don't worry, Mr. Davis, I'm all for role-playing in bed if that's what you're into."

He clears his throat, and then I grab his hand, pulling him out of the shop, loving the fact that she thought I was his girlfriend.

We walk just a little more and come upon a row of the most charming Airstream food trucks, and then even my stomach starts to growl. We stride up and down, trying to decide what to choose, considering each one of them has several things that sound completely amazing. The number of choices seems to be a little overwhelming for Kennen, so we end up in front of the Meltdown on 30A.

The aroma of grilled cheese must hit both of our senses quickly, because at the same time we both shout, "This one."

Everything on the menu is making our mouths water, so we decide to get two different kinds and share them. Kennen picks the "Sloppy Melt," which is made up of sloppy joe beef, American cheese, and Funyuns. After much consideration, I end up choosing "A Bunch Of Baloney," which includes fried mortadella, American and cheddar cheese, mustard, and potato chips.

Once our order is ready, we go sit under one of the trees on a cute green bench and open our foil packets. We pull apart our sandwiches, and the cheese oozes and stretches out of each one with mouthwatering perfection. We devour our first halves and then switch foil packets to share the different amazing flavors.

I close my eyes and can't help but let out a small groan. "There is nothing like a handcrafted grilled cheese by a local chef on a sunny afternoon."

He nods in agreement and then gets up to go order a drink while I sit there spellbound by my lunch.

When he returns, he's got a massive smile on his face, a drink in one hand, and the other one behind his back. "I wanted to get you a souvenir to commemorate this special occasion."

I look up at him curiously, placing my sandwich down and wiping my hands on a napkin. "And what occasion is that, exactly?"

"Our first official date with you being my girlfriend, of course." He gives me the sweetest wink and then throws a rolled-up shirt at me. I unroll the shirt and instantly know this will be my new favorite shirt ever.

It's a teal blue shirt with a dark brown and a light orange square grilled-cheese graphic with the bite out of the corner, and on top of the sandwich it says, "I had a meltdown on 30A" with "Seaside, Florida" underneath. The play on words, of course, reminds me right away of Kennen, making me laugh. I quickly get up and wrap him in a bear hug and plant a playful kiss on his cheek.

"This is by far my most cherished gift I've ever gotten; I love it so much, Kennen, thank you." I hold it to my chest and can't wait to add this to my collection.

We finish our lunch, and then I lead him over to a local gallery that I stopped by the other morning when I came out exploring on my own. I met the sweetest lady named Judy, who owns the shop, and we talked for well over an hour about all different kinds of art, the ocean, and life in general.

"I can't wait for you to see this gallery, Kennen. They have all different forms of art, from paintings and hand-blown glass sculptures to custom jewelry pieces."

I love that he's smiling at me right now, knowing that this is right up my alley. "I actually used to paint quite a bit when I was young, before all of the mathematical madness kicked in, that is."

I stop walking for a minute and grab his hand. "Really?

I had no idea you were into art. That's so great, Kennen."

He looks over towards the gallery for a minute and then back at me. "Like I said, that was a long time ago, and I haven't picked up a paintbrush since." He smiles lightly at me and then pulls my hand to have us start walking again.

When we get inside, I see Kennen's eyes light up, which brings an unexpected excitement to me, as I wasn't sure if it would be too chaotic in here for him to enjoy it.

Judy notices us come in and walks up front to greet us. "Brielle, what a pleasure to see you again. And who is this strapping young gentleman you brought with you?"

How can you not love this town, where everyone is so friendly and actually remembers your name (or nickname in my case at the coffee house earlier) after one visit?

She gives me a warm hug and then holds her hand out to Kennen, who proceeds to grab it and bring it to his mouth to kiss the top of it.

With a flush now in her cheeks, she turns back to me. "Oh, my sweet girl, this one is a keeper for sure."

Kennen and I both laugh and then begin to walk around with Judy in tow, going over some of the art with Kennen that she proudly showed me previously. Kennen seems really focused on the section of paintings she has displayed, carefully taking in the detail of each one and smiling.

After we are done admiring the art, we end up by the display case in the center of the room where she keeps her custom jewelry for sale.

Her face suddenly lights up. "Oh, Brielle, I must show you the most beautiful ring that I got in yesterday afternoon as part of a custom collection made by a well-known jewelry designer from New York." She smiles at me as we walk over to her. "As much as you love the ocean, based on our conversation the other day, this one instantly made me think of you, my dear."

She pulls out the most stunning engagement ring I have ever seen. It resembles the shape of a wave made of 14K white gold, with a two-carat round diamond in the middle that has several smaller diamonds, blue topazes, and sapphires curling around to the left side of the diamond and then moving down over to the right. The transition from dark to light hues reminds me of the ocean as it moves up to form a wave, while the diamonds mimic the water as it transforms into a whitecap.

I am completely mesmerized by this ring. "Wow, Judy, this is absolutely breathtaking." I can't take my eyes off this amazing piece of art. "What I love most is the symbolism of using a wave as an engagement ring."

Kennen looks over at me curiously. "How so, Brielle?"

"Well, as a wave builds up, sometimes it crashes, and sometimes it gently flows down. Yet in the end, it always blends itself back in with the rest of the ocean, finding its peace and rhythm once again." I smile at him and then continue, "Just as how making a commitment to someone means that you are willing to be there alongside them not only through the good times, but through the rough times also and everything in between…always coming back together as one in the end."

He looks down at the ring and then back up at me again with a warm smile on his face. "I love that, Brielle."

I hand the ring back to Judy. "Thank you for showing that to me. It really is lovely."

We finish browsing our way around the gallery, then say our goodbyes and make our way back out into this quaint little town.

I grab Kennen's hand, leading him up the steps and

onto the welcoming porch of the town's local bookstore next. As we walk inside, we can't help but grin at each other. The aroma of paperbacks, and the tall bookshelves overflowing with dreams just waiting to be read, instantly fills our souls with happiness.

After spending some time looking through all the titles, we find our way over to the staff's favorites section and both choose a new book to purchase as a future beach read. Then hand in hand, we walk outside carrying our latest treasures.

## CHAPTER 17

I can't believe I have a girlfriend again after keeping people away after all these years. So much for staying strong and controlling myself. There's no way I wasn't going to give Brielle a chance, though, knowing how strong the connection we have is, and how much she genuinely really seems to care about me. I feel like she is the first person to ever really accept and understand me for who I am. I also absolutely love the fact that my mind is so focused on her that everything else has seemed to fade into the background for once.

After our trip in town earlier today, we ended up coming back to the house and grabbing our beach gear to go out to the beach to relax for a little while. I have to say that the beach is really beginning to attach itself to my soul, especially having Brielle there to share her love of the sea with me. We brought our new books with us and lay down together on the blanket, Brielle using my chest as a pillow and my arm wrapped around hers. It was silently peaceful.

For dinner tonight, we decided to grab a rideshare and check out the next town over, as Brielle found some amazing oyster bar she really wanted to try out.

Ditching her classic T-shirt tonight, she decided to try to drive me insane again, this time wearing a short yellow sundress with ruffles at the bottom and spaghetti straps with a very revealing V-neck. I'm trying to focus my eyes on hers, but it's proving extremely difficult, when I want nothing more than to spend more time exploring her breasts when we're back in bed later on. Neither of us were able to hold off very long earlier with as much buildup as we have had lately.

She's smirking at me when I finally look back up at her.

"Don't worry, we'll make it an early night, as I haven't forgotten about the additional rounds you promised me earlier, Mr. Davis."

Where the hell is this waiter, anyway, so we can hurry up and get this dinner over with already.

She laughs, probably knowing exactly what I'm currently thinking, and then grabs the menu and asks, "Are you good with just ordering a couple of dozen oysters, or would you like something else to go with it?"

I slide closer to her and run my hand up her thigh, brushing the edge of her dress, "Order as many oysters as you like, Miss Bisset. As you and I both know, it has long since been proven that they are natural aphrodisiacs that create increased sexual energy and sperm count." Then I move my hand further up her dress, grazing her upper inner thigh.

She drops the menu, sucks in a quick breath, and then takes a sip of her water. "Oh, I'm all for the increased sexual energy; however, you'd better keep your boys under control unless you plan on marrying me someday, mister," she says, holding up her hand, pointing out her empty ring finger, and laughing.

I grab her hand and gently rub her finger, suddenly remembering that she once had a ring there until that scumbag cheated on her. I'd love to see him and let him know what I really think of him hurting her like that, but the other part of me would also like to thank him. Otherwise she wouldn't be sitting here with me, talking about being in my bed again tonight. The thought of her being with anyone else, let alone being engaged to someone, after the connection we made this morning, brings a sudden ache to my heart.

The server finally arrives and takes our order, but before he leaves, he lets us know that they are hosting a trivia game here tonight and asks us if we would like to participate. Apparently, there's a grand prize of a free beer and branded T-shirt, which is all it takes for Brielle to hear before she signs us up for another interesting evening.

Giggling, she looks at me. "It's time to let me show you off a little bit, especially since there's a T-shirt at stake."

Oh, man, I'm so done for, as how can I possibly say no to that face when it just totally lights me up inside.

"Alright, but here's the deal, if we win, I get the shirt and you get the beer, okay?" I give her a wink, knowing she's obsessed with these crazy shirts.

She folds her arms across her chest and pretends to pout. "Fine, I guess you need to add it to your collection more than I do anyway."

I lean over and give her a quick kiss. "You're so damn cute, even when you pout, my Ula."

After a short time, our dinner arrives, and we enjoy the fresh oysters and each other's company. We see the trivia host start to set up in the corner of the bar area, and then an assistant walks around with game cards for all the participating teams.

Once we have ours in hand, Brielle lights up with excitement. "Are you ready to kick some trivia ass?"

I laugh. "How is it that I keep letting you talk me into

doing all of these insane things, anyway?"

"It must be my irresistible charm, I suppose."

Irresistible is an understatement, but I don't want to let her know that quite yet, so I just nod in agreement.

The host begins going over the rules, and then we get the game started. We are competing against five other teams around the bar. Luckily, we don't have to get up in front of anyone, as we just use the cards to record our answers for each round.

We get through each of the five rounds easily, causing Brielle to squeal out wildly with each round we make it up the leaderboard. We are, however, tied with a couple on another team, so it all comes down to a final tiebreaker question. They ask us to have one person from each group come up to the area where the host has been conducting the game, and of course Brielle instantly nominates me.

I'm beginning to think that she has a thing for tormenting the hell out of me at this point, but I suck up my antisocial vibes and take one for the team by going up there. The guy from the other couple comes up to join me, and we give each other the stare down like we're about to start the final round of a heavyweight championship boxing match. If he thinks I'm walking out of here with Brielle and no shirt in hand, he's got another think coming. I break eye contact with him to look over at Brielle quickly, and she blows me a kiss, then gives me a wink. I give her a smirk in return and then focus back on the host, who explains how this is going to work. He will call on each of us to answer, and whoever has the closest correct answer will win the game, which sounds simple enough to me.

The host speaks into the microphone. "What is the length of the state of Florida from north to south in miles?" Then he turns to my opponent, who gives an answer of six hundred and seventy-five miles.

I chuckle, as I know he's not even close. Then the host turns to me for my answer.

Feeling confident about my answer, I try to throw a little humor into it. "What is four hundred and forty-seven, Alex."

The guy looks at me and laughs. "Riiight…well, that is actually the *exact* length of the state of Florida, and we have our winners, folks."

The crowd joyously starts clapping.

My opponent gives me a look of defeat, knowing he just lost by knockout, and walks back to his table, his head lowered in shame. When I turn back to look at Brielle, she's already running up to me. When she reaches me, she leaps right up, wrapping her arms around my neck with her legs around my waist, and gives me the sweetest kiss.

With her smile beaming at me, she says, "I'm so proud of you, love."

It feels so good having someone as amazing as her being proud of me, even if for such a simple thing as winning trivia night at a bar.

The host clears his throat, getting our attention, and then chimes back in on the microphone. "I tell you what, guys, should we find out if this genius over here can answer one more bonus question *exactly* correct again?"

The crowd erupts in hoots and hollers, signaling that they're all for this.

Of course, Brielle and I look at each other and start snickering at the fact that he just called me a genius.

Brielle slides down and stands by my side, wrapping her arm around my waist, giving me a squeeze.

The host looks back over at me again. "If you can also tell me the exact number of miles of beaches for the whole state of Florida, we will also pay for your dinner tonight."

I catch our server's attention and ask him to bring me up our bill. When he has it prepared, he walks up to me with it, and I take the bill for our dinner and hand it right over to the host.

"That would be six hundred and sixty-three miles of beaches. The entire state is made up of 54,136 square miles of land area, and 4,424 square miles of water area…oh, and please leave an extremely large tip for our server when you pay."

The crowd looks at the host, waiting for his response to see if my answer is correct, as he just stands there staring at me in disbelief until he finally speaks up. "The miles of beaches is exactly correct, as for the rest of the facts he stated, well, I'll have to rely on one of you with a cell phone to confirm, lol."

The crowd erupts in thunderous applause and whistles.

He shakes my hand, pats me on the back, and then hands me a T-shirt that says "Shucking Off at the Down and Out Oyster Bar."

I look over at Brielle, who's just read the shirt, and she has her hand covering her mouth, trying to contain her laughter. "Oh, my gosh, you are so wearing that to our first board meeting when we get back to New York."

I tilt my head back with laughter, as I can only imagine what the board would think of Brielle and me if we both walked in wearing our latest T-shirt finds.

I grab her around the waist with both of my hands and pull her into the most passionate kiss I can, never feeling fuller of life than I do right now.

Once we're done kissing, I look down at her. "Hey, we also get a free beer. Do you want to stay and drink it?"

She smirks at me, then leans up to my ear. "You should

have them give it to the poor guy you just KO'd in the last match. You still have several rounds to go with me tonight when we get back, and I won't be as easy on you as he was."

I instantly snatch her up in my arms, causing her to squeal, and then tell the host to give the other guy my beer as I walk straight for the door of the bar. I order a rideshare and realize that this car can't get here quickly enough.

Luckily it's a quick ride back, as it takes everything she and I have to keep our hands off each other while in the car.

When we get inside, she starts running up the stairs faster than I have ever seen her move before. Unfortunately for her, I can run faster and take two steps at a time, catching up with her once she hits the kitchen area on the second floor.

Wrapping my arm around her from behind, I cause her to suddenly stop short and start laughing. "Where do you think you're going in such a hurry, Miss Bisset?"

She spins around so that she's now facing me and somewhat out of breath. "I was just trying to hurry and get up to the bedroom. Why?"

With a look like I'm about to devour her, I start moving closer, trying to minimize the gap currently between us, and she starts backing away. I don't stop until she backs right up into the refrigerator. *Perfect.*

I put a finger under her chin, raising her face to mine, and get so close to her lips that I can feel every heavy breath she is experiencing as though they were my own.

"Let's get this straight right now. There is nothing about tonight that will be hurried. I plan on taking it so slow with you that you will be begging me by the time I'm done." I kiss her lips so softly, yet I can still feel it when she smiles.

I slowly back up, grabbing her hands in mine as I do, and walk backwards with her over towards the living room. Then I wrap her arms around my neck and mine around her waist.

"Dance with me in the silence again, Brielle."

As we start moving, I can't help but be hypnotized by how beautiful she really is, inside and out. It makes me feel bad for how poorly I treated her when we were in New York.

I connect with her eyes. "I'm really sorry, Brielle."

Tilting her head, she looks at me questioningly. "For what, Kennen?"

"For how I was towards you when we were in the office." I smile and give her a quick kiss on her nose. "It's just that you showed up, instantly turning my whole world upside down, and I didn't know what to think or how to handle it."

"It's okay, as I've already forgiven you, but if you pull that crap again when we get back, I'll make sure that I put you in your place any way I see fit. And trust me, I don't care who's around when I do it." She winks at me and then pulls my head closer down to hers, kissing me with a force to let me know she is being totally serious right now.

As we continue to sway in the silence, I lower my hands down past her amazing ass to where the hem of her dress sits. Then inch by inch, I begin to run them back up underneath the fabric. Once I reach the edge of what feels like lace, I gently run my fingers underneath, taking in every soft, smooth curve of her body.

She gasps. "Kennen..."

"Brielle..." I slide my hands further up now, pulling her even closer into me, and then begin kissing her again.

I need to see more of her, so I carefully pull her dress up over her head and let it drop to the floor. She follows my lead and takes hold of my shirt and begins lifting it up, then has me help her take it off. Her hands go to the button of my shorts, but I place my hand on top of hers, stopping her.

I pick her up, softly lay her down on the couch, and then sit down on the edge next to her. I run my hand into her hair and then slowly trace the contours of her face, her slim neck, and then over the lace of her bra. Taking my time, I continue to make my way down the entire length of her body, taking mental captures as I go. Once I'm done, I repeat the process, this time pressing my lips on every piece of exposed skin available.

She's gasping for breath extremely frequently now. "Okay, I'm tapping out. You win."

Grinning at her, I laugh. "Oh no you don't, not yet."

She grabs the edge of my shorts and pulls me to her. "Yes. I. Am." She reaches behind her and removes her bra and holds it up to me on one finger. "I am officially raising the white flag; therefore in the rules of war, I'm surrendering and cannot be teased any further."

I can't help but chuckle, as she's just so damn cute. "Actually, I think it means that I can no longer fire upon you, nor you fire upon me." Then I move her over enough so that there's room for me to straddle her now.

She covers her face with her hands, laughing. "I had to fall for a walking Wikipedia, didn't I, ugh."

I let out a bellowed laugh. "Yeah, I know. It's usually my least attractive quality according to most people."

I feel her suddenly stiffen below me, and she grasps my face in her hands, looking at me so intensely that I feel like she can see straight through to my soul. "Actually, Kennen, it's my most favorite thing about you." She smiles at me so tenderly now. "Your mind is…" She pauses for a moment, like she's searching for the perfect words she wants to say. "It's brilliantly beautiful."

With that one statement she has just stolen my entire heart, hell, my entire being, and I know I have finally found the piece of me that has been missing my entire life. I found my wave.

## CHAPTER 18

*Brielle*

  *L*ast night was one of those moments in life, like that of a ship finally finding its way back to shore after being lost at sea for so long that you had forgotten what it felt like to dig your feet in the warm sand.

After what I said in response to my heart slightly breaking at Kennen's mention of what people thought of his brilliance, something seemed to shift between us. My sudden urge to rush our time together disappeared, and instead I wanted nothing more than to soak up every minute of passion he was so willingly giving to me. We spent the next couple of hours with our lips pressed together and exploring each other as if not wanting to miss a single inch of our bodies.

We didn't end up having sex last night, though, but we ended up making love instead, several times, in fact. I sigh just thinking about it.

I'm still lying here in bed while my superhero has left to go brave the coffee shop again for me, and I realize that I haven't reached out to Nic since the night we went to dinner with Austin.

I know she's my best friend, and I love her so much, but Kennen and I both agreed that it would be best if we keep our relationship between us until after the merger so as not to cause any issues. Considering that it's taking place tomorrow, I don't feel as bad holding out on her a few more days.

I grab my cell and start typing a message.

> **Brielle:** Hey, girl, how are you feeling, aside from being a few parts short and a bit lighter?
> **Nicole:** You're hilarious, do you know that?
> **Brielle:** So I've been told…but really, how's the healing going?
> **Nicole:** Slow, but it's getting better every day. More importantly, how's everything going on the "workcation"? The last time I heard from you, it was Thursday night and then crickets…
> **Brielle:** I know, I'm sorry. We've been so busy, and time is just flying by.
> **Nicole:** Busy doing what exactly, or do I not want to know?
> **Brielle:** Let's see, I got Kennen on an offshore fishing charter (and yes, we caught dinner), we went into town exploring, and then yesterday I entered us in a trivia game at an oyster bar, and Kennen killed it for us (of course).
> **Nicole:** Wait, what? You can't be serious with anything you just said.
> **Brielle:** Oh, I'm totally serious, and do you know what the best part is?
> **Nicole:** I'm afraid to ask…
> **Brielle:** He's actually having fun and…laughing.
> **Nicole:** Now I know you're full of crap, as in the past eight years, I've not once heard that man laugh.
> **Brielle:** I'm rubbing off on him, I guess, lol.

> **Nicole:** OMG, please do not corrupt my boss, Brielle. He needs to stay focused with everything we have going on at work right now.
> **Brielle:** Silly me. I forgot this poor man isn't allowed to have any kind of life aside from working himself to death.
> **Nicole:** You know what I mean, and work is his life, Brielle. It's just how he is.

What I want to say is "that's not who he really is," but maybe she's right, as I have no idea what he's going to be like when we get back to the normal daily grind at work. I'm sure he'll be even busier after the merger with rollout campaigns and new business, and a sudden feeling of dread fills me. I think back to the other night when I found him so immersed in work that he made himself sick. No amount of business, or money for that matter, is worth living that way. Not that I won't continue to take care of him as it happens, though, as I know his business is like his baby.

> **Brielle:** Right, well, I am going to continue to corrupt him for the next couple of days until we leave, anyway. (Not tomorrow, of course.)
> **Nicole:** Oh, I meant to tell you that his birthday is tomorrow also, so maybe you can talk him into doing some other crazy thing to celebrate after the meeting.
> **Brielle:** Hmmm, how else can I abuse him for his birthday?
> **Nicole:** Brielle…
> **Brielle:** Don't worry, Nic, get some rest, and I'll text you after the merger meeting tomorrow.

**Nicole:** Thanks, and, Brielle, whatever you do, please make sure that merger goes through tomorrow, or we'll both be without jobs and a place to live…

I swallow hard and then throw my cell phone on the bed. She had to go and remind me about that, didn't she. Why is it that I feel like the future of his whole company is being put in my hands, and I've only been employed here for a few weeks?

I get in the shower to go get ready and realize that Kennen can't get back here quickly enough with that caffeine.

We're eating brunch out on the back deck, since we ended up sleeping in again this morning, and going over what we want to do today. I'm in much better spirits now that I've had my frappé fix, and Kennen is sitting here completely beaming at me.

"So, my Ula, what crazy adventure awaits us today?"

I chuckle. "Actually, I thought with the meeting coming up tomorrow that maybe we can just relax by the beach and stay here for dinner."

He takes a sip of his water and then puts the glass down. "That sounds perfect, Brielle. Although, would it be okay if I added one thing to the itinerary for this afternoon for a little while?"

I'm intrigued to hear what this is, considering he hasn't asked to do anything since we've been here. "Of course, what did you have in mind?"

His face fills with a big grin. "Well, when I went into

town this morning, I bumped into your new friend Judy from the gallery, and she mentioned that there was going to be a pop-up art show this afternoon. I thought it might be fun for us to walk around and see what they bring."

I love that he's excited about art again and that it's something we both have in common. "I would love that. Let's finish up and head over there. Then we can hit the beach afterwards for a little while."

"Great, it sounds like the perfect day," he says, then starts eating again.

Once we're done and get everything cleaned up, we head back out into town to go visit the art show. When we arrive, there are a bunch of white tents set up on the brick-lined streets, easily filling the whole entire downtown area.

A woman who seems to be waving at us in the distance catches my eye, and as we get closer, I see that it's Judy. She comes up to me and gives me a big hug again like we've been close friends forever. "Brielle, my dear, it's so wonderful to see you again." She smiles. "I'm so glad you guys were able to make it to the art show, as there are some fabulous artists and designers here today."

"It's so great to see you also, Judy, and we can't wait to look around."

Kennen excuses himself and starts walking over to the first booth, and I have an amazing idea come to me for his birthday.

"Judy, do you know if there's anyone here who makes custom art cases, and where I might be able to buy some supplies?"

She smiles and thinks about this for a minute. "Yes, actually there is. His name is Vince, and you will see his booth not too far away from my gallery. He makes the most beautiful engraved cases out of driftwood."

I am so excited about this idea. "Perfect, thank you. I want to get one for Kennen for his upcoming birthday as a surprise, as he seems to have had his passion for art renewed after visiting your gallery."

She brings me in for another heartfelt hug. "Oh, isn't that spectacular! I also have a whole box full of brand-new brushes and paints in my office that I bought a while back, hoping to start some classes in the gallery, which never ended up happening. Please feel free to help yourself with whatever you'd like to fill it up for Kennen."

"You've been so wonderful, Judy, thank you. That would be amazing." I give her hand a little squeeze. "I'll come back later this afternoon and grab them once I get him back to the house."

With that, we say our goodbyes for now, and I go to catch up with Kennen.

He smiles excitedly when he sees me. "Brielle, come check these out. Aren't they amazing?"

I walk up next to him and see these gorgeous paintings that use different forms of mediums when they're created. The one he's currently standing in front of incorporates real sand and seashells into the design, and it really is beautifully done.

I look back over at him, and when I look into his eyes, I feel like I can see his wheels turning, but in a new way, not clouded and chaotic as they were before.

"Yes, they really are." I take another look at it and then continue, "I especially love the use of the shells, as they have always intrigued me."

He grabs my hand, and we continue walking. "So what's your fascination with shells, anyway?"

"I love how they are all so unique and beautiful, and always wonder what their journeys were like on their way to the shore." I look up at Kennen, who seems to be thinking about this. "Also, legend has it that if you find the perfect shell, listen to its journey, and make a wish under the summer night's sky, it will come true."

He smiles warmly at me. "Is that so?" Then he laces his fingers in mine, and we continue walking.

As we make our way through the booths, we are both becoming increasingly inspired the more artwork we look at. When we get closer to Judy's gallery, I notice Vince's tent that she mentioned to me earlier. While Kennen is in a somewhat deep conversation with one of the local artists, I sneak over to look at the paint boxes he has displayed.

I'm greeted by a gentleman with long salt-and-pepper hair pulled back into a pony, and a beard that is probably just as long.

He smiles as I approach. "Good afternoon, miss, how may I help you today?"

I extend my hand to shake his. "Hello, my name is Brielle. And you must be Vince?"

Eyeing me curiously, he replies, "Guilty as charged, I suppose." Then he gives my hand a sturdy shake.

"Judy sent me over here, as I'm looking for a gift for my boyfriend's birthday, and these are absolutely amazing."

"Why, thank you. Carving new life into pieces of old washed-up driftwood is a passion of mine." He smiles proudly and then waves his arm out for me to look at all his designs.

It only takes me a minute to find my favorite one. "Would you be able to burn a message on the inside of this one for me today, by any chance?" I smile sweetly at him, hoping to charm him into saying yes.

"Any friend of Judy's is a friend of mine, so yes, I'd be happy to do that for you." He grabs the case that I chose, and then goes back to his table and pulls out a piece of paper and a pen. "Please write down what you would like, and I'll have it ready for you before I leave today."

I give him a quick embrace, as I'm so excited to give this to Kennen tomorrow. "Thank you so much. You have no idea how much this will mean to him."

I grab the pen and begin rapidly tapping it on the table, trying to create a quote that will perfectly express my sentiments to him. When it finally comes to me, I write down "Give your worries to the ocean and let the waves set you free, and in their silence, you will always find me. ~ Ula." I smile and then hand it back to Vince.

He reads the message and then turns to look at me. "This is beautiful. He must be quite the lucky man." He gives me a wink; then I pay him and leave to go find Kennen before he comes looking for me.

After a couple of hours of walking around, I turn to him. "Are you ready to go hit the beach with me for a little while before dinner?"

"Absolutely, under one condition, though…"

I am afraid to ask what his condition is exactly. "Hmm, and what would that be, Mr. Davis?"

"That we both have to take turns putting on each other's suntan lotion again," he says, waggling his eyebrows up and down.

I burst out laughing. "Deal." I take his large hand in mine. "Come on, let's go get some vitamin sea."

It was a perfect afternoon relaxing in the warmth of the sun, bodysurfing the waves, and genuinely enjoying each other's company. When we got back to the house, we took a long shower together, washing off hours of salt and sand while continuing to explore each other's bodies. My body has never felt so alive and responsive around someone like this before, and I'm quickly realizing that he is becoming my kryptonite. I blow out a slow breath and get dressed so that we can get dinner started.

We decide to make some of the mahi mahi Kennen caught the other day, and I use the excuse of needing some side items to go back into town so that I can pick up his present on the way back from the local market. I grab some basmati rice and fresh broccoli to make alongside the fish, and then head over to where Vince is currently in the process of taking down his tent and packing up his items.

As he sees me walking up, he lights up with a big smile and grabs the paint box for me. "Brielle, I hope you're happy with how it turned out."

I slowly open the lid of the box, look at the beautiful inscription, and then close the lid, holding it up against my chest. "It's perfect. Thank you again. I really appreciate it."

"You're welcome. Make sure you let me know if he ends up putting any of his future work in a show someday, as I'd love to come see it." Then he returns to packing up his booth.

Incredibly excited, I walk over to Judy's gallery and show her the box, which she absolutely ends up loving, and then she takes me into the back to fill it with some starter supplies. Once she has it filled with several colors of acrylic paints and brushes of all shapes and sizes, she puts it in a gift bag for me complete with tissue paper and a bow.

I smile warmly at her. "Are you sure I can't pay you for all of this?"

"No, no, I'm so happy to finally see it get put to good

use." She tilts her head and then looks at me. "So how much longer will you both be here with us in Seaside?"

"We leave on Wednesday, unfortunately." This causes me to frown slightly.

"Why do you look so sad, dear? Do you not want to go back home?" She takes hold of my hand lightly.

"I'm in between homes right now, and I have no idea what will end up happening with Kennen and me when we get back. Honestly, I just really love it here and wish we could stay." I wince slightly as I realize that I just released all this drama on such a sweet woman.

She looks at me, her eyes filled with complete compassion. "My sweet girl, don't you worry now. It will all work out in the end, you'll see. I can see the special soul connection that you both have, and it reminds me of my late husband and me. And we were married forty-four years before he passed."

"I hope you're right, Judy, and I'm sorry to hear of your husband's passing. I'm sure after being married for so long, you must miss him terribly."

"Every minute of every day, but I'm eternally grateful for all the amazing years we spent making memories together." Her eyes glass over with a shine filled with love.

"Well, I'd better get back before he thinks I ran off on him with some local at the market." I give her a wink. "Thanks so much, Judy. I'm so happy to have met you."

I call out to Kennen when I get back to the beach house, but he doesn't respond. He must be out of sight enough for me to drop the food off in the kitchen and then sprint up to my room to hide his gift in my bedroom closet.

Almost running into him as I'm coming back out of the bedroom, I give him a quick warning look. "You'd better not have been on your laptop working while I was gone, Mr. Davis."

He gives me a big smirk. "And what exactly would you do to me if I was, Miss Bisset?"

"Kennen…" I fold my arms across my chest, giving him a pointed look.

He grabs ahold of me, wrapping me up in a bear hug with his muscled arms I can't get enough of. "I'm just messing with you; trust me, I learned my lesson the other night." Then he urgently places a kiss on my lips to keep me from saying anything more. Before I know it, he smacks me on the ass and then takes off running down the stairs, shouting, "Last one to the kitchen has to do the dishes!"

I can't help but giggle, as I know in the few days that we've been here, I've already created a monster.

We barely get through dinner with our clothes on, as who knew cooking together would turn out to be such a sensual experience for both of us. In the end, he ended up "helping" me wash the dishes by leaning on me from behind and locking his arms around my waist while nuzzling his head in the crevice of my neck the whole time.

With everything cleaned, I spin around while I'm still in his grip and wrap my arms around his neck. "So, Mr. Davis, what shall we do now?"

"Is that a serious question or a hypothetical one?" He raises an eyebrow.

I start kissing along the side of his jaw and slowly down his warm neck, feeling his pulse beneath my lips as I do. "Maybe the more appropriate question would have been, which room do you want to *sleep* in tonight?"

He laughs. "That's what I thought, but actually, I have a surprise for you."

I quickly raise my head to look at him. "Oohh, I love surprises!"

"Why don't you go get more comfortable and then come to my bedroom door when you're ready." He kisses me long and hard and then takes off back up the stairs again, grinning from ear to ear.

You don't need to tell me twice, so I hurry up behind him, excited for what he has planned for us. When I get in my room, I know exactly what I want to wear to bed tonight. Earlier, I had snuck into Kennen's room and snagged his trivia championship T-shirt, thinking I would do the playful yet sexy vibe tonight. I get changed, fluff out my hair, and then go and knock on Kennen's door, lightly bouncing up and down in anticipation of this surprise of his. I hear him call out, telling me to come in, so I open his door and walk in, but I don't see him anywhere.

"Kennen, where are you?" I have no idea where he is, as I don't see him in the bathroom either.

"I'm out on the deck," he calls from outside.

When I open the linen drapes and walk outside, I notice that he has put out a bunch of lanterns with candles, and he has the drapes closed on the sides of the deck, leaving only the ocean view in front of us exposed. When I turn all the way around, I see that he has made up the bed-sized porch swing with a bunch of pillows and a blanket, and he's lying there on his side in sexy briefs.

I'm taken aback by how beautiful and incredibly romantic this all is, and then I look down at myself and wish I would have put on something a little nicer than his T-shirt.

"Kennen, I'm so sorry. Had I known that I was walking out into such an amazing gesture, I totally would have dressed appropriately." I put my hands over my face, feeling completely embarrassed.

He pats the bed, silently asking me to come join him.

I walk over, climb in, and lie facing him. But before I can speak again, he leans over, placing his hand half on my face, half behind my head, and places a soft yet seductive kiss against my lips. After which he backs away a little and starts playing with my hair.

"The only thing you should be sorry for right now is stealing *my* shirt." He gives me a playful wink. "And just for the record, you look sexy as hell right now, so I'm glad you chose to wear it."

"Thank you for all of this, Kennen. No one has ever done anything even remotely this romantic for me. I love it." I put my hand on his chest and start lightly outlining his defined curves with my fingers.

He looks me in the eyes. "You're sincerely welcome, Brielle." He puts his hand on my leg and slowly starts dragging it up under my shirt, sending waves of need up through my core. "All I could think about today was falling asleep outside with you while listening to the waves rolling up on the shore."

Oh my gosh, who is this guy, anyway? I feel like I'm living in some amazing dream that I never want to wake from. I think back to what Judy mentioned earlier about enjoying all the memories she had made with her husband all those years, and I decide not to focus on anything else but being in this amazing moment right now, with the man I know I am totally falling madly in love with.

## CHAPTER 19

*L*ast night was absolutely incredible, making love to Brielle and then falling asleep with her amazing body tucked perfectly into mine all night. I've had more sleep in the past few days since we've been here than I normally get in an entire month at home. I try not to think about it because I know once we return, she'll be staying with Nicole, and I'll be back to living by myself in that big cold apartment. I'm hoping once our relationship is known, I can talk her into staying over a few nights a week at least, as I don't think my heart could handle it otherwise.

I hear Brielle calling me while pushing on my shoulder to wake me up, I suppose. I open my eyes, and she's sitting up on the bed swing, where we ended up falling asleep last night.

I rub my eyes and yawn. "What's wrong? Are you okay?" Then I take a good look at her, and she's smiling, so I know there isn't any emergency. "What time is it, anyway?"

She laughs and pulls me over so that my head is in her lap, and she starts playing with my hair. "Look, Kennen, the sun is about to start rising above the horizon."

I focus on the ocean and see the sky above it beginning to transform with a kaleidoscope of pinks, tangerines, and purples as the sun begins to rise, suddenly changing the color of the water below, as if it belongs in some sort of enchanted location. Aside from Brielle, it's one of the most beautiful things I have ever seen. I'm really going to miss the peacefulness of the ocean when we head back to the discord of the city in a couple of days.

We watch the sunrise together before I ask her to join me on my morning run, to which she replies, "Only if we stop in town on the way back for my morning cocktail."

I laugh, as of course I know that is part of our new normal routine. "You got it, but you're going in there by yourself this time." I give her a faux stern glance.

"Fair enough." She gets up to change and then heads down to the kitchen.

I grab my T-shirt that she stole and put it back in my room, or I know I'll never see it again. Honestly, I may never wash it again, being that it smells just like her now, a sweetness that I crave every time I'm close to her.

I get dressed and run downstairs to fill my water bottle, but she already has it filled and waiting for me on the counter.

"Are you ready to run?" She's got an enormous smile on her face right now.

"Since when did you become such a morning person?" I put my hands on my hips and look over at her.

"It must be all of the great lovemaking and sleep I have been getting the past couple of nights." She gives me a wink and then slaps me on the ass as she walks towards the stairs.

Huh, I could have sworn she said "lovemaking" instead of sex, but I probably shouldn't read too much into that. I know how I feel about her, but I doubt that she already feels the same way about me, especially considering we've only known each other a few weeks.

I tear myself from my thoughts and head downstairs so we can get this run in quick before we need to get ready for the big meeting later this morning.

Unfortunately, as we begin running, my mind immediately goes to thoughts about the meeting and how it will all play out. I realize I haven't checked my emails, or my phone for that matter, for the past couple of days, and I'm starting to panic that I may have missed something important. This is such a major business opportunity for my firm, and I really hope that this "vacation" is enough to convince everyone.

"Kennen, is everything alright? You look completely stressed out all of a sudden." She pauses and looks over at me, sounding somewhat out of breath from running.

I look back at her and see she's stopped, so I do the same. "I'm fine, Brielle. Now come on, hurry up. We need to keep running."

I realize I probably shouldn't have snapped at her, but I have the biggest meeting of my life in a couple of hours, and here I am running on the beach instead of preparing properly. I look over at Brielle when she catches back up with me, and her face has totally lost all the excitement it had just ten minutes prior, making me feel guilty.

If I am going to make this work with her, I need to figure out how to balance having a relationship and maintaining the level of engagement in my business that's required.

I stop running and grab one of her arms, trying to stop her also, but it causes both of us to suddenly crash, sending a million granules of sand flying all around us.

She looks up at me like I am crazy. "Kennen, what the hell was that all about?"

Looking over at her and then down at myself, I realize we are now covered head to toe in sand, which has stuck to the sweat we worked up from the running we've done so far. I start laughing at myself, as that totally didn't go as planned, and we both look ridiculous. Not to mention we still have to keep running covered in this mess.

I stand up and then bend over, scooping her up in my arms, and start heading straight into the ocean with her.

She starts kicking, screaming, and laughing all at the same time. "Kennen, have you lost your mind?"

"Apparently so. Now hold your breath." Before she can say anything in reply, I dive us both into the water, washing away all the warm grains of white sand.

When we rise back above the water, she cradles her arms around my neck and looks straight into my soul like she is once again trying to get a glimpse of what is going on inside.

"I can't read you right now, Kennen. What's going on in there?" She looks at me sincerely like she really wants to know.

"I apologize for being so short with you a few minutes ago." I tilt my head back and close my eyes, trying to let the warmth of the sun help dissolve the confused thoughts in my mind. "Are you sure you want to put up with all this madness that swirls around inside me?"

Wrapping her legs tightly around my waist as we sway up and down within the waves, she looks at me sweetly. "Absolutely. As long as you let me be a part of that madness and allow me to help you when I can, you stubborn ass."

I give her an exaggerated eye roll, a quick peck on the lips, and then pick her up and throw her over my shoulders headfirst into the incoming whitecap of a sizeable wave.

When her head pops back up, she wipes her hands down her face and comes swimming back over to me faster than a sailfish avoiding capture from an incoming fishing line. "Oh, you've just awakened an unforgiving siren, Mr. Davis. You'd better watch your back when I begin to lure you in with my hypnotic ways, or it will ultimately lead to your demise."

I look at her with my eyes full of lust and a grin big enough for her to smack off. "Is that a promise, Miss Bisset?" Suddenly getting splashed with a mouth full of salty water, I decide to take that as a maybe.

She heads for the shore, and I follow behind. By the time we both get out, our running clothes are stuck to us and feeling extremely heavy. I decide to take off my wet shirt and playfully snap it on her beautiful ass as I run by ahead of her.

Before I know it, she runs up behind me and pulls my shorts down several inches in the back, exposing me to whoever may be behind us. Then she starts running backwards past me, removing her tank top and throwing it directly at my chest. I try to grab it and pull up my shorts at the same time without losing my balance for the second time this morning.

When I look back up at her, she's in her sports bra and soaking wet shorts that are clinging to her every curve as she runs. It takes everything I have to try to regulate my breathing and stop thinking about what I want to do to her right now, public beach or not.

By the time we get back to the house after stopping by the coffee shop for Brielle's caramel chocolate-chip narcotic, we need to start getting ready for the meeting. I'm in the shower, washing my face, when Brielle sneaks in behind me, pressing herself into the curve of my back and running her hands down the front of my body.

I let out a quick growl. "Brielle, we're running late, and as much as I want you right now, we'll have plenty of time for celebrating tonight." I turn around and give her a quick kiss.

Extremely smugly, she looks up at me. "Oh, that's perfectly fine, Mr. Davis. I'll be in my shower, taking care of myself, then, if you need me." With that she blows me a kiss, winks, and then walks out of the shower, grabbing a towel as she heads over to her room.

I have a feeling I'm going to be paying for throwing her to the sharks earlier for quite some time to come. I try to hurry through the rest of my shower, but my mind keeps returning to what's possibly going on in her bathroom right now. Damn mermaids…

I decide to put on one of my new suits that Brielle hasn't seen yet. It's made up of a navy-colored jacket and slacks, a bright white shirt, and a sky-blue tie. I lean over, my hands on the bathroom counter, and look in the mirror, blowing out a slow breath. I just need to get through the next few hours and get this deal signed so I can stop stressing about it and move on.

Looking at my watch, I realize that the company driver Austin is sending over should be here in about ten minutes. So I grab my briefcase and walk over to Brielle's room.

"Brielle, we need to head downstairs in a few minutes to catch our ride over to the office. Are you almost ready?"

"I'm coming…calm yourself, Mr. Davis." Then she chuckles playfully.

Apparently, my mind is still in the gutter, as I can't help but notice her usual genius play on words, causing me to grunt.

As she comes around the corner from the bathroom, I

drop my briefcase, probably breaking my laptop in the process. She's got her hair down with those loose curls that I am wild about, and she's wearing a simple yet elegant white scoop-neck dress, with three-quarter sleeves, that is tailored to complement her every curve. It sits just above her knees, and she has her sky-high nude heels on, elongating her legs to all new heights. I've never seen a woman look this professional and irresistibly sexy all at once. It takes me a minute to refocus, as I was expecting one of her clever tees and pantsuits.

She walks over, picks up my briefcase, and then puts it back in my hand, giving it a gentle squeeze in the process. "I think you may need this, Mr. Davis." She looks me up and down and then seduces me with one of her alluring smiles as she walks out of the room to head downstairs.

We're in the foyer, waiting for the car, soaking up a few last minutes of air-conditioning before we head out into the heat and humidity all dressed up, when she grabs my hands and considers my current expression.

"Everything will work out in the end, Kennen. Please just trust in the journey, okay?"

I nod, and then she lets go of my hands and places hers on the sides of my face. Then she leans in and presses her pillow-like lips against mine, causing every part of my being to just melt.

Placing my hands into her hair, I back away slightly, leaning my forehead against hers. I want nothing more than to tell her how in love with her I am right now, but it's not the time to do that right before we head over to this meeting with both of us needing to be focused.

Our moment is interrupted when the driver pulls up to the front door. I follow her into the backseat and blow out a slow breath as I sit down. My stress is kicking into overdrive suddenly, hoping that this crazy plan of hers has actually worked.

As we're driving along, she tilts her head to mine and then whispers in my ear, "Not that you don't look amazing in your black suits, but this one, Mr. Davis, does things to me that I can't speak out loud with current company present."

I grab her left hand, curling it into mine, and place it on my lap so she can feel my reaction to what a simple whisper in my ear from her does to me.

She sucks in a quiet gasp, then whispers again, "Perfect. Now just focus on me during the meeting, and before you know it, you'll be back at the house with me removing every piece of that damn suit you're currently teasing me with right now."

My eyes widen, and I clear my throat, giving her an eager smile. With my thoughts now completely distracted, I realize that shortly after, we have arrived at the AW Advisors office. How does she always know how to read me so well and take care of me just when I need it?

I give her hand one last squeeze and then let go before we head out of the car, and Austin is outside waiting to greet us.

Brielle steps out of the car with all the grace and poise of a movie star, and I can't help but notice how Austin looks at her while she does it. If he tries to make a move on her while we're here this morning, I might have to rescind this contract and knock him out cold.

I quickly get out behind her and get as close as I can without being obvious that she is most certainly off-limits. He seems to be oblivious to this, as when she extends her hand to his, he grabs hold of it and pulls her in for a long hug.

"Brielle, it's so wonderful to see you again. You're looking as stunning as ever," he says as he continues to leave his eyes on her longer than I'm comfortable with.

I feel every tendon in my body tensing up like a tight guitar string and know that the vein in my neck is beginning to pulse at an alarming rate. If I really were Superman, I'd already be firing up my heat vision to take this guy out with one quick glance.

In tune with me as ever, Brielle breaks his grip and then comes right back to my side. "Shall we go inside and get to business, gentlemen?"

Austin smirks at me and then turns back to Brielle. "Yes, of course, follow me, and I will take you both up to the conference room in our suite."

As he walks ahead of us, I turn to her and mouth, "Thank you." Then she casually lets her hand softly brush mine as we walk side by side.

When we get up to their offices, I'm amazed at how different the feeling is in here compared to my offices in New York. You can tell it's Austin's style, as it has the same light and bright yet warm, modern seaside feel of the beach house. When you first walk in, there's a large reception desk made from natural-toned wood with a white marble top, and behind there is a wall of sea-glass-green wavy tiles that remind you of the ocean. I have to admit, aside from all of the glass walls everywhere separating all of the offices, it is a comfortable space to walk into.

He walks us into the conference room, where his attorneys, along with my attorneys, Jack and Carter, are already sitting waiting for us. I look over at Brielle, giving her the "please sit next to me" vibe, and hope that she gets it.

I sit next to Jack on our side of the table, and Brielle still looks unsure of where to sit, so I gently nod my head to my left, and she comes and joins me.

Jack leans over close to me and uses his file folder to cover his mouth as he quietly whispers to me, "Kennen, where have you been? We've been trying to get ahold of you for the past three days."

I immediately shoot him a look with my eyes narrowed. "What are you talking about, Jack? You know I've been on vacation down here, and I haven't gotten any emails or calls from you guys."

He clears his throat, then looks around the table quickly and continues, "Maybe we could step out for just a minute?"

Shit, this can't be good.

I stand up and excuse us from the meeting for a minute, and we walk back over to the reception area and stand off to the side.

I have my hands on my hips now and turn to him. "What's going on, Jack? And it had better not be anything major."

He folds his arms across his chest. "Apparently Austin called a board member the other day with some serious concerns still about where you stand with your current ability to continue as CEO, and how that would affect this merger."

I give him a cynical laugh. "You can't be serious; I just spent a few hours with him a few days ago, and he seemed completely fine and without any concerns." I put my hand up to my forehead, as another damn migraine is already planning its takeover. "What the hell did the board member say in response?"

"Look, I don't know the whole conversation, but the board did approach me and said that they have decided to move forward with taking a vote to see how many are in favor of beginning the process of removing you as the CEO." He rubs his own forehead now. "Before you lose it, remember what we talked about before you left, that with you holding the majority in the company, it will be a long road ahead of them to get it to happen."

I swallow so hard that it feels like I have an apple stuck in my throat. "What does that mean for today, though, in regard to signing the merger?"

He looks directly at me. "I have no idea about what is going to go down in there in a few minutes, as I'm not sure what the board may or may not have told him. When I questioned his attorneys, they said that he still wanted this meeting, so all is not completely lost as of yet." Then he proceeds to look down at his watch. "Come on, let's get back before they start to have any more concerns."

I rub my hands down my face in complete frustration, and then we head back over to the conference room.

When I walk in and sit down next to Brielle, her face is full of concern, and I'm doing my best to hide everything I have going on inside me right now. Of course, she knows me better than anyone and can see right through it.

Austin stands up, getting all our attention, and walks over to the window, looking out for a moment as if in deep thought. Then he turns and looks straight over at me. "So, Kennen, how has your vacation been going so far?"

This guy can't be serious right now. He wants to talk about my vacation when we are about to finalize the biggest deal in both of our firms' histories?

I clear my throat and try to put on a smile. "It's been amazing, actually; I feel like a whole new man." I chuckle, trying to loosen the mood. "It must have been your amazing house. Thanks again for all your hospitality."

"Of course, I'm glad you're enjoying it." Now he walks back over and puts his hands down on top of the chair he was previously sitting in. "So, a new man, huh, in which way would that be, exactly?"

Okay, this prick is just testing me now, and I'm not a fan of where this might be going. I furrow my brows at him and respond, "Well rested, well *loved*, and ready to start this new chapter of our businesses."

Brielle stomps my foot under the table with the end of her spikey heel, causing me to flinch. I'm assuming that was my "watch what you're saying" silent communication warning.

"I see, I'm glad to hear that, as I was a little concerned about a few things I have heard recently." He looks over at Brielle for an extended minute and then back at me.

Why did he just look at her after he said that? I know she would never have said anything negative when we walked out of this conference room a few minutes ago. The one thing that does worry me, though, is what the board may have told him, as I wouldn't put anything past those guys at this point.

He sits back down in his chair and leans over, crossing his arms on the table. "This merger needs to be built on trust from all parties involved, as we all have a lot at stake should something go wrong at any point." He leans his head slightly and then looks at me like he's got laser beams coming out of his eyes. "Would you not agree that honesty and integrity are going to be of upmost importance here?"

"Of course, those are important in any relationship, Austin, and I had hoped we had already established that fact over the past year that we have been working together on this merger." I am beginning to get even more concerned about what his issue is, and he just needs to get to the point already, as I'm tired of playing these games.

"So I had an interesting conversation about the real reason as to why you came down here in the first place, as apparently you aren't known to ever take vacations." He looks back over at Brielle again and then winks.

Why the hell does he keep looking...no way, she wouldn't have told him that I only came down here to try to deceive him and the board into believing that I was admitting to needing to take better care of my health and actually taking time to do so just to close the deal?

I turn to look at Brielle, and it's like it suddenly hits her, and her eyes start to fill with water.

My heart sinks, as I remember them talking while they were dancing together that night at dinner when she was slightly drunk on all the whiskey she had consumed. I can't believe that she would be so reckless and risk saying something that has potentially cost me this entire deal.

Seeing our interaction, Austin continues, "After that bit of alarming news, I called and talked to one of your board members to get their thoughts on this, and I have to say, they were also quite shocked and not pleased in any way." Then he pushes back in his chair and stands up again. "I'm sorry, Kennen, but I don't think this merger..."

I tune out the rest, because I now know that not only has this deal officially been thrown off the table, but my entire career and years of hard work may be going right alongside it.

Brielle puts her hand on my thigh, and it completely goes rigid under her touch.

She must have felt it, as she quickly pulls it away and then turns to Austin. "I'm sorry, Austin, but I spoke out of place then, as I wasn't in my right mind at the time."

He looks over at me and then laughs. "It seems to be a

running theme in your firm, now doesn't it, Kennen?"

I jump out of my seat, and Brielle grabs me, quickly pulling me back down, then she looks back over at him again, pleadingly this time. "Austin, please, you don't understand. He really is so much better now, as he was just overworked and overstressed with the merger coming up. He is absolutely more than capable of successfully running his company and growing together with yours…"

I cut her off sternly before she says anything else that will incriminate me later. "Brielle, don't. Just stop talking. I think you've said enough already, don't you?"

She flinches, and I see a single tear begin to run down the curve of her cheek. Austin also notices, and he has the nerve to come around the table and see if she's okay even though he just totally threw her under the bus.

She looks up at him and wipes the tear away. "I'm fine, Austin, thank you, but would you all please just give Kennen and me a few minutes?"

He touches her shoulder. "Of course. Gentlemen, let's take a break, shall we?" Then he and the four attorneys walk out together, leaving us alone.

I push back with more force than probably necessary and then bolt straight up out of my chair. I start pacing the room for a minute, and then I lean over the table next to Brielle.

"How the hell could you do this to me, Brielle?" I look angrily into her eyes. "Do you realize that not only have your actions cost me this deal, but you probably just ruined my entire career?" I slap my hand on the table as the reality of everything continues to sink in deeper, causing her to jump.

I start shaking my head. "I never should have come down here with you. I should have just stayed in New

York and kept on top of the board instead of wasting my days fishing and fooling around in the sun."

I fall back into my chair and grip my head with both hands, as it feels like it literally might explode due to the pain expanding inside there.

Brielle leans over to wrap her arm around my shoulder, and I gently push it away. "Please, Brielle, I can't handle your touch on me right now."

She stands up then. "Kennen, I'm so incredibly sorry. I never meant for this to happen, and I didn't even remember saying it until he brought it up just now." Tears start streaming down her face like they do on a windowpane on a rainy day. "I won't apologize, however, for the fact that you feel like the past few days of your life have been a total waste to you, as they were anything but for me." She tries to wipe away more of her tears. "I know how much this merger and your company mean to you, Kennen."

"Do you though, Brielle?" I glare up at her.

"I do, and unfortunately they mean more to you than your health, happiness and I ever will." She starts walking towards the door, then turns back around. "And I'm not going to sit here and watch you destroy yourself when you clearly seem to be better off doing everything on your own."

I stand up and start walking towards her. "Good. I want you out of the beach house before I get back there later today, and on the next flight back to Denver, as your services are no longer needed with my firm."

She starts sobbing even harder now. "Is that what you really want, Kennen, to dance in the silence alone?"

I turn my face away, as I can't look at her any longer, knowing I'm breaking her heart, right along with my own.

Taking my silence as her answer, she walks out of the conference room and closes the door behind her. As I see her start to walk away, Austin and the attorneys turn the corner, and of course, he walks up and begins to console her. He looks over at me with one of his cocky smirks and wraps his arm around her waist, pulling her into his side. Then they walk away towards the front of his office.

I close my eyes, rake my hands through my hair, and blow out a slow breath, not knowing how the hell to save any piece of my life right now. When I open my eyes, all I can see is the sight of Brielle completely broken and upset, along with the return of the visions of numbers and chaos that have been missing since earlier this week.

After Brielle left Austin's office, he returned to join me in the conference room, and the tension in there became so thick that it was beginning to stifle my breathing. I tried to explain my position to him, but he had it in his mind that he was done before we even got here this morning.

After the communication of our attorneys on both sides was completed a couple of hours later, we all said our amicable goodbyes, and I called for a rideshare to take me back to the beach house, hoping like hell that Brielle had already left.

By the time I get there and go inside, it sounds eerily quiet and doesn't have the same amazing vibe it did earlier this morning. Slowly walking up the stairs and into the kitchen area, I set down my briefcase on the counter and walk out onto the back deck and over to the railing to take in the sight of the ocean, hoping it will calm my nerves like it did before. But of course it doesn't.

I run my hands down my face and sigh, then decide to go back inside before I totally roast in this suit on a hot summer Florida afternoon. I decide to go upstairs and change before I break out my laptop to see if I can reschedule my Wednesday flight to either tonight or early tomorrow morning instead. I can't get back to the office quick enough to try to clean up the mess that awaits me there.

In my room, I notice a gift bag sitting on top of my suitcase, with a note carefully folded and placed on the top of it. I grab the note, and inside it reads: "Birthdays are like wine; they only get better with age. ~ Brielle, PS: Always remember to take some time to make something beautiful." I let out a light chuckle and then look at the bag, touched that she even took the time to get me something after how things just ended.

When I open the bag and remove the tissue paper, I pull out the most amazing piece of driftwood carved into a unique box. Inside I find several paints and paintbrushes, realizing that she recognized my renewed excitement as we explored all the art over the past few days, and thought to get me into it again after so long.

I'm about to close the box when I notice an inscription burned into the underneath side of the lid. When I hold it towards the sunlight shining into the room, I notice it says "Give your worries to the ocean and let the waves set you free, and in their silence, you will always find me. ~ Ula." I reread it several times, tracing the words with my fingers. I stand up, carefully closing it, then put it on the bed and sit down next to it. Before I know it, my eyes flood with tears, and I can't control the sobbing that follows.

This is by far the most thoughtful gift any one has ever got me. Then I suddenly hear what sounds like glass breaking as my heart completely shatters into a million pieces, taking my soul right along with it.

## CHAPTER 20

How is it even possible for my heart to be aching this bad for a relationship that technically began less than a week ago? Hell, it didn't hurt this bad when I caught my then fiancé cheating on me, and we were together for four years prior to that.

I know what I said obviously didn't help Kennen's cause in finalizing the merger, but I also didn't do it on purpose, nor was it the sole reason. There was never any guarantee that this "vacation" was going to be the cure-all, I just wanted it to be with every part of my being. Unfortunately, this just gave the board additional ammo, and it was all Austin needed to pull the plug at the last minute.

I blow out a long breath. This is such a disaster, and I feel terrible about how much I probably just destroyed Kennen's life. But I'm not going to lie, his words hurt worse than me telling Austin the truth any day. I couldn't believe how cold he was to me, which I guess only proves that I'm the only one who had any real emotions invested after all.

I'm currently walking around downtown Seaside, with my suitcase and carry-on in tow, wandering like a lost puppy looking for someone to adopt me. I know Kennen asked me to get on the next flight to Denver, but there's nothing and no one there for me to go back to, so what would be the point? It's not like I'm a fan of winters and mountains anyway. I'd rather be right where I currently am, by the peace that the ocean brings me and the salt that heals my soul. I just need some kind of sign telling me what to do, as I can't think straight right now. It was incredibly hard to leave that amazing beach house, but most importantly, all the memories that we made there this past week.

My thoughts are interrupted when I look up and see the grilled-cheese food Airstream, ugh. Maybe staying here isn't a great idea after all, as everywhere I look, I'm going to think about Kennen and some moment that we shared together.

I continue walking, as the thought of food doesn't seem at all appetizing right now, and end up in front of Judy's gallery. I notice a Help Wanted sign in the window and can't help but laugh, as you can't get a "sign" more literal than that.

As soon as I enter, Judy notices me and lights up. "Brielle, my dear, did you come to say goodbye before you left for the airport?" She wraps me in her signature hug and then seems to take a long look at me. "Oh, goodness, are you all right? You look horrible, dear."

That's all it takes for me to break down all over again, and she quickly gathers me into her arms and walks me to the back of the gallery where her office is located.

"I'm so sorry, Judy. I had no intention of coming in here for you to experience my sob story." I wipe under my eyes again, and I am suddenly glad that I washed all my makeup off when I got back to the house earlier.

She rubs my back. "Nonsense, you are always welcome

in here no matter what state you're in. But what happened to cause you such heartache, my dear?"

I take a seat in her office, and she sits in the chair alongside mine, grabbing my hand in hers just like the sweet grandmother figure I could really use right now.

I try to calm down enough so that I can talk without choking on my own tears. Once I get myself somewhat under control, I take a deep breath and begin, "Oh, Judy, it's kind of a long story, but the shorter version goes something like this…I've only known Kennen for the past three weeks while I've been working for him, well, did work for him. Anyway, in the past week since we've been here, our attraction and feelings have grown so intense and strong that I think I fell in love with him. That would be absolutely insane, though, wouldn't it? I barely even know him."

I look up at her, and she is smiling at me quite tenderly. "Would it be, though? The first time I took hold of my husband's hand, I knew he was the one."

Huh, this makes me think back to the feeling I got the first time I met Kennen and introduced myself. I remember it as though it were yesterday, as I had never had a feeling so intense flow through me like that before.

I continue, "Well, I thought he felt the same way about me also, but it turns out he doesn't."

She squeezes my hand gently. "I think you might be mistaken, Brielle. I saw the way he looked at you and hung on your every word when you were both in here."

Sighing, I remove my hand from hers, then lean over and place my face in both of them. "The problem is I just ruined a major merger deal for his firm and might have cost him his entire career with the company he created and nurtured from the ground up."

Judy sits up straight in her chair and seems to consider this. "Oh, Brielle, I don't know the details of any of this, but there is one thing I do know, and that is everything happens for a reason." She gets up and wraps her arm around my shoulder, continuing to comfort me. "It will all work out in the end, you'll see."

I have to chuckle at that statement. "I actually said the exact same thing to him early this morning before we left for the meeting, and then all hell broke loose. The next thing I know, he fired me and told me to get on the next flight back home."

Her eyebrows rise at this. "Well, he definitely needs a good swift kick in the behind for saying that, for sure."

I laugh, and it feels so good. "Actually, Judy, the real reason why I came in was because I saw your sign in the window."

"Are you looking for a job, dear? I thought you were just visiting."

I stand up and start pacing her office. "I was, but now that I'm technically homeless and starting over again, I really feel like this is where I'm meant to be, as I absolutely love it here, Judy."

"It's yours, and you can start right now, actually." She places her hand out in front of me to shake on it.

"Really, wouldn't you like to see my résumé or anything?"

"No, thank you, I only hire based on character, as the rest can be taught." She leaves the office and starts heading for the front of the gallery, so I follow her.

She grabs the sign and points for me to grab my luggage as we head back to her office to store them both.

I place my arms behind my head and blow out a quick, loud breath, realizing that now that I have a job, I still need to find someplace to live. "Judy, do you happen to know anyone who may be willing to rent a room to me until I get a little more settled and find something else?"

"Yes, of course, you can stay in my back cottage as long as you need; otherwise it will continue to sit empty." She smiles and continues, "No need to pay rent, dear. Maybe just come say hello and have some tea with this old lady to keep me company every once in a while."

"You'd really let me stay there?" I say, shocked at how generous this lovable woman is.

"Why wouldn't I let my new assistant manager stay there? Besides, don't get too excited, as it's only a tight studio space with a small kitchen and a tiny bathroom." She gives me a quick wink. "Now that that's all settled, are you ready to get to work? I have a lot to teach you before you can help me run this gallery."

I've never met such a kindhearted, amazing person before, and I can't help but walk up to her and wrap her up in a giant squeeze. "You have no idea how much all of this means to me, Judy. Thank you so much."

We spend the remainder of the afternoon training on all aspects of how she runs the gallery. By the time we were done, and after the extremely stressful morning I had, I'm completely drained. I walk back to Judy's property with her, and she jumps right into gathering everything I'll need to get me settled in her cottage. Before I know it, there are clean sheets and towels piled neatly on the end of the bed, and you can hear the click and hum of the air conditioner kicking on.

I sit down on the edge of the bed, slowly sinking into the softness of the mattress, and begin to feel the weight of my sadness pushing me down even further. I'm beginning to experience moisture forming in my eyes again and wipe them with the back of my hands.

Aware of my emotions, Judy gives me a quick embrace and then turns to leave and go back over to her house. "Don't be afraid to let it all out, dear, then get a good rest, and you'll feel much better in the morning."

"Thank you, Judy, for everything." I give her the best smile my face will allow through all this heartache.

Once she's gone, I take a few minutes to make the bed and unpack my suitcase in the small whitewashed wooden dresser that sits in front of the bed. It is a small space, but it's perfectly cozy and decorated with seashells and other fun nautical treasures. There's also a well-loved stuffed chair in the corner, and a small TV on top of a little stand across from it. Next to the kitchen area sits a two-seater little bistro table, reminding me of the one in Nic's apartment.

Oh, my gosh, what is Nic going to think when she finds out about what happened? I've been so upset all day about losing Kennen and what happened with the merger that I haven't even thought about how it will affect her and her position there. I start getting sad all over again, realizing how much I've let her down and disappointed her also.

I have a feeling that this is going to be at least a one-bottle-of-wine kind of evening, and considering I haven't eaten anything since last night, it's probably best if I make a quick trip to the local market and stock up on a few items.

I really do love how conveniently close everything is around here, allowing you to get most anything you may need in a short journey's time. When I get to the market, I grab enough food to get me through the next few days of meals and, of course, stock up on some local wine and cheese. I notice as I am perusing the aisles that they sell little foldable carts with wheels and decide this will come in very handy now that I'm living here, so I purchase one of those also.

As I'm pulling my groceries back towards the cottage, I let the warmth of the evening breeze flow over my face, looking for any reprieve from the sorrow of this day, but unfortunately none comes.

While cooking dinner, I get an incoming text message, and my stomach instantly clenches up. I take a long sip of the sweet Moscato wine and let it run down the back of my throat before I even look at my phone, as I have a feeling I'm going to need it. I close my eyes and take a deep breath, then grab my cell off the counter and open my messages. Of course, it's from Nic…

> **Nicole:** Brielle, WHAT THE HELL HAPPENED?
> **Brielle:** I don't know why you're asking, as you already seem to know…
> **Nicole:** Oh no you don't. You owe me an explanation after you just destroyed the merger and probably Kennen's career. I'm calling, and you'd better pick up…

Great, I can't wait for this conversation. I quickly down the remaining wine in my glass and refill it before my phone starts ringing. As I see her name show up on my caller ID, I'd rather chuck it straight across the room than answer it right now, but then I might damage one of Judy's walls, and I'd really be a monster.

I accept the call, and before I can even say a word, Nic jumps in. "Brielle, will you please explain to me what the hell went down in that office this morning? Why did we lose the merger, and why did I just get a text from Kennen saying I need to hire a temp worker to replace me for the remainder of my leave time?"

She takes a breath and then remains silent, so I take it as my cue to give her my explanation. "Nic, first of all, I'm really sorry about what happened. It was an accident and not at all intentional. Do you remember when I told you that I drank Kennen's glass of whiskey along with my own that night at dinner? Well, I knew I had gotten pretty toasted, but what I didn't know is that I ended up telling Austin the real reason why we took this vacation, and he decided to take that information to the board, and well…the rest is history."

She makes a maniacal laugh. "So what you're saying is that because you couldn't control your liquor, or your mouth apparently, we lost the deal of a century, and Kennen might lose his entire company? I knew this vacation scheme was going to backfire on you."

Wow, I get why she's upset, but really? She's supposed to be my best friend and be supportive, not tear me down even more. "Don't you think I feel terrible, Nic? I was only trying to help the situation not destroy it, as I would never do anything to hurt him…" I feel the tears forming and my throat beginning to close. "I love him too much to do that."

She clears her throat. "I'm sorry, did you just say you love him? Did I miss something here, you've only known him all of three weeks, and suddenly you're in love with him?"

Crap, that slipped out, but I suppose she would have found out at some point. Then again, maybe not, considering I no longer work for him and I'm living in Florida now. "Yes, Nic, I'm in love with him, and I can't explain how it happened so quickly, but it did. If you care about me at all, then you'll be a little more supportive to the fact that I'm completely devastated right now. He wants absolutely nothing to do with me, and I feel like part of my soul has been ripped from my body, leaving me half of the person I was before I even met him."

"Can you really blame him though, Brielle?"

The tears start flooding down my cheeks, and my nose begins to sniffle into the phone. "No, I suppose I can't, but I thought we both felt the same way, and his last words to me completely crushed my heart."

"Look, Brielle, I'm sorry if you are upset and hurting right now, I really am. But from what I know about Kennen after working alongside him over all these years, I would be surprised if the feelings were mutual."

I know she wasn't here with us, so she wouldn't understand, but she has known him for a really long time, and maybe she's right. I really don't want to talk about this any longer, as the constriction in my chest continues to squeeze tighter with every word that's spoken.

At my silence, Nic sighs and then continues, "Okay, fine, what did he say that broke my bestie's heart?"

I try to calm my breathing some and then continue, "He basically told me that he didn't want to see me again and to get on the next flight back to Denver, as my services were no longer needed."

"Wait, where are you? Brielle, you didn't fly back to Denver, did you?"

I allow a slow breath to quietly escape my lips. "No, I didn't, and I'm sorry, but I'm not coming back to New York either."

She cuts in, "I don't understand. Where are you, then?"

"I've decided to stay here in Seaside, as I fell in love with this town as quickly as I fell in love with Kennen, apparently. I don't know how to explain it, Nic, other than by saying it finally feels like home here." Sudden chuckling from the other end of the line fills my ears, causing me to wonder what the hell she could possibly find so funny right now.

"I don't know how you do it, Brielle, letting life lead you wherever it wants you to go, without even giving it a second thought. You always were the free spirit like that, though, and I was always the planner. Which is probably why your life is so much more adventurous than my mundane one is."

There is a definite truth to what she's saying, and I'm completely content with that. I finally feel myself beginning to calm down a little. "We make quite a pair, don't we, though?"

"That we do, Brielle." She sighs. "Alright, let me try to figure out a way to save my job and clean this mess up."

Before we hang up, I have one last thought. "Hey, Nic, when you hire my replacement, maybe you could find a male this time or some grouchy old lady instead?"

Solid laughter instantly erupts this time. "Oh my gosh, Brielle. Fine, no runway models or young chicks with perky breasts, got it."

I can't help but let out a quiet laugh at her response. "Nic, keep me posted on how everything's going, and please keep an eye on Kennen for me, as I'm really worried about him." This brings the sadness rushing back, and I suddenly want nothing more than to curl up in my new bed and call it a night.

"I will. Goodnight, Brielle."

I finish cooking my meal but only end up taking a few bites, as my appetite has long since passed. Then I wash up and crawl into bed, pulling the soft comforter tight around my body like a cocoon, and begin to silently weep.

The first two weeks of my new life here in Seaside have been filled with so many mixed emotions. With it now being the busy season here in town, the traffic in the gallery has been excellent about keeping my mind occupied during the days, but it's the evenings spent alone that have been weighing on me heavily. I'm back to my old habit of staying up late, mostly reading, and engrossed in thoughts of what my life would've been like with Kennen right now had everything worked out with the merger. I haven't heard a word from him since I walked out of that conference room. Each night before I go to sleep, I think about sending him a funny quote or thought like I used to, but he made it rather clear that he didn't want to hear from me ever again.

I'm exhausted, as I keep tossing and turning tonight, and decide that maybe a long walk along the beach will help calm my soul enough to let me come back and get some rest. I end up throwing on one of my crazy tees and some shorts and head out the door.

As soon as the warmth and softness of the magnificent sand we have here wraps around my feet as they sink in, I feel the slightest bit of relief shoot up my veins. I take in a deep breath of the salty air and then head towards the shoreline, slowly making my way along the beach. I find a few beautiful shells that I want to take back to the cottage with me and place them carefully in my pocket for safekeeping. When I arrive in front of the access area of Austin's beach house, I can see the For Sale sign he has on the back deck lit up with floodlights. I decide to turn around quickly and head back, as the sight of that house is too much to take in right now.

I really do love this town and the amazing people who occupy and visit here, but I hadn't thought hard enough about how much I would miss not sharing it with Kennen. The one place I haven't been able to bring myself into yet is the coffee shop, so I did invest in a new frappé maker for the cottage right away.

When I arrive back home and change into my pj's, I sit on the edge of the bed and just let myself fall backward. I lay my arm across my face, covering my eyes, trying to will the sadness to leave, if even for just a little while.

I must have fallen asleep shortly after, as when I wake up, I'm still in the same uncomfortable position I was before, except now every part of my body has cramped up. Stretching out some of the severe kinks, I climb off the bed and grab my cell to see what time it is. It's only six o'clock, but I decide to get in the shower to get ready and head into the gallery early this morning to work on some marketing concepts I have been thinking about lately.

I've never been in the gallery at this time and hadn't realized how quiet it is first thing in the morning. As I walk towards the back office, I notice that Judy must have rearranged the jewelry case last night, as the wave ring that I love so much is no longer being showcased. I make note to ask her about it when she comes in to see if the designer took it back, as it was only here on consignment. When I get in the office, I grab a spare notebook that Judy keeps in her desk to start making some notes of all the ideas I have.

By the time she arrives to open the shop, I've written down several pages' worth of ideas and sketches to go along with them. When I go up front to greet her, I'm instantly filled with happiness, seeing her loving smile shining at me.

"Brielle, my dear, you're here early this morning." She grins brightly at me.

"I know, I woke up early and had a headful of ideas that I wanted to jot down so that I can go over them with you. There's so many amazing things that I think we could do to make this gallery even more magnificent than it already is, Judy."

She pats my hand sweetly. "I can't wait to hear all of them, dear, but first let's sit and have some of the tea and bagels I brought in, so I can let my old bones get fired up for the day."

We walk back to the office and take a seat at a little table she has in the corner by the kitchenette area and enjoy our breakfast. Once she feels revitalized, I go through my concepts with her, all of which she ends up loving.

"These are brilliant, Brielle." Her look of pride warms my heart. "I love how passionate you are about my gallery; you remind me a lot of myself when I first had the crazy idea to go into business to begin with."

She rises out of her chair. "Let's go ahead and get this place open, shall we?"

I follow her out front, unlock the door, and flip over the hand-painted colorful wooden We're Open sign she has hanging on there.

"Oh, Judy, I meant to ask you, what happened to that beautiful wave ring we had from the New York designer?"

With a slight look of sorrow, she turns to me. "One of the locals came in and purchased it last evening. I'm sorry, dear, as I know how much you loved that ring."

Not wanting her to see my disappointment, I smile. "That's wonderful. I'm so glad that someone will be wearing that beautiful piece of art rather than it sitting behind glass all day."

We get the computer for the register logged on, and I walk around, making sure that everything is dusted and looking it's best for a day full of shoppers ahead. It looks like it's going to be another gorgeous summer day outside, which will make for another welcome busy day for us here, and a much-needed distraction for each new disappointment life brings me these days.

## CHAPTER 21

*I* look in the mirror, and all I see is a lost soul with extremely baggy eyes full of pain and exhaustion. If I've been getting a couple of hours of sleep each night in the past couple of weeks since I got back to the city, it's a lot. My days back at the office have been filled with nonstop meetings with my attorneys, trying to figure out a way to stop the board from doing their takeover, along with seeing all my regular clients I already had previously scheduled.

Nicole made good on her promise to find me a replacement for Brielle. A young guy named Marcus, freshly out of college, with a major in accounting. He was more than willing to take this temporary executive assistant position to try to get an in with my firm. He's working out fine, but he's not Brielle by any stretch of the imagination. I really miss the humor and lightheartedness she brought into this office as opposed to his dry humor.

Brielle...no matter how angry I am, I can't stop thinking about her every minute of every day. I haven't heard a word from her in over two weeks now, and the sudden unwelcome silence is killing me. I lie awake in bed with my heart aching and my body missing the warmth of hers curled perfectly into mine. I check my cell each night before I go to bed, hoping to see one of her usual goodnight texts, and the notifications never come. Trying to keep any speck of my sanity still intact, I take out her sticky notes and reread them each night, not knowing if it's actually helping me or making things worse.

I hate that the last time I saw her I said such cruel words to her, causing her eyes to overflow with tears, and not the passion that shone in them just hours before that. Why would she want to talk to me ever again? This thought makes me wonder why I even bother to check my cell, considering I turned around and destroyed her life just as quickly as she had mine. Although, she did it unintentionally, unlike me.

Adjusting my tie, I button up my black suit jacket and get ready to go into the office. I have an early meeting first thing this morning with Nicole, as she texted me last night, asking if she could come in to speak with me. I am hoping that she's not coming in to talk about Brielle, as I'm sure she knows about the relationship we had started by now. She said that it was work related, so hopefully this isn't some ploy to get Brielle and I back together, or worse yet, to chew me out for how I ended things. I'm stressed out enough as it is.

When I arrive at the office, she's already there, looking around the space she hasn't seen in almost a month now since her surgery.

"Nicole, it's good to see you up and about. How is your recovery going?"

She walks over and runs her hand along her old desk. "Hello, Kennen, it's going well, thank you."

I walk over to my office door and hold it open for her to enter. Then once I put my briefcase away, we sit down at my desk and take a long look at each other for the first time in what feels like ages.

Her eyebrows furrow as she looks at me. "Kennen, no offense, but you look like you could be playing the lead role in some end-of-the-world zombie movie."

"That's pretty much how I feel, so no offense taken, Nicole."

Her eyes seem to suddenly fill with concern. "I know you and I have only ever talked about work, but is everything okay with you personally, aside, of course, from the drama going on here at the office?"

I rub my hands down my face and then let out a struggled breath. "Do you know what, Nicole; no, things aren't okay with me in any aspect of my life right now." I grab a Life Saver out of my drawer and place it on my desk, pick up my stapler, and crush the candy until there's nothing left but a bunch of shards, then I point to it. "This right here is what my heart feels like right now, and there's just too many pieces to even try to think about how to start putting it back together."

A look of surprise crosses her face. "Kennen…I'm so sorry. I had no idea. When Brielle mentioned that she thought you had felt as she did, I thought that was impossible with the short amount of time you both knew each other."

This statement makes me want to start questioning Nicole about any conversations she's had with Brielle to find out what else she may have said, or how she may be doing, but I'm not sure if I really want to know at this point. I'm sure she's happy being back in Denver with her old life and not missing the drama left here in New York.

I can feel my eyes begin to glaze over and know that I need to move this conversation onward. "Well, I'm sorry to say it, Nicole, but for once you were wrong. So what was it that you needed to speak with me about today, anyway?"

She clears her throat and then looks down at her lap for a long minute and then back up again. "I was coming in to let you know that my doctor has cleared me to come back to work whenever I'm ready since my recovery is going so well. But I'm not sure that is going to matter now…well, once I tell you what I probably should have told you a while ago."

I'm really glad she is able to come back to work, but I'm afraid of whatever else it is that she needs to tell me, as I'm not sure I could handle any more bad news at this point.

I sit back in my chair and firmly place my arms across my chest. "I have a feeling I'm not going to be happy about whatever you're about to tell me, so please just say it and get it over with, Nicole."

She looks up at me with a nervousness that I have never seen in her before. "Oh my gosh, Kennen, this is all my fault."

"What are you talking about, Nicole?"

Swallowing hard, she continues, "Do you remember how I've been mentioning to you over the past couple of years that I wanted to move up into an accounting position since I finished my degree?"

I think about this for a minute, trying to figure out where she is about to go with this conversation. "Yes, I do seem to remember you mentioning it a few times. Why?"

"Well, it's something I really want. And you knew I was ready for it, but it seemed like you were just being selfish by not letting me advance so that I'd have to stay here and continue to be your executive assistant."

I let out a slow breath, sit back up in my chair, and lean over my desk with folded arms. "Yes, I suppose in a way I was holding you back, and I apologize, as I couldn't imagine not having you on my team as this firm continued to grow, considering you've been with me since the very beginning."

"That's what I thought, and unfortunately, I let the anger about it fester inside me to the point where I wanted you to know what it felt like not to be able to advance your career after putting in years of hard work and dedication." She pauses and looks away from me, then over to the view of the city through the windows.

My stomach drops, and a pain so intense shoots straight into my head. Not wanting to hear anything else come out of her mouth right now, I try to speak, but she cuts me off.

"Kennen, please let me finish." She gets up out of her chair and starts pacing around the office, her fingers intertwined so hard her knuckles are turning white. "I was the one who went to the board and initially put the thought in their minds that you were unfit to continue your duties as the CEO, and of course they believed me without question considering I know more about you than anyone else in this office."

She places her hand on her forehead. "I knew with the merger quickly approaching, I needed to act fast. With that, I decided to push up my surgery date, which was already scheduled for next year, to last month and brought Brielle out here to take me out of the picture temporarily as all of this went down."

I glare at her now with such anger in my eyes that she has no choice but to look at me. "Let me get this straight, Nicole. You were trying to get me fired from my own firm because I wouldn't promote you to another position. Then you lied and used your amazing best friend to cover it all up, which in turn ended up breaking not only her heart, but mine?"

I shake my head. "What the hell is wrong with you?"

A tear suddenly falls down the left side of her cheek. "I know it was a horrible thing to do, and I had no intention of hurting Brielle. I hadn't planned on her coming up with her pretend 'vacation' scheme that the board actually bought, which threw a monkey wrench into my plan. That is until she royally screwed herself and told Austin everything." She stops pacing for a minute. "Unfortunately, I also wasn't expecting Austin to pull the plug on everything, throwing the board into even more of a frenzy without me being here to help redirect it all, thus lessening my chances to position myself where I was trying to get to, to begin with."

I can't believe that after everything I've done for Nicole over all these years (aside from not promoting her, that is) that she would do something so damaging not only to me but to her lifelong best friend. While I do understand why she was upset with me, it doesn't justify her actions, and I've suddenly lost all respect for this woman standing in front of me.

"Just so you know, Nicole, Brielle is ten times the woman you will ever be. Her idea for the vacation was brilliant, as it actually helped me find myself and some happiness again."

She slumps down in her chair and thinks about this for a few minutes. "You're absolutely right about her, Kennen, and I know once she finds out about this, like you, I will lose her also." She suddenly starts to cry at this thought.

What is it about these women in my life and their crying lately that just tugs at my heartstrings? Here I totally cut Brielle out of my life for only telling the truth to Austin, and then I find out that this entire situation would never have happened had I promoted Nicole to begin with. Although, if I think about it, if Nicole wouldn't have planned this whole disaster, I never would have met and fell in love with Brielle. And at this point I don't know what's worse. Ugh, my mind is beginning to spin in every direction possible, and I wish more than anything that I had her here to comfort me.

I walk in front of my desk and sit alongside the edge. "Look, Nicole, I'm really sorry that I held you back all these years, as you didn't deserve that, but please know that it may take me a while to forgive you for the amount of damage that you did to Brielle, me, and my firm."

"Thank you for saying that, and again, I'm so sorry about everything, Kennen." She wipes her eyes, trying to erase the tears she's shed.

We both just sit there for a few minutes in silence, until I speak again. "Alright, Nicole, if you think you might still have the board's ear, I'm going to need your help to try to get us all out of this disaster we find ourselves in."

She looks up at me with a glimmer of hope in her eyes. "Of course, you name it, and I'll do whatever I can to help fix this."

"Good. Oh, and, Nicole, please don't confess all this to Brielle until we know how this will play out, as I can't imagine either of us putting her through any more pain right now, okay?"

"Okay. But no matter what the outcome is, once this is all over, I will tell her the truth. I owe her that and more right now." Her face is full of guilt, and I know exactly how she feels.

"You and I both, Nicole…"

## CHAPTER 22

ONE MONTH LATER

Things at the gallery have been going amazingly well recently. I implemented one of my new ideas I came up with last month, and the response has been so phenomenal that Judy couldn't be happier.

We started hosting "Wine & Pint Painting Nights" once a week, using local artists to lead the class in instruction, and in return, we do a spotlight feature of their work in our newly designed front window display. The artists love the extra attention their work is receiving, and the visitors and locals alike enjoy having something creative and exciting to do.

I have to admit that I finally feel like I found my calling when it comes to my career. With this position, I get to use my marketing and creative talents, along with some event planning thrown in, and I'm having a blast.

I'm also still living in Judy's cottage, as she's in no rush for me to move out anytime soon. We have our daily morning tea and frappé talks about life, love, and everything in between. I'm so grateful for such an amazing newfound friendship with her, and we have become very close, like family, really. She's been slowly trying to help me ease my sadness, yet knows me well enough now to know when I just need to let it remain inside.

I've been taking more nightly walks on the beach, like I am right now, and have acquired quite the seashell collection as of late. I know that I want to create something special and beautiful with them, but I haven't decided what yet. I think back to one of my walks last week when I noticed a Sold sign on Austin's beach house. This made the ache in my heart grow all over again, knowing some other people would soon be creating their own memories in there, as Kennen and I did. I knew it wouldn't take long for someone to snatch it up, though, as it's such an incredible home.

I try to refocus my thoughts back to my shell hunt, as there was a decent-sized thunderstorm this afternoon, which tends to wash up some of the nicer shells afterwards. I'm extremely specific as to which ones I take, as I like them to all be unique and have character. As I am walking along, I realize I'm getting closer to Austin's beach house and notice the faint silhouette of someone sitting on the bottom of the steps that lead to the beach from the back patio. The black darkness of the evening has already arrived, preventing me from getting a good look at their appearance. I'm hoping in some bizarre way it's the new owner, as I'd love to meet the people who ended up purchasing it.

Just as I'm getting close enough to see them, I'm distracted by one of the most beautiful shells I've seen in a long time. It looks to be an old, worn queen conch shell that has been roughed up by the ocean for years on the outside, but when I flip it over, the tones of pink range from dark to light with a glossy shine still to it. I hold it up to the moonlight to see if the conch is still alive in there, but it has long since vacated its home.

This is by far my favorite shell I've ever found, as it kind of reminds me of myself. Outwardly it's beaten and battered by life's uncertainties, yet still beautiful and full of life on the inside. I hug it gently to my chest and smile out towards the ocean until I hear a familiar voice bringing me out of my moment.

"You know, someone remarkably special once told me that if you find the perfect shell and make a wish, then send it back out to sea on a summer's night, your wish will come true."

I turn around so quickly that I almost lose my balance. "Kennen, is that you?" My heart begins beating so fast that I think I might pass out when I see him come into view. I know it's only been a month and a half, but seeing him here in front of me again, I remember just how amazingly handsome he really is.

He walks up to me and gets so close that I can feel the heat radiating off his body and onto mine. Then he runs a hand through my hair so gently and slowly, like his fingers are reminiscing a lost memory. "My Ula, still so beautiful and full of life." Then he looks down at my shell and chuckles. "You weren't planning on sending that one off to sea, now were you?"

I look up at him, not sure what to think right now. "No, this one is coming home with me, as I made my wish when we first got here."

Sensing my cautiousness, he grabs one of my hands in his and rubs his thumb gently over my fingers. "Brielle, I can't even begin to tell you how sorry I am for how I treated you in the office that morning. I would never expect you to forgive me, but I do hope that with time you will consider it." He pauses to look at me. "I didn't have all of the facts at the time, and I suddenly saw everything I thought I wanted crashing around me...and well, I didn't know what to do."

I'm trying not to get emotional, but I can't help a tear that escapes my eye and slowly glides down the curve of my cheek. "Kennen, I know you were upset, and you had every right to be, but your words really pierced my soul. And then when I never heard from you again, well, you crushed my heart right along with it."

He leans his forehead against mine. "I know, Brielle, and I have regretted it every day since. It took me losing everything to realize what was most important to me in my life."

My heart sinks, hoping that he didn't end up losing his company in the end along with the merger. I've barely talked to Nic in the past month, and every time I asked her about work, she would be cautiously vague or change the subject altogether.

"Kennen, I'm also sorry for all of the trouble I caused, but please know it wasn't my intention, as I had my heart in the right place the whole time."

He leans his head back enough so he can look into my eyes and then places his hands on the sides of my face very gently. "Brielle, you didn't do anything but be honest, and I'm incredibly sorry I faulted you for that." He takes a breath so deep that I can feel his chest rise while doing so. "Please forgive me, Brielle."

He's looking at me so tenderly right now that it warms my heart and makes me smile. "I suppose I can forgive you, Mr. Davis."

Before another word is spoken, his plush lips are on mine. It feels so incredible to have the spark we share instantly come rushing back into both of us.

He picks me up in his arms just like he did at the airport that day, and starts heading for the steps to begin climbing.

I look over at him and laugh. "Kennen, where are you going? Austin sold this house already. We can't just go barging in there."

"Shhh, the owners won't even know that we are here if we are quiet enough. I just want to show you something." I can see his smirk with the pale light of the moon shining on him.

Oh my gosh, I have no idea what he's up to, but I can't help but be excited being in his arms again. "Kennen, seriously."

"Shhh, I said to be quiet." He half laughs, half whispers.

He slowly opens the sliding glass door inch by inch, and we walk into the dark game room area, where he carries me up the steps to the second floor carefully in the dark. When we get into the living room area, he gently lays me down, and I immediately sink down into what feels like a pile of clouds, instantly causing my heart to skip a beat. I know this feeling, as I remember it vividly from when we were in his apartment.

I try to adjust my eyes to the darkness so I can get a better look, and sure enough, I'm lying down on his couch that I love so much. "Kennen, I don't understand. Why is your couch here?"

He laughs at my confusion and then climbs on top of me, so he is straddling me now. "I decided that everything and everyone I ever really wanted, and *loved,* was right here in Seaside, present company included."

"Wait. You bought Austin's house? Like for a vacation house?"

He leans down close to me. "This is my home now, and I'm hoping eventually it will be our home, Brielle."

This is all too much to process at once, and then I realize what he said. "Wait, you love me, Kennen?" Looking directly into his eyes, I see that they are as crystal clear as the water that flows along the shoreline just outside this home.

"I love you more than anything else, Brielle, and I can't survive this crazy world without you." He gently lowers his lips to mine and kisses me so softly I feel like I'm melting into the couch even further.

"What about your apartment in New York?" I look at him, still slightly dazed and overly confused.

"Sold it." He leans down and places his warm lips against mine again.

"Oh, my gosh, Kennen, what about your firm? Did the board end up voting you out?"

"Nope, I sold them all of my shares and left." He starts kissing my jaw and slowly down my neck.

"I don't understand. Your company was your whole life. How could you just sell it off and walk away?" I put my hands through his hair as he continues to kiss further down to the dip in my collarbone.

He lifts his head and places his hands back on my face. "My life isn't whole without you in it, Brielle, and you were right, it wasn't worth the stress and pain it was causing…it just wasn't me anymore." He kisses me on the lips again and then looks at me sweetly. "I also seem to remember being told that my palm lines were suggesting a change in direction, so I took that into consideration when I made my decision."

I let out a laugh. "Well, then you chose wisely, Mr. Davis, as you wouldn't want to go against what your lifelines show."

"I choose you, Brielle, above everything else. And I promise I will never put you second to anything in my life ever again."

Another tear escapes my eye, but this time out of pure joy and total happiness. "I love you so much, Kennen."

"I love you too, my Ula." Then he kisses me with such fierce passion that I can suddenly feel the pieces of my heart reconnecting and becoming whole again.

He pauses, then takes a breath and smiles down at me. "I almost forgot; I have one more thing that I'd like to show you." He sits up and gets off the couch, grabbing my hands.

Putting on my best pouty face, I look over at him. "Do we have to leave this couch right now?"

He turns and laughs. "Don't worry, that couch isn't going anywhere for an extremely long time, and I really want you to see this."

I have no idea what he wants me to see, but by the way his face is lit up right now, there's nothing more I want to do than to follow him.

He pulls me up the stairs and over to the room that I slept in when we stayed here previously. "Okay, now close your eyes."

I quickly close my eyelids and hear him suck in a deep breath and then slowly let it out. He opens the door and then carefully guides me into the room. "You can open them now."

I immediately put my hand to my mouth and gasp as I begin walking around the room. He's taken out all the furniture that used to be in here except for the chair and ottoman in the corner, and then turned the rest of the space into an art studio. The most shocking part is the paintings that are in here already, as they are absolutely stunning.

I take a moment to spend time in front of each one of the canvases, and I'm in awe of them. One is of the beach, another is of a mahi mahi fish coming out of the water, all lit up, and there's also an amazing landscape of downtown Seaside.

As I get around the room to the French door area, he has an easel set up with a stool and a little table next to it where the paint box I got him for his birthday sits propped open and full of even more paints and brushes now.

I look over at him for the first time since I walked in the room. "Kennen, these are incredible. I had no idea how talented an artist you are, considering all you said was that you used to paint a little when you were younger. No offense, but I was thinking more finger-painting level, not Van Gogh."

He lets out a chuckle. "Well, these are slightly better than they were when I was six, but thanks for the vote of confidence." He smirks and then pinches my cheek.

"When did you even find time to paint them with everything you've had going on the past month and a half?"

He wraps his arms around my waist, bringing our bodies together, and then looks down at me. "I haven't really slept at all without you beside me in bed, and your card told me to make beautiful things, so I figured I might as well put my restlessness to use."

I let out a small giggle. "I haven't slept either. Wait until you see my seashell collection."

He kisses me on the top of my head and laughs. "I've missed you and your craziness so much, Brielle." Then he backs away and grabs my hand again. "I want to show you the first painting I did. It's my favorite and has the most meaning to me."

He walks me over to his bedroom next door, and when I see the painting displayed above his bed, my eyes instantly fill up with water.

I climb up onto his bed and sit right in front of it, and Kennen follows, sitting behind me.

Wrapping his arms around the front of me, he leans in and whispers in my ear, "This is by far my favorite memory of you, Brielle, as it's the moment I realized that I was starting to fall for you."

I lean my head over until it touches his. "This was the night I made my wish, but I didn't even know that you were watching."

"I know, but I'm not sorry that I intruded on your moment, as it was the most beautiful experience I have ever witnessed." He squeezes me a little tighter around my stomach.

In front of us sits a painting of me on the beach the night we went out to dinner with Austin, and we walked back along the beach. I'm holding my perfect shell out in my hands while I have my eyes closed, making a wish. Every detail is so perfect it almost looks like a photograph. From the reflection of the moonlight on the waves, to the wind blowing through my hair exactly as I remember it did.

"It's absolutely breathtaking, Kennen. How did you remember it so perfectly?" I turn to look at him.

"Photographic memory, remember?" He quickly kisses my cheek. "I made sure to capture it that night, and I've pulled it out of my memory to view every day since."

I turn all the way around, wrapping my arms around his neck and my legs around his waist. I lock my eyes with his for a minute, still in shock that I'm back in this house and snuggled in his arms again.

"I do have one question for you, though, Brielle." He looks at me curiously. "May I ask you what you ended up wishing for, or is that bad luck?"

I move my face so close to his that he can feel the words coming out of my mouth when I speak them. "I wished for your heart to fully heal so that you would be able to find true love again someday." I close my eyes and then place my lips against his, needing our connection at this very moment.

He carefully lowers us down on the bed so he's on top of me again, and pushes a piece of my hair away from my eye so that he can see me clearly. "Thank you for using your wish on me, and for everything else since then."

I wake up to a sunlit room, with Kennen's arm squeezed tightly around me, and I can't help but smile. I slept like a rock, and apparently so did Kennen, because I can barely feel the rise and fall of his chest right now as he continues to peacefully rest.

Glancing over at my watch, I see that it is nine forty-five in the morning, and then jump out of bed, instantly waking Kennen in the process.

"Brielle, what's wrong? Is everything okay?" He is sitting up now and yawning.

"I'm late for work, and since I never came home last night, Judy is going to be so worried about me." I'm frantically running around trying to gather my clothes, which are currently scattered along the dresser, the chair, the floor and across the rest of the room.

"Wait, where are you working, and where are you even

living?" He stands up, trying to find his own clothes.

I start jumping into my shorts. "I am the assistant manager at the gallery, and I'm living in Judy's cottage behind her house. If it wasn't for her, I have no idea where I would be right now."

He smiles at me. "Remind me to thank her later."

I grab my phone and call the gallery, hoping she'll answer the phone before we open in fifteen minutes. Luckily after the sixth ring, she finally picks it up. "Judy, hi, this is Brielle. I'm *so* sorry that I'm running late this morning. I overslept. I'll be in shortly, but I wanted to let you know that I'm okay…" I look over at Kennen quickly, and then refocus back on my phone conversation. "Actually, I'm better than okay. I'm great."

"Oh, Brielle, my dear, thank you so much for calling. I was so worried. But my heart is full knowing you got some much-needed rest, and you are doing so well. Take your time, and I will see you when you get in."

I blow a kiss into the phone. "Thanks, Judy, you're definitely my angel in disguise. I'll see you soon."

Kennen walks up to me and tries to grab my shirt out of my hand. "Do we have enough time before you have to leave for work, Miss Bisset?"

I quickly snatch it away. "No, Mr. Davis, we do not, and just so you know, I'm blaming you for my tardiness today." I move past him, giving his toned ass a quick glance, and then walk over to his bathroom to continue getting dressed so I can go home and get cleaned up for work.

By the time I get there, it is already ten thirty, and the gallery is already in full swing. I see Judy over by the register, ringing up a customer, and I give her a quick wave before I head to the office to put my purse away.

When I come back out, the customer has left, and Judy

walks up to me and pulls me in for my daily embrace, which I lovingly return. "You look like a whole new woman, my dear. That must have been some amazing sleep." She gives me a wink, and I can't help but laugh.

I clear my throat, but before I can answer, the door chimes, and in walks Kennen. Well, he couldn't have timed that any better if he tried.

He walks up to us, flowers in hand. "Ladies." He grabs Judy's hand and kisses the top of it and then hands her the flowers. "Judy, I can't thank you enough for taking such great care of Brielle while I—"

Blushing, she cuts him off, "Had your head up your ass, perhaps?"

Kennen and I both look at her with eyebrows raised and in total shock.

I can't help but laugh, and then Kennen joins in. "Yes, exactly that, Judy."

She takes a minute to smell her flowers and then looks back up at Kennen. "Well, don't let it happen again. Oh, and, Kennen, try not to make my assistant manager late with your extracurricular activities next time, please." She gives him a smirky wink and then walks to the back to put her flowers in water.

I push him playfully in the chest. "You'd better go before you get into any more trouble, Mr. Davis."

He pulls me over to him. "I can't believe you told her the details of why you were late."

I laugh. "I didn't have to."

I see Kennen eyeing the painting section of the gallery. "Go ahead, Van Gogh, take a look at all of the new ones we've gotten in since you've been here, and let me get to work."

As Kennen admires the artwork, Judy approaches me

with a warm smile on her face. "So everything worked out in the end, did it?"

You couldn't slap the enormous smile off my face right now if you tried. "Yes, it did, and better than I could ever have imagined." I bump shoulders with her. "Thank you, Judy, for being here for me through all of this."

She looks over to where Kennen is and then turns to me. "What did he ever think of the gift you gave him, dear, as he seems exceedingly interested in the artwork still?"

"Oh my gosh, Judy, you should see the paintings he's created already. They are incredible." My heart swells with pride. "Once he gets settled into the house, and if he's comfortable with it, I would love to have him teach one of our painting classes so we could display his work out front, if that would be okay with you, of course?"

"I would absolutely love to see that happen, dear. There's nothing more rewarding, owning this gallery, than watching aspiring artists grow." Then she gives my shoulder a quick squeeze.

## CHAPTER 23

Kennen

All it took was seeing Brielle shell hunting along the beach last night to solidify the fact that I absolutely, one hundred percent made the right decision giving up my old life to create a new one down here with her. I had to inwardly chuckle when she spotted me and then got totally distracted by that old conch shell she found.

We're currently in my new living room, lying on our favorite couch, reading books together. Well, let me clarify, she's reading, and I can't seem to keep my eyes off her. It's amazing how comfortable and natural this all feels right now, and I'll do everything I can to make sure that never changes.

I'm pulled from my thoughts when I hear her cell ping with a text message notification.

She grabs her phone and then smiles at whatever she's reading. "It's Nic. I can't wait to tell her about everything that happened."

I suddenly feel a knot clench in my stomach and wish that Nicole didn't have to tell her about everything she did, as Brielle is so happy right now.

"Brielle, please just go easy on her, okay?"

Confused, she looks at me, but before she can respond, her cell rings, and she answers it right away. "Hey, Nic, how are you feeling? I hope the recovery is still going well."

I love how her first concern is always for everyone else, as she's so selfless, and I hope to learn from her to better myself in that regard.

I listen as Brielle speaks again. "Oh, really? I'm so happy that you are loving your new position at the firm. Kennen told me that you were able to stay on after he left and that you're in accounting now. That's amazing. I'm so proud of you." She looks over at me with an excited smile on her face.

Suddenly her smile begins to fade, and a look of worry replaces it. "What do you need to tell me, Nic? Is everything okay?"

I can feel my heart rate begin to rapidly increase, and I'm not even the one getting the bad news this time.

Before I know it, she's jumped off the couch and pacing the room. "Nic, how could you do that to us? You've worked for him for over eight years, and we've been best friends since we were kids. Does none of that even matter to you?" Her hand is flying around, and she's yelling now, and it's probably the Italian coming out in her.

"I do understand why you were upset that he held you back all of those years." She looks over at me with her eyebrows tightly drawn together.

I tilt my head back against the top of the couch and begin rubbing my forehead. So much for our relaxing afternoon, ugh.

"Of course I'm happy that it worked out in the end for all of us, but still, Nic, what if it didn't? That was a very risky stunt you tried to pull off." She flops down on the couch next to me, and I place my hand on top of her thigh and begin to rub her leg to try to keep her calm.

Huffing and looking defeated, she continues, "Yes, I still love you, but, Nic, it's going to take me a while to completely forgive you, okay?" She leans over, laying her head in my lap, and continues listening to Nicole while she's looking up at me. "Yes, I was very surprised to see him, but in an amazing way, unlike this call, unfortunately."

Ouch. She's actually taking this call better than I thought she would, but probably only because, as Nicole mentioned, everything did work out for each of us in the end. I start running my fingers lightly down her leg and start to inch them towards her inner thighs, causing her to take in a quick breath.

"I'm extremely happy for sure, and yes, we'd love to have you come visit." She's trying to focus on her conversation, but I can tell I'm distracting her (intentionally of course), trying to get this afternoon back on schedule.

"Sounds good, Nic. Look, I need to go and absorb all this and grab a bottle of wine. Can I call you back another time?" She sits up and kisses me while she still has the phone to her ear. "Thanks, bye." She hits the end button and drops the phone on the couch, then climbs onto my lap.

"I can't believe you never promoted her, Kennen." She harshly pokes me in the chest. "Why did you forgive her so quickly after she literally tried to sabotage you and everything you worked so hard for?"

"Selfish reasons, mainly." I start playing with her hair, as I can't get enough of how soft it is. "Look, she was my right-hand person from day one, and we worked so well together. I wouldn't have gotten to where I was today…well, two weeks ago technically, if it wasn't for her."

She smiles considerately at me. "Was there more than

one reason for forgiving her, as you said reasons?"

I pull her face within an inch of mine. "Because I got the best part of this whole deal thanks to her fiasco." I gently press my lips to hers, loving how sweet tasting and smooth they are.

She backs her head away just slightly. "Oh, and what might that be, Mr. Davis?"

"A new house on the beach, of course." I wink at her; then she gives me a death glare as she pinches my leg before she climbs off my lap and walks away.

"Luckily for you, the couch is comfortable, as that's where you'll be sleeping tonight, Mr. Davis…by yourself of course." She smirks and then takes off running up the stairs.

I laugh and can't help the enormous grin forming on my face right now. Life is definitely good.

## Epilogue

### ONE YEAR LATER

I'm so excited to finally have Nic here with us at the beach house for the weekend. Since she took on the new accounting position at Kennen's old firm, she's been working nonstop and hasn't had a chance to breathe, let alone fly down to see us.

We're all on our way over to the Down and Out Oyster Bar, where Kennen ended up winning the trivia game last year, to take a private oyster-shucking class. Unfortunately, once they found out that Kennen was, in fact, a genius, they banned us from all future trivia games. It's still one of our favorite spots to eat, though, so we go and make bets amongst ourselves as to which team is going to pull off the victory.

I can't wait to see Nic take this on, as it's totally not something she would normally be into. Kennen thought it would be a fun way to immerse her in our new Seaside culture, and I wholeheartedly agreed (mostly because I'm looking for some good social media material to blackmail her with, should the need arise again in the future)

We also have Judy riding with us since she's become our

adopted grandmother of sorts, and we love spending time with her as much as we can. She's currently in the front seat of the rideshare, looking back, questioning Nic about all things arts and culture in the city. Kennen and I are watching in amusement, as Nic isn't really into the arts much.

"So, Nic, are you ready to go shuck some oysters?" I try to save her by changing the subject, then give her a playful wink.

"Umm, no, not really. Unless I end up finding a pearl, then that would be pretty cool, I suppose." She shrugs her shoulders nonchalantly.

Kennen feels the need to chime in with technical data, of course. "Actually, Nicole, pearls are found in *Pinctada maxima*, or 'pearl oysters,' and are pretty rare. The oysters we will be shucking tonight won't contain any future jewelry pieces for you, I'm afraid."

Nicole looks over at me mockingly. "I still can't believe this is who you, of all people, Brielle, fell in love with."

Kennen and I both laugh, and I give him a quick peck on the lips. "His brilliance is what I love most about him, Nic." Then I lean over and snuggle into the delicious curves of his broad chest.

"Oh my gosh, you two are killing me over here with all that crap." She covers her eyes with her hand, trying to be dramatic, causing us to laugh even harder.

Judy chimes in again, "Nicole, my dear, is there anyone special currently in your life?"

We all look over at Nic, who glares at us and sighs. "No, Judy, it's just me in my little New York apartment, and that's exactly how I like it."

"That's because you work too much, dear. You need to live a little more, as it's not good for you. Right, Kennen?"

She gives him a wink, causing him to grin.

Nic laughs. "Oh, Judy, if you only knew Kennen before Brielle entered the picture, I would be a party animal in comparison."

Kennen and Nicole exchange looks like they are about to throw down, and I burst out in laughter. Luckily, we pull up to the bar before anyone starts throwing any more jabs.

When we get inside, we are greeted by Jake, the owner, who leads us all to the back room they usually use for party reservations. He's got a couple of tables pushed together in the center of the room, covered in brown butcher paper, with plates, oyster knives and paper towels in front of each chair.

Kennen and I sit at one side of the table, and Judy and Nicole on the other, which gives me the perfect view to watch them both try to shuck oysters. We get our drinks, then settle in and wait for Jake to come back with the oysters and our lesson instructions.

Judy turns to Nicole. "Care to make a little wager, my dear, as to which one of us can shuck the most oysters first?"

Kennen chokes on his sip of water, and I laugh so hard that my eyes fill up with water. How can you not love this woman?

Nic turns to look at Judy now. "You cannot be serious right now?"

"So can I count you in, then, Nicole? If so, let me know what you would like if you win." Judy carefully places her slightly aging hands on the table.

Nic seems to consider this for a moment and then looks at Judy. "You know what, you're on, and if I win, I get to pick one of those unique small glass sculptures from your gallery."

"A girl who knows what she wants. That's a very admirable quality, Nicole. It's a deal. Let's shake on it." She holds out her hand to Nicole, who happily grabs it and shakes.

"Wait, you never said what you get if you win, by some miracle." Tilting her head, she smirks at Judy.

Oh boy, Nic doesn't know Judy like I do, and she hasn't realized it yet, but she just lost this bet before it even began. As Kennen squeezes my leg under the table, I try to stifle my laughter so as not to interrupt this moment.

"If I win, which I will, my dear, you have to go on a date and have some fun this weekend before you leave, with a suitor of my choice." She winks at Nicole and then takes a long sip of her white wine.

"Oh no, no way is that happening." Nic starts shaking her head.

"Good, then you'd better not lose, my dear." And with that, the conversation is over, and Kennen and I can't hold it together any longer.

Jake walks up with a bucket of oysters and an apron for each of us. The blue aprons have the bar logo and the phrase "Shuck up or shut up" screen-printed across the top portion, which of course I absolutely love.

"Oh, this just keeps getting better, doesn't it?" Nic says as she holds the apron up in front of her.

Kennen helps tie mine in the back for me, and I do the same for him, then we're all set to get started with our lesson.

Jake grabs my knife and one of the oysters out of my bucket to demonstrate. "Okay, folks, so this little fella right here is an oyster, and this here is called the hinge of the oyster. The outer bottom part is called the cup." He's pointing out each piece of it as he explains. "Now, what you want to do is put the oyster on your plate, carefully insert your knife into the hinge, and wiggle it around some until it loosens enough that it pops open for you. If it doesn't, you might need to twist the knife some like you would with a key in a lock. Once that opens, go ahead and continue to work your way around the hinge and through the muscle until it's totally free from the top." He pauses for a moment and looks around the table at each of us. "Everyone good on what to do so far?"

Nic is watching him so intensely that I'm surprised she's not taking notes. She has a lot invested in winning this bet, because the last thing she wants to do is go on a date with one of Judy's friends' grandsons more than likely.

We all nod in agreement, and he continues, "Once you have the top shell off, go ahead and set that aside, and then clean out any residue that may have gotten on the oyster during the shucking process. After that, you can place it on the ice trays I'll bring out, and enjoy it with your favorite topping." He looks around again and sees that none of us have any questions. "Great, well, I'll go and get them for you, then. Be right back."

Nic grabs her knife and holds it up, looking at Judy and saying, "You're going down, grandma..." causing the rest of us to instantly erupt in an explosion of laughter.

I try to catch my breath and then speak up. "Best. Night. Ever."

Kennen leans over and places a sweet kiss on my cheek and then whispers close to my ear, "You have no idea how much I love to hear you say that, Miss Bisset."

All it takes for my entire body to fire up is having him whisper in my ear. Hell, it could be any set of random words and it wouldn't matter.

I turn so that I can get closer to him now. "Oh, this

night is only getting started, Mr. Davis." And I teasingly kiss him right below his ear on the edge of his jaw.

He clears his throat. "You're definitely right about that one."

We end our private conversation as Jake returns with a few staff members carrying our buckets of oysters and ice trays with toppings.

Once we are all set up, we each grab our first oyster and place it on the plate. With that, Kennen does a countdown, and we all dig in. It's definitely harder than Jake made it look, so it takes us each a few oysters to get the hang of it. I can't help but glance up at Nic and Judy every so often to see how that's playing out. So far it looks like Nic is in the lead by three oysters, and Judy seems totally unfazed as she takes sips of wine in between shucking each one.

Kennen notices me watching them, and then starts shaking his head, snickering. "Should we make our own wager on this?"

I chuckle. "Nah, this bet is perfect as is."

I look Judy in the eye, and she winks quickly, then dives right into her bucket of oysters, shucking the remaining ones in less than two minutes flat.

She turns to Nic. "Do you need help with the rest of yours, my dear?"

Nic's mouth drops open; then she turns to look at Kennen and me, and then back at Judy again. "What the hell just happened?"

Judy proudly chimes in with, "My husband was a fisherman for over thirty years, my dear. I have shucked an oyster or two in my day." She grabs her glass of wine and takes a long sip, then carefully sets it back down. "I'll be in touch in the morning with the time and location of your date, Nicole, and don't even think of skipping town, as I have friends in New York too, you know."

"I can't believe I just got swindled by a sweet, *innocent* old lady." Nic lays her head down on her arm that's resting on the table and sighs.

Judy and I high-five across the table, and Nic notices. "Hey, did you know about this, Brielle?"

I casually look at her and then smirk. "Payback's a bitch, isn't it, Nic? Have fun on your date tomorrow."

Kennen lets out a bellowing laugh, and then Judy and I join in.

We finish shucking our remaining oysters and get them all set up on their trays as the staff returns and clears off our mess. They give us each a warm wet towel to clean our hands, and we get excited for the dinner that we all worked so hard to prepare.

Jake comes back out a moment later and hands me another oyster on a plate with a clean knife. "I owe you one from the demonstration I did earlier. I wouldn't want Kennen upset with me for shorting you of any additional aphrodisiacs." He gives me a playful wink.

I chuckle. "No, we wouldn't want to do that, now would we, Kennen?"

I look over at Kennen, who is suddenly quiet, and I'm wondering what is going on in that beautiful mind of his.

"Kennen?" I place my hand on his forearm.

"I'm sorry, no, we most definitely wouldn't want that, so shuck it up, Miss Bisset." He turns in his seat to wrap his arm around me and give me a quick kiss, then takes a long-drawn-out sip of his water.

I grab the knife from Jake and place it into the hinge and start trying to pry it open. This one seems a little tougher than the others. It's either that, or my hands are just tired from the other eleven I already did earlier. I finally hear it pop, and then carefully make my way along the rest of the edge. When I finally open it up, I almost drop the knife on my plate.

My heart begins to flutter faster than a hummingbird's wings as total confusion sets in. My head quickly snaps over to look at Kennen, and I can see a shine already forming in his eyes. He withdraws his arm from around my back and then carefully removes the breathtaking wave ring made by the New York designer from the oyster shell.

He pushes his chair back, then gets down on one knee and gently takes hold of my left hand. I can feel the trembles surging through both of us, like an earthquake repeatedly rocking the earth's core.

"Brielle, we've definitely shared times that have built us up, and unfortunately some that came crashing down. But there is undoubtedly no one I would rather dance in the silence with for the rest of my life." He takes a minute to catch his breath, and then he locks eyes with mine to continue, "You are my wave, Brielle, and I would love for you to be my wife."

A single tear escapes my eye as I place my hands on either side of his face. "Kennen, my love for you is bigger than the ocean itself, and it would complete my soul to ride the waves with you for the rest of our lives." I slowly lean in and tenderly kiss his lips. "I love you so much, Mr. Davis."

He carefully slides the ring onto my finger and then looks back up at me, happiness pouring through those brilliant eyes of his. "I love you more, Mrs. Davis."

The End

## ACKNOWLEDGMENTS

Creating this book has been one of the biggest dreams that I have ever taken on and accomplished. I'm truly humbled by the amount of love and encouragement that I have received from all my family and friends throughout this process. Without each of you, this never would have happened. So, from the bottom of my heart, thank you!

To everyone who has taken the time to read and share this novel, it means so much to me as a debut indie author to have your support. My hope is that Kennen and Brielle's journey left you slightly emotional, full of laughter, and maybe a little bit flustered along the way. Putting my dream out there for you to read has been both extremely exciting and completely nerve-racking at the same time. Thank you for all your kind words and reviews, they mean the world to me.

I would also like to express my heartfelt gratitude to *USA Today* Best-Selling Author G. Michael Hopf, who not only selflessly shared his wealth of knowledge and experiences of writing with me, but became the amazing mentor and friend I needed to see this book become a reality. How he put up with my endless texts and questions during the creation and publication of this novel is beyond me, but is appreciated more than he'll ever know. A special thanks to his wife, Tahnee, for all of her support also. I'm so grateful to have your family in my life, thank you all!

To my wonderful editor Pauline Nolet, (who is probably

now sporting a head full of gray hair after correcting an obnoxious number of grammatical errors along the way) thank you. My goal is to not make you suffer quite as much on my next novel...no promises though, sorry! You've been amazing to work with, and I look forward to having you be a part of future adventures with me.

How spectacular is the cover of this novel, you guys? I've had the amazing honor of working alongside Drew Button, of D. Button Ink, for over four years now on different projects. He's extremely talented in many different forms of art, and his creativity often leaves me speechless. It's always fun when we get to collaborate, and this time was no different, as he totally nailed my vision for this cover. Please take a minute to visit his Instagram account @dbuttonink and show him some love. Thank you, Drew, I absolutely love my cover...you rock!

I wish that I could personally acknowledge every single person who has influenced and encouraged me over the years, but this novel would end up being an obnoxious number of pages. However, there are a handful of people who need special recognition: my mother, Roberta, and stepfather, Wayne; my Big D, Tom, and my stepmother, Nancy; and Sandi (who will always be like a mother to me). To my awesome siblings, Gail, Allie and David, you're the best, and I love you guys so much! A shout-out to my cousin Michelle, who shares a passion for writing with me, I can't wait to read your novel someday. To one of my longtime besties, Jen, I love you bunches, girlie.

I'd also like to thank Mary for guiding me on some of the legal questions that I had within the storyline, as it was definitely helpful and appreciated!

Life has been slightly crazy for everyone over the past couple of years to say the least, and I couldn't have made it through them without my "mom squad." Jody, Liz, Loan, and Muska, I can't thank you enough for all your love, support and friendship that you give to me each and every day. You've been here for me through so much…you ladies are the best!

To my amazing kidlets, I love you more than you will ever know. I can't imagine my life without you guys in it, and I'm so proud of the humans you are becoming as you grow and go through all that life throws at you. A special thank you to my daughter for being my biggest fan throughout the process of writing this novel. All of the late nights you spent awake with me and endless chats about my characters and plot lines will be memories that I will cherish forever, thank you, Boo.

I had to save the best for last…my hubby, Scott. Thank you for sharing your love of deep-sea fishing and Java Chip Frappuccinos from Starbucks with me, both of which inspired scenes in this novel. I know it wasn't easy having me spend countless late nights (and obnoxiously early mornings) locked up in my office so that I could follow my dream of writing this book, thank you. I wish I could be more productive in the daytime, but that's not how my creative brain works, so again I appreciate your sacrifices while I met and completed my goals. Thank you for always being by my side as we ride the waves of this crazy life together.

## About Elaine Patch

Elaine Patch lives in sunny California with her family and spends her days in the marketing, graphic design and photography worlds. In the late-night creative hours, you will find her writing romance novels while jamming out to her favorite playlists. She's a total book nerd, but her soul will always belong to the ocean. *Brilliantly Beautiful* is her first novel.

For more information about the author,
please visit her website at:

**authorelainepatch.com**

Connect with Elaine on social media:

www.instagram.com/authorelainepatch
www.facebook.com/authorelainepatch
www.twitter.com/authorEPatch

Made in the USA
Coppell, TX
20 July 2021